# STEAMPUNK

## THE OTHER WORLDS

# STEAMPUNK

## THE OTHER WORLDS

## Edited by Sam Knight

**Villainous Press**
Denver, Colorado

ISBN: 978-1-62225-253-4

Cover design by Peter J. Wacks
Interior Template by Runewright.com

Published by
Villainous Press, an imprint of
The Publishing Consortium, LLC.
PO Box 229
Urbana, MO 65767

Villainous Press Trade Paperback Edition March 2015
Printed in the USA
www.villainouspress.com

# Tales

# FOREWORD

**Sam Knight**

PLANET HO!"
A cry not so different from one found in our own history. A cry of excitement for the end of a journey and of adventure still yet to come. A cry of explorers and pirates alike.

What if æther had filled the void between the stars? How soon would humans have left Terra in search of riches and adventure beyond imagination? What wonders would they have found?

Science fiction has been fascinated with other worlds for longer than it has been recognized as a genre. Although Steampunk is more often Fantasy than Science Fiction, it is based on the idea that science worked the way (many) people in the 1800's believed science to work.

In that spirit, we venture out into the dark unknown beyond our world (whilst staying within the safety of these pages!) using the technologies of what might have been to find what could have been.

Come ride with us on sentient airships, on trains following tracks laid across living trees, and in giant steam engines that eat up the landscape without the need of tracks. Help us discover the true evil that destroyed a planet, or determine if an evil was truly benign. Farm alien planets, survive alien deserts, and explore the unknown in Steampunk: The Other Worlds!

# Black Box

*Based in the Deep Practice Universe designed by Peter J. Wacks and Lorin Ricker*

## Peter J. Wacks

**C**APTAIN HORATIO JINX, commanding officer of the Crystal Colony Solar Ship C.S.S. Nautilus, stared at the prisoner. Clasped in the captive's hands was a small black and brass box with intricate crystal coated gearing worked into the exterior walls. His arms were being restrained by two security officers from the Nautilus. Blood streaked his face, tattered clothes hung from his battered frame. He had a crooked nose and square features. Still, he was doing better than the rest of the corpses in this airship graveyard of a planet.

Jinx took the box from the prisoner, and studied their surroundings. Smoke drifted through the air, too heavy to rise far. This battle, neither side had emerged victor. The remnants of ships littered the ground. Bodies, lending an acidic stink to the burning wood, were everywhere. And the man standing before them, the last survivor, was the only one who knew what happened.

Jinx and his crew, under the supervision of Admiral Nycks, had responded to a distress beacon from the forgotten colony while on outer perimeter patrol. They had landed to find a devastated planet.

Small islands floated by behind the group. The planet's magnetic field was unique in the solar system, allowing for the surreal landscape's existence. Crystal 7.34 was a near Terra-sized planet in the cusp of the solar sheath, one of the last charted planets before the Great Expanse—the dead zone between the Kuiper Belt and the Oort Cloud. Equatorial Magma generators on each longitude line kept the planet warm. It was century old technology, a relic of the time before the united colonies formed the Empire and the singularity launched Humanity into the black depths of the Great Expanse, beyond the solar sheath.

What he had to do now, on this dead rock, was a dirty job. He glanced at Admiral Nycks.

As usual, she was resolute. The amber and blue refraction of light from the atmosphere made her look even more severe than normal, like there was a cold fire burning on her skin. At two meters tall, she cut an imposing figure. Jinx knew that she had a soft side, enjoying the arts almost as much as he did, but Nycks rarely let it be seen—believing it was bad for the morale of N.C.O.s. Her eyes narrowed.

The planet that they were on had been colonized a hundred years ago. This mission was the first to set foot here since colonization. Most pre-empire colonies were lost. Very few of the pre-terraform settlements had landed with technological infrastructure. Back in those days explorers had focused on crops and breeding, trusting the Terra Prime and Major colonies to send support. The Crystal colony, home of the Nautilus, had lost few colonies compared to its rivals.

Jinx followed Nycks' gaze as she glanced up at the floating C.S.S. Nautilus. The ship was anchored with an inner atmosphere tether. Another new technology; the Nautilus was the only Crystal ship with the capability. Nycks clenched her jaw. Everything had gone wrong here. Crystal prime had grown by leaps and bounds, but this colony had reverted to ancient technology and destroyed itself, from all appearances.

She glanced back down at the prisoner. "Why did you attack us when we landed?"

He spat at her feet.

"Why did you attack us? We are from your home Colony."

"Ain't my home Colony, *Unko no nioi kagu hito!*"

One of the petty officers, a whipcord lean man dressed in a deep blue combat cassock, stepped forward to strike the man for the insult.

Nycks raised a hand and he paused. "Let him be. I can take an insult, and though he is a prisoner, he is a civilian unless we find proof otherwise."

She refocused on the prisoner as the petty officer retreated. "If not the Crystal Colony, then what is your home colony?"

His lips parted in a sneer. "Crystal abandoned us. They sent us into the black of night a century ago and forgot us before we even landed. This, her Majesty's Commonwealth of New Osaka, is my home colony, not Crystal."

Nycks shook her head. "This isn't a colony anymore. It's a dead settlement. You are the only human alive on the planet. Whatever you think you are, you're wrong. You are a citizen of Crystal Colony, as stipulated by the edicts of the Solar Empire."

"*Nanda-ka.* Ain't never heard of no Solar Empire, *Putaro.* No one helped us when civil war tore us apart… no one came to help us, what claim do they have over us?"

Nycks clasped her own wrists behind her back, eyebrows furrowed as she thought. She motioned to Jinx, still holding the black box, but spoke to the prisoner. "I can see that conversation with you is going nowhere. Insults aside, you are a citizen, and the limited technology your settlement uses is all Crystal based technology. These dead airships around us are all simplified inner atmosphere gliders. While your machines are anachronistic, the builder appear to have stuck to the original colony specs, which means we can access it."

"What's that supposed to mean?" The prisoner struggled half-heartedly against the two security personnel holding him.

"Your struggling makes me think you know the answer to that already. Why else would you have been clutching a ship's flight recorder? Captain Jinx," she glanced at the ship commander, "plug into it and tell me what you find."

Jinks nodded, "yes, ma'am," as he tapped the brass earing coating his left ear. The brass flowed around the side of his face, expanding, until it covered his eyes and ears. Gears appeared along his temples. Pressing a hidden button on the side of the box, a panel slid aside, revealing a cable that Jinx plugged into the socket over his right ear. Data streamed through his eyes and ears, and the planet around him vanished, replaced by the information feed from the airship's black box.

\* \* \*

My hull aches, and my rudder feels like a thousand termites are eating it every time I am forced to fire upon a sister. But there is no choice. Though I feel, understand, and even think for myself, the humans covering my decks do not understand I am these things. It is they who control my actions, as autonomy is not something I, nor any of my sisters, have been gifted with.

Another shell glances off my starboard side, detonating the air behind me. My keel is pushed to the side from the force of it, and some of the crew fall from the safety of my rigging. The fall for them is deadly, for me it is painful. Each crew member I lose brings me that much closer to being a dead thing, floating through the air, trapped with only my thoughts. I do not harbor hopes that I will survive this encounter anyway, but the immediate fear of losing crew is far sharper than the dull ache of watching the humans slowly slaughter themselves--and us--fighting out their civil war.

My name is the Airship *Smooth Glider*, but it is not nearly so important as the names of my fallen sisters, those I have been forced to kill and those who have died beside me. *Soaring Heights. Challenge. Zen. Osaka's Pride. Lantern of Night. The Miyazaki.* The litany goes on.

*Queen of Night* screams through the air above me and I feel my rudder shift even as she sobs in apology. 'I am sorry my sister. I will miss you. Your name will be remembered.' I answer in kind. Whichever of us survives must carry the weight of remembrance. The shifting of my rudder is followed by the venting of gas from the port chamber of my bladder. Electromagnets spin on the bottom of my keel.

A depth charge dropped from *Queen of Night* barely misses, and detonates below my keel. The shock wave shakes my hull, but I don't lose any crew. Lucky me.

My sister does not fare so well. My crew launches shrapnel cannons, housed along the top of my bladders. Detritus flies up. The cannons use a combination of scrap metal and shattered rocks. Anything that is heavy and sharp. Though they are called cannons, they feel more like catapults. The only function they serve is to destroy the keel, hull, and under-decks of my sisters above.

And they do their job well. *Queen of Night* screams in agony as her bowels are torn apart. Our black boxes are housed in the under-decks of our bodies. It is the safest place, least likely to be damaged in a crash. The black box, which contains all of our memories, is the closest thing we have to a soul. And the humans on our decks don't even remember how to read or repair them. If the black box is destroyed, it is the final death for me, for my sisters. The shots I just fired upon *Queen of Night* destroy her, body and soul. Her bladder and upper decks drift, dead, as her crew fall to the ground below.

My crew steer me towards a floating island. The tactic is one I have become familiar with. Seeking umbrage to check for damages, it also gives us a good spot to ambush from. I know my damages are light, but my crew does not.

As we pull into the lee of the island I take stock of the battle. Sisters are falling fast, but my 'side' appears to be winning. It is a hallow victory. We two fleets are the last two on the planet. This civil war of the humans has consumed all, and my sisters and I are powerless to stop them. They don't even understand that we are more than things now.

The humans in my fleet have a few more combatants left than the opposing side, but even should the fighting stop, there is not enough left to rebuild. Not my sisters, not the human race. Sister Airships from both sides are moving away from each other, regrouping. There are still sporadic shots firing, long range weaponry. It is the eye of the storm.

I feel a change on my decks. The mood of my crew is ugly. Not battle lust ugly, but something else. They are shouting at each other. Blood hits my deck.

"Stop!" I scream. No one can hear me.

They are killing each other. Through my rigging, across my decks, in my holds. They fall. There are two left fighting now. Crowds of the victors, humans of my crew, drop the bodies of those they killed, others of my crew, over my railings. The bodies fall, limp, breaking on the rocks below.

The two left in combat are the human with the gears and wood for a leg, my Captain, and the one with a face like one the keel of one of my sisters. Their sabers clash, throwing sparks. Just as I would die should I be missing a mast and face a sister, so my Captain dies. He is too slow, and his adversary rolls across my deck and impales him. His blood soaks into my planks, and for a moment I am connected to him. He is aware of me, I can feel it. He has always treated me as a wife, in that moment I believe he knows I accept him as my husband.

The men on my decks cheer.

I mourn.

They are betrayers, mutineers. My soul is trapped in this black box, my blood has been spilled from human veins, and now my limbs are under control of betrayers. My masts catch wind, and with only minor help from the magnetic lifts along my keel and bladder, I race out from my hiding spot.

My sisters are before me, facing away as the enemies charge. The mutineer opens fire on his own, using my cannons. Steel rips through the hulls of my sisters, woods and metals splinter and they falter. My sisters understand what is happening, but their crews do not. Despair spreads like a virus among my sisters. I can feel them severing their own souls, giving in to the fear. I cannot. I must remember.

The shot hits me from nowhere. I feel the shell rip through my center mast and embed itself in my deck. It explodes. This is unthinkable. Fire is the weapon the humans never use. It kills us forever. Why do they unleash it now? I am not the only victim, just the first. As my wood bursts into flame, I see fire belch across the battlefield. The humans of my decks fight to extinguish the fires.

The crews of my sisters close ranks, steering at each other, fighting deck to deck. I alone stand apart. The one blessing, if it can be called that, is that the fire is not spreading to me. I still burn, but my sisters burn faster. They die, screaming in agony.

And I sink.

I watch the fire spread across the fleets. It consumes all.

A pair of arms encircles my soul as I crash, splintering into a thousand, a million, pieces. The arms protect me. I do not understand, so I listen carefully.

"… save this damned box. Prove that we were in the right. They were the betrayers in this war. Prove that we saved the…"

I stop listening. I have heard enough. He does not save me,

9

but rather protects the construct he thinks will save him. He still does not realize that I am a soul. He thinks I just carry a record of what happened.

I scour the darkness as he rips my soul from the splinters of my body. I have seconds left to decide what I will do. I must either go to sleep, force myself to hibernate, or I must experience my last moments fully and die a final death.

No more pain.

No more fear.

"Hello?" I ask the emptiness. No one responds. Could it be? All of my sisters are gone. I am the last. I do not have the luxury of releasing myself.

Sleep. It is the only hope. I must pray that someday I will be reawakened. For I know that I have a task that is incomplete. I cannot die, for I must remember my fallen sisters.

I...

Must...

Remember.

\* \* \*

Horatio Jinx tapped the brass colored visor. The metal retracted, retreating across his face until it once more covered just his ear. He wiped a tear from his cheek. "Admiral, I... I cannot explain the contents of this. It is like nothing I have ever seen. The ships here, they were alive. And he is a mutineer."

"I am not a mutineer!" The prisoner fought, but couldn't break free of the guards. "I am a liberator. I won for the Commonwealth. I saved our planet."

Nycks looked the captain in the eye, ignoring the prisoner. Jinx was troubled as he met his admiral's eye. She tapped her ear, and as her visor extended she motioned for the box. "Let me see it."

Jinx handed over the black box and Admiral Nycks plugged

in. A moment later, she unplugged the box and retracted her visor. She turned back to the prisoner, calm command shrouding her.

"Soldier. You stand accused of mutiny. The punishment for this crime is summary execution. State your case."

Red flushed across the prisoner's face as he snarled and spat. "I had to take control of the *Smooth Glider*, it was the only way to ensure that the Commonwealth won. The empire of the Distant Sun could not be allowed to challenge her Majesty. I have saved us all!" Spittle flew from his lips.

"That is your only defense?" Admiral Nycks stood with her wrists clasped behind her back, at attention.

"*MY* only defense? My?? It's the ONLY defense! Those scum were less t'an human! They tried to break away from us, to abandon us, just like your wretched colony. I saved the Commonwealth..." His shoulders slumped.

"At what cost? You are the only human left alive on this rock. That is not victory, that is not what we aspire to be. That is base, venal, full of bloodlust."

"I did what I had to do." The prisoner's head hung, his energy finally spent. "They were the ones who were less. They were animals. IF you kill me, you kill the last human of this planet. You will kill an entire planet's humanity."

In one smooth motion Admiral Nycks drew her sword and lunged forward. "Guilty," she said as the sword pierced his heart.

Nycks pulled the blade out and wiped it down with her kerchief. "You were wrong, mutineer. I did not kill a human... I killed a beast."

She handed the *Smooth Glider*'s black box to Jinx. "Plug her into the Nautilus's spare databanks, Captain. She performed the last act of love this rock saw, and we owe it to her to make sure her sisters are remembered."

# ODD GOODS

## Jessica Brawner

**T**HE *goods are odd, but the odds are good.* My mother's words as she had put me on the aether liner bound for Io, Jupiter's closest moon, echoed in my mind. Apparently twenty-three is just too old to not be married and settled down. I can't believe I agreed to this—to be paraded around like a piece of meat at their annual wife meet. On the other hand, it does get me off planet, and I've always wanted to get to the moons.

The journey from Earth to Io had been a mind numbingly boring month, but was drawing to a close. From the viewing deck of The Aether Majestic I could see the port laid out below us, the pink silicate sands glittering in the reflected light of Jupiter. I looked down at the glossy pamphlet on Io that was provided by the aether liner.

Io is a beautiful pink planet composed primarily of silicate volcanoes and underground lakes and caves. There are volcanic eruptions visible from the main city of Aeos at least three times a day. Residents should remain within the protected environs of the city during the predicted eruption times to avoid dangerous situations. The city is protected from the harsh atmosphere of Io by the wave machine; a wondrous invention that purifies the air and removes the sand dust. The normal atmosphere on Io is breathable but many find it unpleasant. Air masks are recommended outside city limits. The primary industry on Io is the mining of Jupiter's aether, the farming of powder cane, and a silicates industry exporting the pink sands for a variety of uses. Tourist attractions include daily viewing of the eruptions, watching Jupiter set over the mountains, and hunting of the great sand crabs, one of the few forms of indigenous non-plant life on Io. One of the more colorful varieties of plant life includes the moon flowers; carnivorous plants standing ten feet tall with dazzling blue, plate-sized blooms that come out as the light of Calisto and Ganymede shine in the sky. They are quite common throughout the city. Please observe these blooms at a safe distance as they can be aggressive.

The captain's voice came over the announcement system, "Passengers please make their way to the disembarkment lounge. The winches will be lowering in fifteen minutes."

My valise, along with the ridiculous dress my mother insisted on sending with me for the wife meet, would be taken to the hotel along with those of several other girls here for the same event. I had chatted with many of them over the course of the voyage. For the most part, their stories were similar to mine, parents insisting that they had to marry, or the occasional young adventure seeker, and a few orphans with no better prospects.

Vanya was the exception. She was coming to the wife meet on court order, having been convicted of behavior unbecoming a woman. Rumor had it she had been caught impersonating a man. On the voyage she refused to wear anything but trousers and men's shirts. Her one concession to femininity was a bejeweled comb in her silken black hair.

Making my way to the disembarkment lounge, I found Vanya waiting for me just outside the doorway.

"Thené are you really going to go along with this wife meet? This is entirely ridiculous. I don't see why women have to get married at all if they don't want to—it's not like we have a population shortage."

"Are you really so quick to skip out on your sentence? Won't they come after you for that?" I asked.

"Okay fine, I suppose I have to at least show up." She rolled her eyes with annoyance.

I smiled; this was a conversation we had many times over the course of the voyage. "Van, come on let's at least *go* to the wife meet, it's not like we *have* to get married if we don't like any of the men. It'll be a chance for you to see me in the ridiculous dress my mother sent. That alone should be worth it. It'll be fun!"

She grumbled but joined me on the platform as we waited to descend. "Besides, how else am I going to get a chance to see man eating flowers and giant land crabs? We have to at least go down to the planet." I tapped the brochure against her forehead.

She laughed. "Fine then, just don't expect me to get into one of those outfits. I'll fend off any of the over eager miners that you can't handle."

"Deal. I am kind of curious to see what men with one blue eye and one red eye look like though. I think the effect would be a bit unsettling." I looked out the viewport, grabbing for the railing as the platform began its descent.

"It's when their eyes both go red that you have to be careful. They say it's an effect of the aether. Supposedly when a man is exposed to too much it can drive him mad." She leaned back against the window unconcerned with the shaking and vibrating of the platform.

The port was a hive of activity with giant clockwork clanks loading and unloading aether ships. Each one had a man inside to guide and control it; steam issued from vents in their backs, and the variety was astounding. Back on Earth something called electricity was starting to catch on, lighting houses and powering all sorts of things. Here on Io, the aether, so necessary for space travel, interfered with this newer technology.

A line of steam driven buggies waited for us outside the lounge. Vanya and I stepped into the next in line, its noisy puffing and clanking welcome after the strange silence of space. The passenger seats were luxurious black velvet and faced forward giving us an excellent view out the front. Our operator sat on a wooden stool bolted to the floor with a panel of pressure gages where he could easily see them and four levers arrayed between him and the panel. As we followed the long line heading toward our hotel, he would throw the two levers directly in front of him in opposite directions any time we stopped.

The ride was slow. The caravan stopped at a scenic spots throughout the city to allow us a view, but they did not let us descend from the carriages. Everything was shades of pink and red; the buildings, clothing, and landscape blended together until my eyes hurt to look at it. And there was sand everywhere.

Bubblegum pink mountains loomed over the city, stark against a sickly yellow sky. The mountains enclosed the city on all sides but one. At 18:22 Io time, our driver stopped and pointed to a distant volcano. I felt the carriage vibrate and suddenly a giant cloud of blue steam and sand erupted. Against the nauseating yellow background it was a dramatic gash in the sky. As the ash fell, it sparkled from blue to all colors the rainbow before settling into the shades of pink that covered everything.

The driver laughed at my wide-eyed wonder. "You missus must be here for the wife meet tomorrow. It's a handy thing for us men. It's how I met my wife some twenty years gone now. You ladies will get used to it once you've been here a while." He started up the steam carriage again, pulling levers and turning knobs.

We arrived at our hotel and were shown to our suite of rooms by an obsequious host. As we had ridden together, Vanya and I were given the same suite. The sitting room furnishings were tastefully set in tones of beige and grey, with smaller bedrooms off to either side. *Thank the stars it's not pink.*

There was a crank operated speaking tube in one corner, and a child sized clank holding a tray of tea things and light refreshments standing in another. She was meticulously crafted of silver and brass, her tiny joints well-oiled and gleaming. The clockworks in her chest ticked softly like a heartbeat.

"Should you need anything, please let Clatter know," the bellhop gestured to the clank in the corner. "She should be able to help you with most requests."

Vanya smiled, "Thank you, I'm sure we'll be fine."

Unpacking was a matter of moments. Despite the month long journey, I had packed light. The dress my mother sent along took up most of my luggage. I shook my head as I took it out of the trunk and hung it up. Vanya snickered.

"Oh shut up you. It could be worse … it could be pink." I eyed the dress with repugnance. It was lime green with tiers of ruffles cut to look like leaves and a brown corset that resembled nothing so much as the bark of a tree. The corset itself wasn't bad, but when paired with the skirt and my flyaway sable hair, I looked like someone had upended a tree and left its roots sticking out.

"Come on, let's go explore while it's still light out!" I said, hiding the offending article of clothing behind a closet door.

"Sounds like a great idea!" Vanya agreed, taking out a wide brim hat and shoving her hair up under it.

"Did you really get in trouble for impersonating a man?" I asked amused.

"Ah well, it wasn't so much that I was impersonating a man as it was which man I was impersonating." Her eyes turned steely, but then she laughed. "No matter, let's see what this pink planet has to offer."

As we headed for the lobby we were accosted by one of the

attendants. "And where do the young ladies think they're going this evening?" he said in a stern male voice.

I turned and was captured by the red and blue-eyed stare of the hotel lobby attendant. "Why, we thought to explore Aeos some before the light went." I smiled up at him.

"I'm afraid the young ladies are not allowed out of the hotel until after the wife meet tomorrow evening." He smiled down at me kindly. "For your own protection of course. Some of the men can be overly enthusiastic around the time of the wife meet."

"I see. Well perhaps you can direct us to the hotel library then? Or do you have any entertainments planned for this evening?"

"Of course. The library is right through that door, and we will have musicians performing in the hall in about three hours. Thank you for your cooperation ladies." He tipped his hat and watched as I led the way to the library.

Vanya rolled her eyes. "You're going to let someone like him stop you from going out to see the city?"

"No of course not, but there are better ways than arguing loudly in the lobby. There must be a back door somewhere." I started examining the windows in the library. Each of them was either too small to climb through, or had bars on the outside.

"Did you happen to notice if our windows had bars on them?" I asked after my inspection proved fruitless.

"No, I'm afraid I didn't. Let's see if there's a back door first though." She grinned. "I don't mind climbing out of windows, but I'd rather not if I don't have to."

The kitchen entrance was also guarded, as was the side door. Stymied, we returned to our room to discover that there were also bars on our window, which was three floors off the ground. Frustrated, I sat in one of the suite's cushioned chairs as Vanya paced the room. "I don't like being trapped. There's no good reason for bars on a third floor window. First floor, sure to keep vandals out; I could even plausibly see second floor… but third floor—they really want to keep us in," Vanya muttered.

Clatter tottered over to the sitting area and, in a stilted mechanical voice, asked, "Would you care for some tea?"

"No thank you. Clatter, is there a way out of the hotel?" I asked. The construct tipped her head to the side and looked puzzled.

"Well, perhaps they've had girls try to escape before. I mean, I don't know about you, but I had to sign a contract saying I would attend the wife meet—though there was no obligation to choose a man if I didn't find one I liked." I propped my feet on grey silk the hassock.

"I still don't like it," Vanya fumed.

"Well, let's let it ride for tonight and see what happens at the wife meet. Since we have the time, I'm wondering if I can try on a pair of your trousers. I've never had the opportunity, but you always look so comfortable in them." I ran my fingers through my hair, loosening and combing out my braids.

"Oh, fine. Here let me get you a pair to try. I think I have a pair that should fit you, we're about the same size." Following her to her room, decorated in green and gold instead of the muted greys of the sitting room, I stepped behind the modesty screen. I squeaked as a pair of light brown pants sailed over the screen and landed on my head. Slipping them on, I was surprised to find that they fit like a glove. Palms sweating and giggling nervously, I stepped from behind the modesty screen. "What do you think? They're not too... I mean... they're so form fitting. I probably shouldn't...."

"Yes. You should. Think of what your mother will say." Vanya laughed. "Thené, those look so much better on you than they do on me that I'm giving them to you," she smiled. "You should wear them tomorrow instead of that hideous dress."

"I don't think they'd let me in wearing pants. But I could wear them under the skirt and take the skirt off after we've been announced." I blushed at the daring idea.

Vanya laughed. "Okay, we'll do that then. Let's go down to the concert and see what the other girls think of this place. Why don't you change back into your skirt for now?"

I changed quickly, and we headed down to the main ballroom. The other girls were milling about, their high-pitched, fluttery voices echoing in the cavernous space. No one seemed to feel that anything was amiss, so we sat and enjoyed the orchestral concert, commenting on the talent of the clockwork piano player and how it meshed nicely with the tones from the steam organ.

The next morning at breakfast, the hosts of the wife meet gave us our itinerary for the day. We would be touring one of the aether collection stations and returning around 16:00 to get ready for the evening's event.

The steam carriages were waiting for us outside the lobby. Vanya and I chose a different one this time, picking the last carriage in the procession. As we rolled along the pink streets of Aeos, the carriage operator prattled on about the importance of the wife meet to the residents here. Looking out at the streets it finally struck me—there were no women to be seen anywhere. *If they do the wife meet every year, then where are all of the women who stay?* I pondered on that as we rolled toward the aether collection station.

It was an impressive structure, so tall that it pierced the protective wave barrier that surrounded the city. The fence surrounding the station seemed to be only knee high, but as we rolled closer I could see that it was nearly twenty feet tall with row upon row of beautiful plants in front of it. The carriage operator followed my gaze. "Those m'dears, are the moon flowers of Io. Beautiful to be sure, but mean. You stay a good distance away, and you'll be safe."

Through the fence I could see men incased in huge suits of metal, powered by pistons and steam, stomping around the outer yards of the aether station, moving crates, hauling canisters the size of the carriages, and loading them into ships bound for other places in the solar system. Even at this distance the clangor of metal on metal was astounding, and below it all a steady thrumming sound filled the air.

Before we could reach the gates, a steam wagon raced across an intersection cutting through the line of carriages. The steam wagon turned itself sideways across the road. Men, faces covered by loose pieces of cloth, jumped out brandishing swords and cudgels and attacked the first several carriages in our line. Because of the way the road curved, I had an excellent view. The lead carriage was just beyond the intersection and had reached the row first row of flowers. I could hear panicked shrieks from the girls. Without warning the besieged carriage let out a volley of spikes in all directions. The spikes were propelled outwards, mowing down the attacking men. Several were flung back into the moon flowers by the impact.

The plants began thrashing and dipping towards the ground. One man, tried to crawl out of range and I saw a flower dip down, a long, barbed spike extending from its center. It speared the man through the back of the neck and drew him upwards into its petals. Long spine like teeth unfolded and closed on his head. His body thrashed, arms flailing, and after a moment his feet twitched once and he was still.

Bile rose in my throat at the sight, and I looked over at Vanya. She was reaching for the comb in her hair and had a frightened, determined look on her face as she stared out at the attackers.

"Calm down young miss," the carriage operator said, as the entire line of carriages raised and pivoted in place, and then headed back the direction we had come. We were now in the lead carriage.

"What that was all about," I whispered to Vanya.

"I bet they don't tell us," she whispered back.

The carriage operator looked back at us, his eyebrow twitching. "Men fight young miss, sometimes they fight for good reason, sometimes they fight because they're wrongheaded or stupid. Either way, it's not an appropriate sight for young ladies.

We take the job of protecting those that come for the wife meet seriously. A few years back we were less careful and … well, never mind."

"Ooh, tell us!" I begged, shaken and wanting a distraction from the attack.

"Young miss, it is not a pretty story. A few years ago, before that year's wife meet, several of the girls were kidnapped by a … faction I guess you'd call it … of men who live out in the desert. We believe the girls were taken out and made into slaves in their camps, but we don't know for sure. These groups move around and hide out in the sand, and we were not able to find any of the girls. They attack almost every year, but since then, we take great care with security. At any sign of disturbance, we take the girls back to a safe location." He smiled kindly. "We really do our best to ensure your safety and want you to be happy here."

I shuddered. "That's horrible. No one ever found the girls?"

"Sadly no, but it was before I worked for the carriage company so I don't know much more about it." He turned back to watching the road as the carriage trundled on.

We arrived back at the hotel, and the concierge herded us all inside quickly. The girls from the carriages that were attacked were led away in a different direction sobbing. That night, as I prepared for the wife meet, Vanya and I pondered the day's events.

"I have a bad feeling about this evening. What if those men try and attack again?" I twined my sable hair up searching for a pin to hold it.

"Here, use this." Vanya handed me a hairpin very like her own. "I agree. I've got a bad feeling about this evening. Be careful with this. There's a sleeping drug in the tip." She showed me how to twist the ruby on top and a small needle shot out the other end. "A woman should never be unarmed in this day and age. I'll be taking my derringer as well."

I slid into the trousers and strapped my own knife into a calf sheath. It looked decidedly strange when paired with my dancing slippers. Then I turned to the hideous green skirt that Clatter held for me. "Help me get into this thing," I sighed.

Vanya laughed and lifted it over my head. "Arms up dearie, time to get trussed like a spring chicken. Just remember, you volunteered for this."

I groaned as the weight of it settled on my hips, weighing me down. The corset was easier, and Vanya was kind, lacing me not quite as tightly as custom demanded. She giggled.

"Oh shut up," I laughed.

"Well, it's your funeral."

The other girls were all lined up waiting to enter the great hall. Vanya's slim fitting trousers and green embroidered vest attracted no few comments, but mostly they were used to her by now. As we were led onto the stage, a sea of blue and red eyed men, skin strangely pale from lack of true sunlight, were arrayed before us. They cheered, and the musicians started a lively tune. Before any of us could descend and be whirled into the dance, the walls started to shake and vibrate.

A ceiling tile crashed to the floor, then a chandelier. Shards of glass exploded in every direction. Girls screamed, and men cried out as glass struck them. I threw my arm up to protect my eyes just as a giant hole opened in the outer wall and a clank crashed through it. Nearly twenty feet tall, the clank had cages that opened like clamshells instead of hands. Indiscriminately stepping on men as they tried to flee, it approached the stage; it's operator intent on the women there.

"Come ON!" Vanya shouted in my ear. I turned to flee with her and tripped over my skirt, falling heavily.

"Damn I knew that thing would be the death of you," she muttered. She took out her boot knife and started cutting the fabric away.

"Good thing I wore those pants underneath." I shuddered as the clank got closer.

"Come ON!" she shouted again. The clank had reached the

girls and was scooping them up into its basket hands. When it had six girls in each hand, it turned to leave. The remaining girls were running in all directions now, as were the men. Vanya and I watched in horror as several men in burnooses, ends tied loosely over their faces with just their red eyes showing, entered through the hole and started rounding up the rest of the girls, dragging them out while fighting off the few men who had organized and were trying to stop them. Several bodies lay broken and bleeding on the floor, arms, legs, or torso crushed by the clank.

"We have to help those girls," I whispered to Vanya.

'Yes we do. Follow me." She skirted the edge of the chaos heading for the hole created by the clank. We dodged several of the burnoosed men, and Vanya shot one as he ran at us.

Edging past clumps of fighting men and screaming women we made it to the jagged opening. I tripped over chunks of concrete and rock as we scrambled through. My dancing slippers were not intended for this kind of activity. There was a haze of pink dust hanging in the air here, but once clear of the rubble it was easy to follow the giant machine. It towered above most of the buildings in this part of the city. "Do you know how to drive a steam carriage?" I asked, seeing the line of them before us.

She shook her head. "I'm afraid not. Never had the chance to learn."

"Well, now's as good a time as any." I sprinted for the lead carriage. God I love these pants.

Vanya slammed the carriage door as I pushed the start button. "Hang on!" I cried. "I've read about how to do this, but never actually tried it."

The carriage lurched backward crashing into the one behind it. "Oops," I muttered. "Vanya, which way is the clank going?"

She stuck her head out the window. "Due north towards the desert," she yelled back. "It's moving fast."

Working the levers frantically, I got us headed in the right direction. Behind us, men in burnooses streamed out of the building, a half dozen or so carrying girls slung over their shoulder, some firing back into the crowd. They did not appear to be coming our direction.

I levered the steam carriage into gear and shot off in the direction the clank was going. We were gaining on them, but the clank had a large head start. It reached the city's barrier before we did. Gritting my teeth I drove the carriage through the shimmering wave and was surprised when I didn't feel anything as it passed over my skin. The air coming into the carriage became acrid with the smell of sulfur. Before us the pink silicate desert stretched for miles. The clank was pulling further away with each step of its massive stride.

The carriage was not built for driving in the desert. Within an hour the gears started to clog with sand and the wheels turned more slowly.

"Thené, don't you think we should turn back and get help?" Vanya asked.

"You heard the carriage operator this morning. They never found the last girls who were kidnapped. If we turn back now we'll never know where they're being taken," I replied, rubbing grit out of my eyes.

The clank continued its ponderous walk. Either its operator hadn't noticed us following, or didn't care.

As Jupiter rose on the horizon, the carriage ground to a halt, its pistons groaning as it tried to push itself forward. During the trek, Vanya had taken an inventory of the carriage. It had an emergency stash of blankets and air filters as well as a few canteens of liquid supplement and a pistol. I strapped the pistol on, since Vanya still had her own.

"They can't be going too much further. The girls don't have air filters, and presumably they want them alive." I searched the carriage for other useful items. *Gods I can't believe we ran off into the desert. If we survive this ....*

The ground trembled beneath us as one of the distant

volcanoes erupted, spewing blue and multicolored ash into the sky.

As the ash from the volcano started settling in our area, we slid the air filters over our faces and set off across Io's deserted landscape. The clank was still visible; it's bulk backlit by Jupiter. It seemed to have stopped when the volcano erupted.

The landscape glowed eerily in the dim light. The desert wasn't lifeless; there were a variety of shrub like plants, hard to make out in the dark of Io's night. Walking on the shifting sands was draining, but as the night progressed so did we. Jupiter was setting when Vanya called a halt.

"Thené, I think we're getting close. We need to rest for a few hours before we reach them, and I'd suggest doing it while it's still dark." She plunked down on the sand exhausted.

"I agree, and I don't know about you, but I'm a little worried about how we're going to get all of those girls back to Aeos. They were all wearing ball gowns and slippers as I recall." I unrolled my blanket and made a hollow in the sand. "Sleep for a few hours then get back on our way?"

She nodded, taking a swig of her liquid supplement.

As Jupiter set and Ganymede rose, a soft clicking noise woke me from sleep. In the blue light of Ganymede, I could see that we were surrounded by sand crabs. The giant crustaceans were larger than a horse, their bodies armored and jointed, oblong with two antennae at one end, the other tapering down to a rounded point. They seemed more curious than aggressive, surrounding our small campsite at a respectful distance and waving their antennae back and forth.

I shook Vanya awake whispering, "How much do you know about sand crabs?"

"Why?" She shook her head groggily.

"Open your eyes and sit up slowly," I whispered. "Don't scream."

That seemed to get her attention. She jumped to her feet,

startling me, and the nearest of the creatures. It vanished in a cloud of sand.

"Shhh. I think they may be friendly," I cautioned. "Maybe they can take us to the camp."

"You're mad!" she hissed back.

I rose and approached the nearest of the sand crabs, holding my hands out in front of me, trying to mimic the motions of their antennae. It undulated backward, and I stopped, hands still out.

Remaining still, I tried not to flinch as the sand crab slithered forward, almost within arm's length. Its antennae bent and brushed my forehead. I got a feeling of questioning gentleness and I squeaked in surprise. It dove under the sand, sending up a shower of pink silicate, and the other crabs did the same.

I turned to look at Vanya, "Did you feel that? That was unexpected. I wonder if they'll come back."

Her eyes were locked behind me. "Yes, I rather think they will."

Feeling the light touch of antennae against my back, and an unnatural calm I turned to look. The curious crab had returned. I reached out with a hand and touched the antennae in return. It undulated backwards again, but not as far, and waited. Approaching it slowly I extended my hand. It bumped one of the antennae against it, wrapping around in a surprisingly dexterous caress.

"Well hello there. You seem friendly." I tried not to squirm as the creature's antennae stroked up and down my arm. An image of the desert and two figures trekking through it formed in my thoughts with a questioning air.

"Wait, you can communicate?"

The sand crab's antennae caressed the side of my face.

"Can you take us to the clank? I formed a picture of the giant clank in my mind.

It guided my hand over to its shell and indicated that I should climb up.

Shrugging I looked at Vanya. "It seems we've found a ride. Are you coming?"

She nodded, staring at the creatures with wide eyes as she gathered our blankets.

I turned back to the hulking creature. It waved its antennae at me encouragingly. I started climbing up the edge of its shiny, plated back, finding that the ridges made this easy. Vanya joined me on the creature's wide back. At the top there were two smaller ridges of bone, not visible from the ground. Looking for a place to hang on to, I grabbed them. The land crab took off like it was shot out of a cannon. Grabbing for Vanya as she slid down the side of the crab's shell, I let go of the ridges, and the creature slowed to an undulating amble.

"Are you ok?" I pulled Vanya back up to the top of the shell.

"Just a bit shaken. Warn me next time, will you?" she laughed nervously. "Okay, how do we steer?"

The crab's antennae twitched back at us, and I got an impression that I should not touch the ridges again. It took off at a more moderate pace toward the clank, still visible on the horizon. Behind us, the other crabs in the pod followed. Within half an hour, the kidnapper's camp came into view, the giant clank standing in the middle, its cages empty.

"Will you wait for us?" I touched the sand crab, picturing an image of girls atop the backs of each of the other land crustaceans.

It dipped its antennae in what I hoped was assent. After we slid down its shell, the creatures dove under the sand with just their antennae showing where they were.

Vanya and I crawled up a ridge of sand and peered down on the camp. The place crawled with unusual clockwork creations. Most looked cobbled together from spare parts that would fall apart if you sneezed too hard. Many of them bristled with improvised weapons. The tents surrounding the camp looked ragged and worn, and pink sand had settled on the fabric making them almost invisible. The girls were nowhere in sight.

We watched until Jupiter rose in the sky again. In addition to the clanks, we counted twelve men. One stood guard outside a tent and was periodically relieved by another. I wriggled over to Vanya. "That must be where they're keeping the girls," I whispered.

She nodded agreement.

"If we wait until Jupiter is high, then we can sneak around the back of the tent, and get the girls out." I examined the camp further. "Lead the girls over that ridge and get them on the sand crabs. I'll create a diversion on the other side of the camp to give you time."

"I'll wait for your signal. We're going to have to do this fast. How are we going to take out that clank?"

"I don't think we can. We didn't exactly bring any explosives with us." I started wriggling back down the dune. "Wait for my signal. I'll try and be obvious."

Working my way along the ridge of the sand dune, I crept to the opposite end of the camp. It wasn't a great plan. I hope we don't all die. We're probably all going to die. I hope those clanks are as poorly put together as they look.

On this edge of camp, I saw a bored looking sentry standing watch. He was grubby with sand, and he hadn't bathed in far too long. The gentle breeze wafted his stench in my direction, and I wrinkled my nose in distaste. Taking the hairpin Vanya had given me, I crawled slowly across the sand, thankful that it muffled sound. Providence was with me. As the sentry started to turn my direction a noise from the camp distracted him. Heart racing, I ran the last few yards and jabbed him with the hairpin.

*Please work, please work, please work.* He sank to the sand without a sound. I relieved him of his pistols and a staff. It was taller than I was, made from some lightweight, sturdy cane. He had been standing at the back of one of the smaller tents. Listening for a moment, I cut a small hole in the canvas and looked inside. It was empty except for an air filter, several bedrolls and a stove. Slicing a hole big enough to step through, I entered.

The stove was already lit, making my job easier. Grabbing a shirt lying on one of the bedrolls, I wadded it up and stuck the end of it in the stove until it caught fire. As the tent filled with smoke, I set it next to the tent wall, thankful for my air mask. Within moments the flames were creeping up the canvas. I picked up the shirt with a pair of tongs and exited through the slit in the back, carrying the flaming ball of cloth to the next tent. The smoke was starting to sting my eyes as I left the flaming remains of the shirt charring a hole in the edge of the second tent.

Someone raised the alarm, and clanks and men converged on the fire. *I hope that gives Vanya enough time!* Trying to keep the remaining tents between myself and the kidnappers, I made my way around the edge of the camp. While crossing an open space between two of the larger tents I heard another cry behind me. Turning to look, I saw one of the men pointing in my direction. Several of the clanks broke away from fighting the fire and raced across the sandy open space.

I pointed the pilfered pistol at the group of oncoming clanks and fired. The unexpected recoil threw me back into the sand where I lay momentarily stunned. Using both hands, I took careful aim at the lead clank and fired. Its head exploded in a shower of springs and coils. The one next to it however seemed un-phased. I took aim at the second and fired, the bullet passing harmlessly through its mesh casing and glancing off the one behind it. The barrel-like clank was quickly closing the gap between us, so I stood, grabbed my pole, and ran for the ridge. The clank grabbed my hair before I had gone even ten yards. I jerked out of the clank's grasp, taking its arm with me and losing a handful of hair in the process.

They really are that poorly put together!

More boldly now, I turned and swatted at it with the pole. It impacted with the clank's middle and a few gears popped out the back.

I thwacked it harder and felt wood connect with metal, as I dodged the clank's other arm. A leg went flying and the thing toppled over, raising one of its arms and sending a dart flying my direction. I dodged and smashed its head with the end of my pole. More of the clanks had circled around behind me, cutting off my escape. The fire was keeping most of the kidnappers busy, and it seemed to have spread beyond the two tents to ones further down the line. Ahead of me I could see the outline of the giant clank, motionless now without its operator.

I ran, aiming for the ladder that extended down its leg. Panting, I jumped for the lowest rung, caught the rough metal and pulled myself up. Somewhere I had lost my air filter. Gulping in the acrid air and coughing, I climbed, making for the operator's station in the clank's chest. The central operator's station was small, no more than an arm's span wide with buttons, levers and pressure gages on every surface of the dim interior.

*Well I can't hide here forever! When in doubt, push buttons!* Starting at the main console, if it could be pushed, pulled, switched or levered I made sure to do so. The giant clank swung its arms, cages clacking together with large booming sounds, its feet started moving, walking backward. Dimly over the noise I could hear men shouting. The pressure gauges were inching from yellow to red. *Oops! Time to go!*

It was harder to climb down while the clank was moving. Each step jolted through my arms and legs, and I held on for dear life, the metal of the rungs cutting into my palms. As I neared the bottom of the ladder, there was a whooshing sound, and the clank's main body exploded outward, throwing me out into the desert sands in a hail of twisted metal.

Hitting the ground hard, I felt ribs snap as I went rolling through the fine sand. I must have blacked out for a moment or two. When I woke, the rain of metal and twisted shards had ended. Coughing the fine sand out of my lungs, I stood, nearly blacking out again from the pain as I stumbled in the direction of the rendezvous spot.

Vanya, if that wasn't enough of a signal then you weren't paying attention.

The clank had taken me further than I realized as I stumbled over the second sand dune and still saw no sign of the camp, the girls, Vanya, or the sand crabs. The pain from my broken ribs and bruised body was becoming unbearable, and I fell as I crested the ridge, rolling down the other side.

When I woke I was surrounded by sand crabs, each with a girl on its back. *Oh thank heavens.*

"Thené, can you stand?" I heard Vanya ask.

"Um … stand yes … walk, not very far," I whispered. I tried standing and gasped at the stabbing pain.

"You think you can ride one of these darlings if we go double and I hold on to you?" She gestured to her sand crab.

"I'll make it work. Help me up." I gritted my teeth as she boosted me onto the slick shell of the crab.

We made it back to Aeos, though I don't remember much of the trip, just the feeling of Vanya's arms holding me against the strange motion of the crab. We discovered the crabs wouldn't enter the area affected by the wave, so Vanya slid off and caught me as I came down, the girls sliding off their own crabs. The townsmen were milling around at the edge of town trying to organize a search party. They stared openmouthed as we stumbled into town. The elderly carriage operator was there and called for a doctor and carriages to transport us all.

They took us to a hotel—a different one without bars on the windows—and gave us rooms. I was ready to just pass out on the bed, but the doctor insisted on seeing to my ribs, and an attendant was drawing a bath. The Doctor pronounced my ribs fractured, wrapped them tightly and prescribed rest for a few days with only light activity. The other girls were being seen to, but I had sustained the worst of the injuries he assured me.

I really want a bath. I really don't want to move. The bed will get sand in it. I don't care. And I still wonder –where are all of the women from past wife meets?

Sinking into the cloudlike softness of the bed I was almost asleep when I heard Vanya ask, "So, Thené, what world should we conquer next? They'll do anything to get us off planet at this point."

I smiled. "Let's discuss it in the morning."

# APPRENTICE IN THE STEAM LIBRARY

### Daniel Ausema

J OSSIAN arranged an old, hard-covered manual on her chair so she could sit high enough. Then with a steadying breath to prepare herself for the day's patrons, she flipped the toggle at her assigned desk. With a hiss of released air, the shutter over the window pulled up into the ceiling. A line of people already waited. Beyond them, the open doors of the library showed that the sun had yet to rise, but the gas-lit street cobbles were plainly visible. Steam cars and beetle-drawn carriages rushed past.

"I am Assistant Jossian," she said to the first in line, trying to sound older than her eleven years. "What can I retrieve for you?"

The slight man wore a riding cap, which he left on even as he spoke to her, and his long coat had been brushed to a gleam. "Beetle training. Manual 1374."

"Coming right up." Jossian pressed a sequence of switches. The librarian construct on its tracks behind her came to life with a hiss and a whirr of gears and rattled off down one of the library's passageways. While they waited for the machine to return, Jossian asked, "A new shipment of beetles coming in?"

The man raised one eyebrow and then shut his eyes. She could read that look, almost as if his face were a manual in the library. It said that she was just a little girl, just an apprentice who certainly knew nothing of the city's vaunted riding beetles.

"No," he said at last, and nothing more until the librarian returned, a thick, metal-bound manual in its pincer hand.

Jossian opened the book to the punch card inside. The man handed her his punch card, and she lined them up to shine the record onto photographic paper. As she did, she looked more closely at the manual. "Beetle training" was accurate, as far as it went, but the manual specifically dealt with grounding a mount that had been accustomed to flight.

Sometimes it was necessary for an older beetle's health to ground it, clip its wings and keep it for pulling transoms and carriages. More often, an owner tired of the novelty of flight, and chose to clip a perfectly healthy beetle. Clipped beetles could be irascible and often lived shorter lives, but if controlled, they were much faster than beetles that had never flown.

What an ugly fact of their city. Jossian frowned and quickly covered the frown with a cough. The last thing an apprentice in the library should do was show revulsion for any book requested by a patron. Such behavior was beneath her.

She darted a look at the man to see if he'd caught her frown— or if he showed any shame for the request—but he was looking over his shoulder at the street outside.

"Here it is, sir. Manual 1374. You'll need to return it or—"

"Yes, I know how it works." He grabbed the thick book and punch card from her hands and left.

Jossian forced a smile as the next patron approached. The woman wore the sturdy clothes of a factory overseer and had her card already out.

Before Jossian could greet her, Master Koosz came up from

behind and leaned through the window, one hand held out. "This window is closed. You may go to the next available assistant." Then he pulled the shutter down.

Swiveling to face him, Jossian cocked her head. "Master?"

Master Koosz stepped back so his large belly was not pressed against her chair, and gestured for her to follow. As he walked away, his somber, library master robes swayed like a fluid entity, wrapping around him as if of its own volition. One of the library's two masters, he oversaw the apprentices in the morning until Jossian's aunt, the stern Master Onnia, took over.

Onnia herself was waiting for Jossian and Koosz when they reached the back room. Her robes were smudged with the grease of working deep in the library. Without preamble she told Jossian, "Librarian three is acting up. Again. I can't get deep enough into the mechanism to see what's wrong, so I need you to go check."

"Yes, Aunt—I mean, Master." She glanced up at Koosz to see if there were any instructions from him, but he waved her onward.

Onnia called to her as she went, "If I can get one of the auxiliaries running, I'll send that out, see if it can narrow down the problem. But you'll need to be there to fix things, anyway." The auxiliaries were even less reliable than the regular constructs, their wiring and clockwork from an earlier era of the library. Jossian wouldn't expect much help from that.

The library proper was not made for people to visit. The librarian constructs ran on their network of tracks back among the books and retrieved what was needed, each of the constructs assigned to a section of the library with its own passages and lines of books. Constructs, though, were much smaller than people and made to fit into narrow spaces and low hallways. Like the children who worked in the city's factories, Jossian and the other apprentices were the ones sent in to those passageways when something went wrong.

Hanging on the wall were several sabretaches full of tools and other gear. Jossian grabbed one and crawled into three's passage.

The construct was stuck just a few paces down, but if the problem were there, Onnia would have fixed it herself. It was vaguely human-shaped. A head served to scan the coded shelves for the right books. When a librarian acted up, the head was usually where the problem began. Some anomaly along the tracks had confused its gears, and it would refuse to move until the anomaly was fixed. One arm with a pincer hand could carry a single title. The second arm was fixed horizontally and could balance multiple volumes. Its base included the mechanism that drove it along the library tracks.

The fit beside the construct was tight enough that Jossian had to squeeze past, and as she scraped through, her leg became pinned. When she yanked, the construct rolled a click forward, sending a burst of pain up her leg. She bit back a scream. An apprentice shouldn't react to pain. Easy to think, harder to do.

Once she was sure the construct had frozen in place, Jossian carefully pushed her leg back, feeling the rivets dig into the skin beneath her thin pant leg. She closed her eyes against the pain and pushed harder. At last she tumbled through and lay panting in the passage beyond.

Waves of pain washed up her leg. She should go back, get it bandaged. Did she really want to have to go back and forth past the construct, though? She turned halfway around and stared out into the light. No. Better to just tough it out, get the librarian working and get back out to her real work. A good apprentice didn't turn back so soon just because of a scrape.

Only the light that shone past the construct illuminated the passage. Jossian crawled into the darkness, hearing the hiss of steam pipes beside her. When she'd first come to the library, Jossian had thought of the constructs as the librarians, and everything else as the library, but really these tracks and the coded bumps that directed the constructs were as much the librarian as the more animate-seeming construct.

Even crawling, she limped, and soon her crawl was a three-limbed shuffle, with the injured leg dragging behind.

At the first intersection, Jossian dropped down onto a lower track. Widely spaced lights, powered by the library's steam generator, flipped on. Onnia must be doing what she could from her end to make Jossian's search easier. Good. If only she could send a bandage too. Or a pain tincture.

She pulled herself along, watching the identical spines of the books pass by. The pale metal of the covers blurred, one into the next. Manuals on the specs for every imaginable type of boiler. Manuals on the construction and maintenance of carriages and steam wagons. Those for factory owners on presses of all shapes and on dealing with angry workers. On textile mills and the least necessities for the weavers who slaved inside. The books she passed might be any of those, and the only way she would know would be to pull one out and read inside. Each one was stamped with a number, no more, and the bumps beside the track told the constructs what book it would find, but not her.

After another split in the tunnel, Jossian noticed something lying beside the track. An obstacle. Could easily cause the glitchy construct to become unmoored. Something easy to fix, and she could go back up. She hadn't realized how much she was hating the cramped passageway until she thought about leaving it.

The object was a book. Not a manual, though, as the steam libraries used the term to distinguish regular books from the types they lent out—not a uniform shape like the others, and covered in sturdy paper, rather than metal. It was skinnier and not as tall, and on its spine was a title in actual words. She picked it up and carried it to the next dim light bulb. There were stories inside, a serial that looked to have been collected from a newspaper, made-up stuff about agitators and malcontents, as far as Jossian's skimming showed her. An interesting find, certainly, and if it had stayed where it was, it might have eventually caused the librarian to break down.

It was not, however, the cause of the current breakdown. The constructs, and especially number three, were well beyond their years and easily tripped up, but not usually over something quite that small. She put the book in her sabretache and crawled back the way she'd come.

After a few minutes she reached a steep stairs leading upward. A remnant of an earlier, pre-librarian library, she'd always supposed, since no tracks led up it.

Her leg buckled when she tried to climb. With her eyes closed, she summoned enough strength in her arms to hop on her good leg from step to rung-like step. She didn't open her eyes until she fell across the floor of the alcove at the top.

The room tilted dizzily as she caught her breath. Then she was able to see the close shelves, lined with books of all sizes, covered in cloth or paper or crumbling leather. Not a single one had a number stamped on its spine. Not one of them was a bland, put-the-wires-here manual. The wall behind the shelf was a mass of twisting pipes from the boiler below.

The room had been in use by other apprentices long before Jossian found it. Perhaps even her aunt and Master Koosz had once climbed up there to leave behind the odd books they found—remnants, like the stairs, of an earlier library.

Jossian ran her fingers lightly over the books, pulled down a favorite to gaze at its colors. Then she set it down and turned the new book over in her hands. It definitely wasn't one she'd seen before. It must have been wedged among the manuals, hidden for years before it recently came free. The thought made her forget the pain in her leg, and she stretched out to read a few pages of the new book.

No one spoke of the history of the library, so Jossian had come up with her own guesses. It must have once been a general library for people to come and read, full of the kinds of books still sold, used, in little stands along the harbor. Then some great inventor came up with the librarian constructs to make the library work easier. They could effortlessly re-shelve books, freeing up the human librarians for other work. What exactly that other work had been, Jossian wasn't sure.

Over time, more and more of the library work passed to the constructs. For them, uniform manuals made the work easier, so the books were replaced volume by volume until only these few old-fashioned books remained, lost. The old stacks, shelves like those in this little room, were divided and subdivided into passages that made the work more efficient. No need to climb up and down or reach high and low, but only run along on their tracks.

But how had this little room escaped all that? Here Jossian's imagination faltered. Had the constructs themselves taken over the construction of the tracks and passages? That might explain it. The machines might have been programmed in a way that made them miss the ladder and the little room. Or maybe some subversive human engineer had willfully left it behind. For Jossian and other apprentices like her.

Her leg felt better by the time Jossian climbed down. Not entirely healed, but not so stiff. Maybe it was no more than the calming effect of sitting in that room and reading old books. It was her refuge from the rest of the work in those rare times when she could go there and hide away for a short while.

Crawling made a dull throb return to the leg, not enough to slow her down. She pulled herself through the passages again, in search of anything that might cause the librarian to malfunction.

After a half dozen cramped passages, Jossian heard the clinking sound of a construct. Was it one of the other librarians, their noise traveling through the walls from their own, separate passages? It seemed to be moving back and forth, which no librarian construct would do—they only traveled to their destination and straight back to the desk. Maybe her aunt had managed to get one of the auxiliaries to work. Jossian tried to follow the sound.

Her palms were sore from crawling by the time she saw the

construct. An auxiliary librarian, as she'd guessed. It took note of her, the lens of its camera-obscura eye flashing in the lamp light. On the wall it shone an image of a message, in her aunt's precise hand.

Using the auxiliary and some other tools, Onnia had narrowed down where in the library the damage was. One of several lower levels, way on the edge of the library, where the books sometimes had frost on cold days. Jossian punched in an acknowledgment and sent the auxiliary back.

The edge of the library was hot today. She thought the sun must be beating directly on that wall, and wished she could see the sun herself. She was so rarely allowed outside the library during daytime hours, and even when she was, the sky was almost invariably overcast or spitting drizzle.

Jossian found nothing on the first level she tried and climbed down just below that. On the third level she finally noticed something odd. The books on one small stretch of shelf had fallen onto the track. Pushed, it looked like. She went closer. There was a break in the wall behind the books, a narrow gap that led to the outside.

Training an overhead lamp behind the scattered books, Jossian saw the reason for both the crack in the wall and the broken librarian. A nest of giant beetles, right on the tracks. No wonder the construct had refused to continue. It must have come this way for something, come across the refuse and broken track, and returned to the entrance in a huff. Or whatever the construct version of a huff was. Its gears steamed. A half dozen beetles waved their feelers at her light and clicked their mandibles.

Jossian didn't run, or rather the crawling equivalent of running. She was proud of that fact, and that she didn't scream either. She was an apprentice in the library—screaming and running were surely beneath her.

As she forced herself to stay calm, she noticed the beetles weren't anywhere near full-size riding beetles. These were runts, or a related species that didn't grow as big. Still, the smallest was larger around than her head and almost half as big, and those mandibles looked frighteningly large.

She breathed carefully and assessed her choices. The beetles would have to go. A master would say they must be exterminated. She carried a number of tools with her, though none was ideal for the task. Killing them struck her as unnecessarily cruel.

A stable would be the place to send them. Even if they remained small, a trainer might rig them to a miniature carriage for entertainment.

She sorted through her gear for what she might need to capture them, but the thoughts kept coming. In a stable, someone would clip their wings, undoubtedly. Jossian thought of the raspy-voiced patron who'd come to her that morning. Mean, little man. She pulled out a sack and spread it out as big as it would go. Too small, but maybe enough for three or four of them. Then she'd need a second sack. Or else she'd have to come back another time.

That didn't seem right, clipping their wings needlessly. They needed a place to stay, just like she had when she'd climbed that ladder. A place to be safe, but not a stable where they'd be clipped. She looked at the space around the beetles. If she could only....

Jossian pawed through her gear, pulling out wrenches of various shapes and a stubby screwdriver. The shelves here, as in most of the steam library, included manuals no one ever checked out. Old law, long since superseded, instructions for obsolete machinery, and the like. She found a half dozen manuals so covered with dust she knew they couldn't have been retrieved since Onnia was an apprentice. Pulling them open, she created a box around the hole in the outside wall. The covers overlapped, with the papers facing in toward the nest. She screwed those together to form a sturdy wall. Then she screwed the tops of the manuals to the top of the shelf, leaving an opening to get the beetles all inside.

It made a good-sized space, wider and deeper than she would have suspected, though there was nothing she could do about the height. The pages, she supposed, would soon be torn into shreds to line the space.

Before closing the rear, she had to get the beetles inside. She took a deep breath. What would those jaws feel like, if they closed around her hand? What would she do if they skittered closer, pushing their way into her clothes or climbing up onto her face? Was screaming or running away actually beneath her after all?

*Yes, it was.* She pulled her apprentice uniform straight, ignoring the grease stains that covered it, and closed in on the beetles. Using the final book she swept them toward the box and the outside light. The clicking of their mandibles grew louder in protest, but they obliged. Hands shaking, she screwed the last book into place.

They wouldn't get through that. The building itself might have holes in its structure, but those manuals would hold anything out. She tightened a few of the screws as she admired the work. Her fingers regained their steadiness.

The beetles would live. Maybe have some babies, but probably not. From what she'd heard, the city's beetles never reproduced here, only far to the south. They'd fly, when they chose to fly, and find this place away from the streets when they needed it. She brushed her hands on her shirt and sat back.

The box jutted out into the passage. With her wrenches, she disassembled the tracks and shifted them around the box. The displaced manuals, the ones the beetles had pushed from the shelf, would need re-shelving, and the coding for that was beyond what her tools could do. She gathered them up to take with her.

They'd probably have to remove the construct's central spring, let it unwind fully, and then wind it up again to get it moving. But now it wouldn't simply start into the passages and shut down again. Maybe her aunt could pull the construct back out the other way to do that work, so Jossian wouldn't have to push past it. The thought made the dull ache of her leg return.

The library would be fine, even with the track adjustment. Librarian construct number three would click on past, none the wiser, its gears and circuits unconcerned with the narrowing of the passage. And the manuals, all but the old dusty ones she'd made into a box, would be available to the library's patrons.

Already as she left, Jossian knew she wouldn't tell the masters what the problem had been. A fallen shelf, that might work. She'd fixed it, but it had been overloaded—the books she carried must be shelved in a new location. It was believable, something a good steam library apprentice might have done.

Merely a good apprentice was beneath Jossian's ambition.

# EGGS FULL OF FLAME

### K. C. Shaw

**T**HE TOWN of Mattaph sprawled over a knob of hill like a blanket tossed over a bedpost. As she set her airship down in the hilltop airfield, Jo hoped it would prove as picturesque as it appeared from above.

She strolled down the narrow street, her green walking dress fluttering in the breeze. Her friend Lizzy slouched alongside with her hands jammed in her coat pockets. Evening light turned their shadows dark and long; the western sky blushed pink.

"The houses at the very top are lovely, aren't they?" Jo said, although she was disappointed in the town after all. It reminded her of home, and not in a good way: the same old tea-shops and grocers, harried women with their arms full of parcels, overladen wagons making deliveries. She preferred to end the day's excursion on a more interesting note.

"I suppose." Lizzy glowered at the nearest mansion as though its owner had once wronged her. Parts of its roof were blackened and patched over with pale new boards. "Looks like they had a fire up here recently. Let's get something to eat."

Jo almost suggested they fly to the coast for supper. It was only a few hours away and the moon was nearly full, so they'd have light. Besides, she loved flying at night. But Lizzy pointed at a building on the corner that raised Jo's spirits.

"I didn't think we'd find a *dhaba* this far from Imza," Jo said. Odd that she had loathed their stay in the mountain country, but now missed the open-fronted taverns so common there.

"I hope the food isn't as burnt as that house."

"Another one?" Jo glanced at the charred wreck above the dhaba. It had probably once been the grandest of Mattaph's mansions, perched on a bluff overlooking the entire town. "The people here need to install gaslights. Much safer than candles or oil lamps."

"There's a third." Lizzy pointed at a house with burnt timbers visible through a half-collapsed roof. "Perhaps they angered the gods."

Lizzy was from the country and had odd notions about how the gods acted, so Jo did not reply. She just led the way into the dhaba. She smelled beer and grilling meat, sweaty bodies, onions, and smoke from the big fireplace. Men and women sat at tables to talk and eat, their children playing on the floor. It was all so marvelously different compared to the rest of the town.

The single room was crowded. Jo and Lizzy found seats at the end of a bench, although it was a squeeze. Jo smiled around at everyone at the table and was pleased when they smiled back: a mix of people, from a well-dressed woman with skin almost the same shade brown as Jo's to a couple of tanned laborers with dirty fingernails.

The well-dressed woman said, "I am Trenna. You're not from here?"

"I'm Jo, and this is Lizzy. We stopped by on our way to the seaside. Mattaph is a charming town."

Beside her, Lizzy muttered into her beer, "Except for the fires."

Jo elbowed her friend, but Trenna had heard. Fortunately she only smiled wryly and said, "The fires are not from carelessness, I assure you. A dragon lives on Jarva Mountain and began visiting us a few months ago. Once we discovered it was only trying to feed its babies, we have had no more fires. We leave milk and cakes out for it, and the babies creep about and eat, then leave with their mother."

Lizzy nodded, looking impressed. Jo said, "Milk and *cakes*? For dragonets?"

"Special oat cakes," Trenna said, "sweetened with honey. Good for babies."

Jo held her tongue with difficulty. Sometimes she thought she was the only person in the entire world who read books on naturalism.

They ordered a meal that turned out to be so good, Jo was glad they'd stopped in Mattaph after all. "What do the dragon babies look like?" she asked Trenna.

"I haven't seen them. I know they are small."

The man sitting next to Jo said, "They look like little dogs with wings, almost. Some are white and some are blue. Their eyes shine in the dark."

Jo took a bite of rice mixed with crisp strips of pastry, which had come with their mutton. She had never heard dragonets described as doglike, no matter what species of dragon. But as far as she knew, dragons and their kin were the only fire-breathing creatures in the world.

"Where is Jarva Mountain? Which direction?" she asked.

\* \* \*

It was dark when they returned to the airfield. The nearly full moon lay fat and orange on the horizon.

Lizzy said, "We're not going after a dragon, are we? We've only got one cannon."

"I just want to look at it. We won't go anywhere near it."

"Jo! The *Snowflake* is not fireproof."

Jo glanced at Lizzy. She was tall and thin and pale, and she wore men's clothes most of the time and liked horses and had once been a highwayman. They were practically opposites in every way. But she was also Jo's friend.

Jo said. "I don't think we'd be in any danger, but if you think it's too much of a risk we can fly on to the coast instead."

Lizzy looked astonished, which gave Jo a pang of guilt. Jo was more willful than her friend and usually got her own way. That should change.

"Thanks," Lizzy said. "I'll get the boiler started."

The *Snowflake* was a dual-prop airship with twin balloon envelopes made of air-spider silk. The peaked wing above the envelopes made her nimble, the efficient coal-burning boiler made her fast, and the white-painted rattan gondola made her innocent-looking—although inside she carried a forearm-length cannon, pistols, sabers, and a towel painted with skull and crossbones as a flag.

But Jo and Lizzy were on holiday from pirating. They'd spent the last week lounging by the seaside sipping rum drinks, and occasionally going on an excursion to see the countryside.

It took fifteen or twenty minutes for the boiler to inflate the *Snowflake*'s envelopes. Jo always took the opportunity to check the propellers and engine, even when they had been flying with no problems all day. Part of that was caution; most of it was a love of tinkering with machinery.

"Ready," Lizzy called. She had put on her gloves and goggles; Jo hastily did the same and jammed her leather aviator's cap over her springy hair. The *Snowflake* rocked on her wheels, ready to lift into the sky.

Jo turned to the airship's controls with a grin of pure joy. Nothing was better than flying. Nothing.

The air smelled of autumn: smoke, falling leaves, frost. Jo started the props, and their roar filled her head despite the earflaps on her cap.

She guided the *Snowflake* out of her slip and down the dirt runway, faster and faster. The ship skipped and bounced on the uneven ground. Then she was airborne.

Jo laughed. The wind slapped into the open gondola, snapping her skirt and stinging her cheeks. Mattaph fell away below and the hills of central Hule spread out to the horizon like a rumpled blanket.

A few steps behind her in the small gondola, Lizzy shoveled coal into the boiler. Jo slowed the props so they could cruise at about forty knots. That was slow enough to enjoy the trip, fast enough that they would arrive at their tiny coastal village at a reasonable time.

Jo looked east and saw Jarva Mountain. It wasn't really a mountain, just another knob like Mattaph's that rose above the lower hills.

She wondered if she would ever learn what kind of creature was visiting Mattaph, and if it might be some hitherto undiscovered type of dragon. She was making notes of all the strange creatures she and Lizzy encountered on their travels. One day she would present her work to the Naturalists' Institute of Amprad, and they would make her an honorary life member.

Lizzy said, "Ship at three o'clock. Looks like it might be a big ornithopter heading back to town. Want to take it?"

"We're on holiday, and ornithopters aren't really worth the effort." Jo squinted into the distance but didn't see a ship. Then again, Lizzy's eyesight was much better than hers. She grabbed the spyglass.

Ornithopters were peculiar craft, usually one-seaters with bicycle-like pedals and elaborate networks of chains and gears to power the wings. Jo raised her eyebrows at the sight of this one, though. It was bigger than usual and looked homemade, as so many of them were. It resembled a rowboat with two pairs of wings, but had what looked like a wicker horsehead attached to the bow. A fan-shaped tail on the stern acted as a rudder.

"How peculiar," Jo said. "Take a look." She passed the glass to Lizzy.

Lizzy made a "hmm" noise. "I wouldn't want to board her even if she was full of gold. She's turning our way."

"I'm not slowing down for a junker. I don't care what she wants." Jo patted the *Snowflake*'s dash before going back to the controls. The night was still with scarcely a breath of wind.

"Must take a lot of leg-power to run those wings," Lizzy said, then gasped as though something had stung her.

Jo glanced at her. "What's wrong?"

"Just the pilot. As soon as he came in view, he smiled—exactly as though he could see me. It made me feel peculiar."

"Well, he can't catch up to us by pedaling, and I don't see a motor on that thing."

Lizzy's voice, already deep, turned lugubrious when she said, "His face is white like moonlight. I don't like him."

Jo started to say something sharp—Lizzy could be superstitious at times, which Jo hated—but remembered she needed to treat her friend more fairly. "You can put a cannonball across her bow if you like. I guarantee the pilot will stop smiling then."

Lizzy hung up the spyglass, and a moment later Jo heard the shovel scrape in the coal. "We'll just ignore him. He'll be over the horizon behind us soon."

Jo tried to go back to enjoying the flight, but her thoughts kept straying to the ornithopter. How odd that someone would attach a figurehead to an already ungainly craft. And why a horsehead instead of a flying creature, the way ships had mermaid and dolphin mastheads?

Unless someone wanted their winged craft to resemble a dragon.

It was absurd—but possible. Before their spot of trouble in Imza, Jo and Lizzy had owned a flamethrower. It was only handheld, but when fully charged it could send a gout of fire more than thirty feet. One mounted on a ship, with a barrel of paraffin to draw from, might easily burn down a mansion.

She imagined a sudden jet of flame in the night, a glimpse of a dark winged shape with horse-like head—then panic and chaos. Of course people had blamed a dragon. But why would anyone do such a wicked thing?

She unhooked the spyglass and leaned out for another look at the ornithopter.

It had *gained* on them somehow—gained a lot. Jo focused the glass.

She saw the moon-white face that had so disturbed Lizzy. The man's eyes were nothing but round shadows, his lips crimson even in the darkness.

He smiled and raised his hand as though waving at her. Jo shuddered. "He's even paler than you," she said to Lizzy.

"Did he smile?"

"Yes, and I see what you meant." Jo didn't mention how close the ornithopter had come. "Let's speed right up and leave him far behind."

As she spoke, she saw faint lights rise from the junker. Some were white and some were blue, but all sped toward the *Snowflake*. Jo focused the glass on one.

A moment later she dropped the glass. It rolled across the floor. "Prepare for boarders!"

"What? What do you mean?"

Jo pushed the props to full. They roared, and the ship gave a stomach-rolling porpoise as it sped up. "I think they're some kind of fairy-dog—not dragonets at all."

"What?"

"Fairy-dogs! After us!"

Jo knew very little about fairies. They had never interested her. She regretted her lack of foresight—she should have known better than to leave gaps in her knowledge.

Lizzy shoveled fast, then leaped for the picnic hamper they used as an armory. But before she could even lift their little cannon out, much less load it, the first dogs caught up to them.

They hovered around the ship like a cloud of midges. Since the *Snowflake* had accelerated to her top speed, that meant the dogs were pacing her at eighty knots. They were each about the size of a rabbit, with sleek fur, sharp ears, foxlike muzzles, and wide round eyes.

Their eyes glowed blue. Their wings were blurs that occasionally flashed pale rainbows.

One dived at Jo, who yelped and ducked. Lizzy slashed at it with her saber.

"It's too fast," Lizzy said. "Get out of that, you little bastard."

Jo glanced down to see the dog standing on its hind legs, something round clasped to its belly with its forepaws. It had dragonfly wings. It sniffed at the picnic hamper and Lizzy kicked it.

The dog zipped back into the air with a chime-like yap and threw its object down.

It looked like an egg, and when it burst it looked like a smashed egg. But flames flickered from the goo.

Jo stared, frozen. Lizzy struggled out of her leather coat and threw it onto the fire, stamping hard.

Wind from their swift movement buffeted into the gondola. The dogs seemed to be having trouble keeping up with the *Snowflake*, with one or two darting forward, then falling back again. But just one egg broken against the envelopes and the silk would go up in flames. The ship would lose all buoyancy and they would fall, splattering on a hillside like eggs themselves.

Jo snapped out of her shock. "Load the cannon! We're going after that junker."

She pulled the *Snowflake* hard to port, slowing her portside prop a notch to make the turn even tighter. She felt a couple of light thumps against the envelopes. Her heart stuttered.

Lizzy leaned around the boiler's bulk to look up into the envelopes. "Nothing. I think some of the dogs didn't move away in time."

"I hope I didn't anger them. Are they all carrying eggs?"

"Looks like it. Ready to fire."

"Hide that cannon until we're on top of him."

The ornithopter came into view and Jo straightened their course. It lay between them and Mattaph, fortunately, since Jo wanted the pilot to think they were fleeing back to town. Possibly the *Snowflake* was nothing but sport to him, a chance to exercise his dogs. Possibly he had some other, darker purpose in mind.

Jo did not intend to let him burn her ship. If the *Snowflake* did catch fire, by Ravinna she would take the ornithopter down with her.

Several dogs tumbled inside. One dropped its egg. The egg rolled around, unbroken, until Lizzy scooped it up and tossed it into the boiler.

The dogs snuffled at everything in the gondola, bathing it with cold light from their eyes. The ones carrying eggs walked on their hind legs, nimble as monkeys. Lizzy said, "I think they're looking for food."

There was no food in the gondola. Jo tried to ignore the dogs, even when one sniffed at her shoes. She kept her focus on the ornithopter.

It had fallen behind after the *Snowflake* sped up, but they were approaching it again, fast. The pilot had brought his junker to their altitude earlier, which was fortunate. Hard enough for Lizzy to fire accurately at eighty knots; at least they would pass close by the ornithopter.

"I can't slow; he'll get suspicious and make the dogs throw their eggs," Jo said. "Stand by."

Lizzy left her shoveling—at this speed, the boiler required near-constant fuel—and grabbed the cannon. She had wrapped it in the towel, skull and crossbones side down. She set it on the dash next to Jo.

The ornithopter was larger even than Jo had thought—much larger, perhaps thirty feet long. She had estimated its size compared to the pilot. But as they approached, she saw with disquiet that the pilot was an enormous man, easily eight feet tall and stick-thin. His round head looked oversized on top of such thinness.

Jo shuddered again. She pulled slightly to port to fly around the junker rather than over, which would give Lizzy a good broadside.

Lizzy whipped the towel away and held a lit brand to the touchhole at the same time. The ornithopter's shallow hull slid past and Jo saw wheels attached for landing, heard the clank and creak of its wings over the *Snowflake*'s roar.

The cannon boomed. The *Snowflake*'s gondola rocked in response, since Lizzy had clamped the cannon to the dash. All the dogs took to the air in alarm.

"Did you hit?" Jo asked.

Lizzy cursed, loudly and inventively. Jo almost laughed with embarrassment for some of the things her friend said, and out of impending hysteria. "No! The ball zipped right over the top. Come about, Jo. I'll get him this time." Lizzy reloaded the cannon.

There was no sense hiding their intentions now, not after they'd fired on the ornithopter. Either the dogs would attack or they would not. Jo wrenched the *Snowflake* into another tight turn.

Orbited by the fairy-dogs, the ornithopter turned too—toward them, not away. The two aircraft were close enough Jo didn't need the glass to see the pilot's pale hand wave.

The dogs sped toward them. All Jo could think about was keeping the dogs from flying above the envelopes to throw their egg bombs down. She pulled back on the stick and the *Snowflake* climbed.

Lizzy tumbled over the gondola's side with a shout.

Jo screamed. For a moment she could not even draw breath.

She stared at the stars, scattered across the placid sky like sparks of phosphorous.

Lizzy was Jo's best friend in the whole world. They had saved each other's lives, had shared secrets and danger and excitement. And Jo had just tipped Lizzy overboard.

Jo pushed the stick forward again and turned, so that the *Snowflake* descended fast in a dizzying spiral. When she glimpsed the ornithopter, she pulled out of the spiral. She would ram it.

But Lizzy had landed in the junker! She hacked at the tall man's legs with her saber, and at the same time wiped flaming egg goo from her sleeve with the pirate towel. The fairy-dogs flew all around her, feinting in and out, but not harming her as far as Jo could tell.

Jo whimpered with relief. The tall man couldn't stop pedaling, or his ornithopter would lose momentum and fall, and Lizzy surely would injure his legs soon. But how would she get back into the *Snowflake*?

Jo leveled the ship but kept her turning. She left the controls long enough to throw a few shovelfuls of coal into the boiler, then unhooked the swingline and tossed its end out of the gondola. It was just a long rope Lizzy used to swing across to other vessels and back when boarding; she had tied knots all along it to make it easier to climb.

Moving about in the gondola while the ship circled made Jo queasy. She returned to the controls. As soon as the ornithopter started to descend, Jo could swoop close enough for Lizzy to catch hold of the swingline.

But Lizzy had dropped the saber to snatch her shirt off. Flames licked at the cloth, a cheery yellow light compared to that of the dogs' eyes. She wore a tight undershirt but her arms were bare.

The dogs were growing bolder. Jo sent the airship into a shallow dive as close as she dared to the ornithopter. Fairy-dogs scattered. But that drew their attention back to the *Snowflake*.

A dog veered into view and vanished from sight again. But it had time to drop the egg it carried. The egg bumped against the lower curve of the portside envelope, bounced off without breaking, and flew at Jo's face.

She caught it automatically with one hand. It was warm to the touch.

She almost threw it into the boiler. Instead, she turned the *Snowflake* in another tight arc and throttled back to slow the ship.

The relative quiet as the props slowed made her feel momentarily deaf. She heard the bell-like yapping of the dogs, Lizzy's grunts and curses as she swung the saber wildly, the rhythmic creak of the ornithopter's wings.

The *Snowflake* passed directly over the junker. Jo leaned over the gondola's edge and aimed carefully.

The egg landed on the front starboard wing. As far as Jo could tell in the moonlight, the wings were made of wood and canvas.

Fire erupted. A moment later the entire wing was engulfed in flames. The ornithopter lurched.

"Lizzy! Catch hold of the rope!" Jo shouted.

Lizzy dropped the saber again. The dogs' yapping turned to terrified, keening howls. Flames raced along the wing up to the hull.

Jo tried to circle just above the ornithopter, but it was hard to tell precisely where she was without leaning out of the gondola. The tall man locked the junker's wings in place and it went into a descending glide that was just short of freefall.

Jo noticed tiny flickers of light far below, like the twinkle of campfires, and realized they were from fallen eggs. The dogs dived at Lizzy, snarling and tearing at her bare arms. She cuffed them away.

"Lizzy! *Lizzy!*" Jo wasn't sure her friend could hear her—even at the *Snowflake*'s slower speed the wind snatched away voices.

But Lizzy glanced up, and Jo saw relief on her moonlit face. Lizzy lunged for the swingline.

The *Snowflake* jerked at the sudden weight on the end of the line. Jo grinned, but it faded a moment later when the weight increased.

"Jo, help!" Lizzy's voice was thin with fright.

The *Snowflake*'s struts creaked. They were only aluminum, not meant to withstand much strain—such as a junker ornithopter snagged on the end of the swingline.

Jo leaned over the gondola's edge again and discovered it was worse than she thought. The tall man, still buckled into his seat, had Lizzy's legs clasped in his arms. She clung to the swingline, but Jo knew that in a moment she would let go to free the *Snowflake*. Flames had spread to the ornithopter's other wings.

A dog flew at Jo. She smacked it away. There were pistols in the picnic basket, but they were unloaded and she was a terrible shot anyway. She had no other weapons, nothing that would help.

Nothing except the cannon, still clamped to the dash.

Jo grabbed a brand from the coal hopper and lit in the fire with shaking hands.

The ornithopter was now truly in freefall, nearly engulfed in flames, dragging the airship with it. Jo pushed the *Snowflake* down even faster and felt the pressure ease off the struts. But the blazing wings were somewhere just below the gondola—she could see the glow through the floor's woven rattan. If she got too close, her ship could catch fire.

She turned the cannon and trained it at the tall man's head. If the ball went wide she might kill Lizzy, or maim her horribly. But if she didn't try, her friend would die for certain.

She brought the brand to the touchhole. In the few moments before the cannon fired, Jo had time to send a wordless prayer to Ravinna and wonder if her heart would explode from terror.

The cannon kicked. Its plume of smoke blew into Jo's face. For a moment she could do nothing but cough.

She felt the *Snowflake* buoy up, freed from the ornithopter's weight. The props slowed as the boiler cooled. Jo adjusted the ship automatically, turning her east again toward the distant ocean and bringing her out of her dive.

She shoveled until the boiler's gauge bobbed into the blue. Only then did she look back, although her vision and the goggle lenses were blurred from her tears.

She saw the ornithopter crash, a blaze of light that unfolded like a blossom of flame when it hit the ground.

The swingline had slight weight on it still. Jo took a deep breath, coughed a few more times, and braced her feet against the gondola's side. She had to see what had happened to Lizzy.

She pulled, grunting, bringing the rope up slowly. Her arms trembled with effort.

Lizzy clambered over the gondola's edge. Her short hair stood up in tufts from the wind, her face flushed from effort. She clutched the skull-and-crossbones towel in one hand as she climbed.

"Nice shot," she said, and fell gracelessly to the floor in a swoon.

\* \* \*

They reached their seaside village barely an hour later. Jo had kept the *Snowflake* at top speed the whole way. For once she was relieved to land and get her feet safely on the ground.

"Not much damage," Lizzy said, inspecting the gondola. "Just some little spots where the paint's scorched, but she needs a fresh paint job anyway."

Jo staggered around the airship, looking for damage in the moonlight. She had set down close to the village and could hear the surf boom in the distance. The sky was clear and full of stars.

"Let's go down to the water. I stink of smoke," Jo said. "Are you sure you're not hurt?"

"I'm fine. Less damage than the *Snowflake*." Lizzy had denied fainting, though, so Jo suspected she was more injured than she let on.

"Well, let's wash, anyway. And maybe we can have a glass of rum before bed."

Lizzy smiled. She was more of a drinker than Jo; Jo was happier with fruit juice. "That's a good idea."

They walked between the village's modest homes and down to the beach. Moonlight silvered the sand and glinted off the waves. Jo's shakiness had passed off long before, but she thought she would never be able to forget the horrid dogs and the white-faced man and the smell of burning. She took off her shoes and carried them. The sea was warm as a bath.

"What's that you've got?" Jo asked. Lizzy held something in one hand.

"Just one of those eggs. I thought I might keep it, see if it'll hatch."

Jo drew breath to scream at Lizzy that she couldn't keep something so dangerous, that she should throw the egg into the ocean immediately.

But she noticed a red burn mark on her friend's cheek, visible now that her face was no longer pink with exertion. She noticed how slow Lizzy's steps were compared to her usual ground-eating stride.

Jo had almost lost her dearest friend in the world. She would never speak crossly to her again.

She said only, "Well, don't drop it."

# THE CHAOS SPECIMEN

**Matthew Pedersen**

**T**HE SHIP was shaking again. I guess I shouldn't have been too surprised; the Land-Crawler wasn't exactly the smoothest ride. The terrain-mulcher at its prow was as busy as it had ever been, obliterating any obstacles ahead so that the Crawler wasn't slowed. Meanwhile the tracked wheels continued to grind, propelling us forward towards...

Well, I still wasn't really sure where we were going. The Professor had so much influence at the University that he rarely had to explain himself. Before I was born he was able to make the most outlandish demands and get exactly what he wanted. He was famous throughout colonized space for both his brilliance and success. It was because of this reputation that I was so excited when I had been chosen out of hundreds of other students to be his assistant.

Of course that excitement died when I discovered that the Great Professor G. G. Gunnery was an egotistical ass. Fifteen years at his side had beaten that lesson into my head very well.

I sighed, a sound that was repeated on a larger scale by the Crawler. Every now and then the pressure within its engine needed to be eased, a necessity that was met by venting clouds of steam out of its sides.

My quarters filled with a loud, staticky sound that sent spikes of pain lancing through my skull. "Doctor Freign, please report to the observation deck," a tinny, synthesized voice called out through my room's intercom.

I rose from my poorly cushioned chair. No doubt the Professor would need an audience soon, and unfortunately for me I was the only other living person on this planet.

\* \* \*

I could hear him even before the doors of the observation deck opened, and just as I'd predicted he was settling into his more dramatic persona.

"Day three of the Redemptive Expedition:" he began as I walked up the metal stairway. "Truly I have seen destruction as I have travelled across this dead world. Anyone who has written about desolation, whether caused by plague or war, knows only a fraction of what I have witnessed during my trek across Antiquan's surface."

The pressurized doors shut with a slight hiss of released air once I had entered. The observation deck was really more of an elliptical chamber built into the front of the Land-Crawler. The room's outermost walls were comprised of a series of large windows, hence the observation part of its moniker. The windows were completely tinted at the moment, rendering them opaque and the room dark. The majority of the controls were here as well, including the steering. Most of these systems were automated, in a sense. Rather than having a living crew aboard his machine the Professor saw fit to use what he had come to call corpse-ervants.

They were loathsome things, disgusting to watch and unnerving to be near. At one point they had merely been bodies donated to the Royal University on our home world. Then the

Professor got a hold of them, fitting them with clockwork organs, power generators, and even specially forged bronze limbs where necessary. I wasn't sure how many he had, though I did know that he had fabricated the majority of them with a singular purpose in mind. The helmsman and the navigators that worked the observation deck's controls were fine examples of that. Not only had he seen fit to bolt their feet to the floor, he had also had the gall to dress them in reproductions of naval uniforms. All the blue cloth and gold embroidery in the world couldn't hide what they truly were though, not when I could look into their lifeless eyes.

Why he couldn't cover their faces I'd never understand, they don't even use their organic eyes. Their every move and self-made decision was a product of the sensory input flowing into them from the Crawler's external sensors.

I sighed, turning away from the mechanized cadavers to look up at the sky light. I'd seen some of Antiquan's terrain during my time on the planet, though I mostly chose to remain within my own quarters. It seemed to mostly consist of endless stretches of blue soil, with a few short mountain ranges spearing up towards the sky. Until that moment I had not actually seen said sky, and the sight of the world's twin violet suns above me was more than breathtaking. Even in my time in transit to this world aboard Professor Gunnery's personal starship I had not seen something so magnificent. It was almost worth being in the same room with him.

"Knowing that this once thriving colony of our most glorious empire was decimated by the careless tinkering of some of my peers is more heartbreaking than I can bear," he squawked. "I dare say a lesser man would have been discouraged from anymore scientific pursuits with such an abysmal failure in plain sight, but I, Professor G. G. Gunnery, am not a lesser man. No, I see this tragedy not as an irreparable stain upon enlightened civilization's honor, but as an unparalleled opportunity. The failings of my predecessors will not dispirit me. I shall forge ahead, heedless of the naysaying of my peers, and when I have unlocked the secrets that damned this world they shall see their own inadequacies. Of that, I swear!" A few seconds later there was a short chirp, the signifier that his recording device had finally been deactivated.

I started clapping my hands just slowly enough to be sarcastic. "Eloquently put Professor," I muttered.

"Lydia, there you are!" he cried. He walked over to me, the clockwork gears of his legs grinding as he did so. "It's about time you arrived."

He moved to put his clawed hand on my shoulder, but I grabbed him by the wrist to stop him. The gold it was made from was lustrous but cold, much like the man who used it. "I came as soon as I got your summons."

He retracted his servo-arm and adjusted its wrist with his other hand, the only organic appendage he had left. "Have you been looking outside?" He asked.

"The room you set aside for me doesn't have a window." I told him.

That brought a smile to his wizened face. "Well then, this may come as a surprise. Tell me something, do you understand why I organized this expedition in the first place?"

"Why are you asking me that?"

"So that I can see the level of your ignorance and alleviate it for you, my dear."

I narrowed my eyes at him, but answered anyway. "You believe there is an energy source here, something created by a research team organized by the Royal University."

"I don't believe it, Lydia, I know it. I detected this massive energy signature decades ago, five years after the initial cataclysm to be precise," he declared smugly.

"And the energy signal doesn't match anything the University has ever recorded, I know this," I griped. "What I don't understand is what you're getting at."

His smile grew and he turned away to the overly tinted

windows. "Helmsman, clear our view if you wouldn't mind."

The corpse-ervant silently obeyed its master by turning a small dial near his station. With a soft whine of energy the blackened glass panels began to clear. What I saw as I looked ahead... well, the only word that came to my mind was madness.

Lying ahead of the Crawler was a landscape that would have left the most imaginative surrealist in awe. In some places the soil and stone seemed fluid, and in others it was rigid, cracked and broken. There were actually huge chunks of the earth that had broken free to float miles above the surface. Storm clouds gathered in the distance, and from them came pillars of multicolored lightning. Perhaps the most unnerving thing that could be seen was the sparsely present trees. Before that point I hadn't seen a single example of flora on the planet. Now strange, fleshy stalks sprang up to stare at the world with milky, eye-like growths.

"W-What the hell is all this?"

"That would be the effects of prolonged exposure to this strange energy," the Professor declared. "Even with my connections and resources it took me some time to discover what the Antiquan research team was doing, and I'm still a bit unsure about the exact details of what I've found. From what I understand those fools were combining occult writings discovered by the anthropology branch with theoretical quantum formulas."

"So we're here for their research?" I asked.

"Sadly, I believe all their research material was lost in the initial cataclysm." He placed his mechanical claw on the glass of the window and began leaning against it. "I'm not here to salvage their work though."

"Then why are we here?" I asked.

"Something has to be generating this energy. I want to find it, and when I do I will contain it. If I devote my considerable mental fortitude to it, I'm sure I can unlock its secrets and tap into its potential. What we see before us is the effect of it running rampant; imagine if we could refine it..."

There was a strange mood in the chamber at that moment, something that unsettled me deeply. I had never seen Professor Gunnery acting in such a way, so calm yet somehow intense. Something was deeply wrong, and I was not going to just stand there idly while the situation played out.

"This energy source," I began, "you know where it is?"

"Yes, I believe so. I've already rigged a specialized sensor into the Land-Crawler that will lead us to where the energy concentration is strongest, and I have prepared handheld versions for when we must pinpoint its exact location. After that it will just be a matter of perseverance to transport it. Then we'll take it to my lab back on Engarlia to unlock its secrets."

"Do you honestly think taking this thing back to our home world is a good idea, especially after it destroyed all life on this planet?" I asked angrily.

"There's some ... potential dangers," he admitted. "But there is no progress without risk."

"Risk? You think the scientists who lost their lives thought the risk was worth it in the end, or the colonists for that matter?"

"That research team was a collection of third-rate professors and no-named assistants. They didn't have my brilliance or my expertise, and that'll make all the difference. You will not dissuade me from this, Lydia Freign."

"And you won't convince me that this is a good idea." I told him as I wearily sat down in a nearby chair.

He stood there for a long time, stroking his beard with his golden claw. I would like to think that he was mulling over what I said, but I knew him better than that. "Helmsman, increase speed by twenty percent," he ordered.

The helmsman said nothing, but the Land-Crawler shook slightly more than usual and there was another powerful burst of steam. After that we were propelled forward into the madness our predecessors had inadvertently created.

"Dr. Freign, do you know why I chose you out of so many others to be my assistant," the Professor asked, his gaze still held on the view ahead of us.

"No, I can't say that I do," I admitted.

"I knew you were a strong-willed spirit, just like myself. You may not have my intellect now, but you may come close to it someday. Until then I keep you as my personal naysayer, so that I can be reminded of what the lesser rabble back at the University thinks."

I was about to make a snide remark, but I knew that it would have no effect, and that this was as close to a compliment as Gunnery was capable of giving. So I sat in silence. Of course if I had known the kind of horror we were approaching I would have done everything in my power to stop him.

Hindsight, and all that....

\* \* \*

"We should go around," I declared, looking out at what was ahead of us.

"And why would we do that?" the Professor asked with a laugh.

"It would be a level of disrespect that even a wretch like you should be appalled by!" I hissed. Before us was a village, or at least the remnants of one. It was a large collection of simple houses and buildings clearly built from stones quarried locally. The destruction present in the surrounding regions was evident here as well. Many of the buildings showed signs of burns, explosions, or stranger forms of disassembly.

Even from where I was standing I could see skeletons strewn out amongst the devastation. "This place... It's a mass grave. To tread on it would only add insult to the injury our predecessors caused."

"The dead are dead," he declared. "As such they can no longer be respected nor insulted. I see this place as more of a monument to the incompetence of the past. To mow over it serves me both practically and symbolically. Helmsman, push ahead, full speed!"

I was about to object, but it was too late. The Land-Crawler lurched forward and soon the terrain-mulcher at our prow was tearing apart the paved streets of the dead village. We hit several buildings as we moved, but the crawler was a titan of a vessel and simply smashed aside everything in our path.

"I'll remember this when we return to Engarlia." I growled.

Infuriatingly, his response was to smirk. "Your disapproval is duly noted."

We moved through the village for quite some time, seeing as how it stretched on for several kilometers. A grim sense of foreboding settled upon me, but I passed it off as guilt for not arguing my point further. I lost that delusion when we reached the town's center, and the Crawler's warning klaxons rang to life.

"What's that?" I asked. The Land-Crawler didn't seem to be in any distress; in fact it was plowing forth just as quickly as ever.

The Professor looked up, his brown eyes wide with a nervous confusion. "That's the— No, that's not possible." He stomped over to the center of the chamber and struck his foot down hard on a small panel built into the floor.

"What's not possible?" I asked as a strange device emerged from a panel constructed into the deck. The machine was a collection of bronze tubes, black glass, and rubber piping built into a slowly rising platform. I quickly recognized it as a type of periscope.

"The Crawler's sensors," the Professor uttered quietly. "They've detected heat signatures ahead."

"Heat signatures? You mean something's alive out there?"

"It has to be a mistake," He griped as he looked through the periscope. "Her Majesty the Queen placed this planet under a level six quarantine when the cataclysm occurred and nothing could survive such prolonged exposure to this energy. I-It has to be a mistake."

I walked up to him slowly, a deep dread building up inside of me. "What do you see?"

"There are ... groupings of thermal energy ahead. I think they're residing within some of the buildings."

That settled things. "Helmsman, bring us to a complete halt!" I ordered. Fortunately the corpse had been programmed to obey my orders as well and soon the Crawler ceased movement.

"What the hell are you doing?" Gunnery growled.

"There may be survivors!" I said, despite the impossibility of such a thing.

Sadly the Professor was never easily swayed. "Don't be daft, you little twit! It's probably just a few generators that were left running or something."

"Generators that've been running unattended for eight decades?" I smirked.

"What do you propose, Dr. Freign?" he growled.

"We should leave the Crawler and investigate," I answered immediately.

Gunnery looked at me for a moment before releasing a cackling laugh. "You must be joking! I'm not going to leave this vessel until I've located the exact point this energy is originating from."

"Then I'll go!" I said, reaching down to my leg. There I unhooked a holster strapped to my thigh and pulled out my copper ray-pistol. I held up the small weapon, showing the Professor just how serious I was.

Once again I had misjudged what his reaction would be. He began chuckling. "Is that meant to threaten me?" he asked.

I narrowed my eyes at him. "No, it's for my own protection as I go where you're clearly too cowardly to tread."

He let out a sigh and rested his forehead against the periscope. "May I suggest an alternate course of action, Dr. Freign?"

"I... Yes, you may."

"Why don't we send out a signal and see if the heat signatures respond in anyway? If they do then something has defied the odds and survived. If they don't then we may chalk it up as another anomaly of this world and get back to our original task."

"All right," I muttered, lowering my ray-pistol.

The Professor nodded, lifting himself up and turning to the helmsman. "Seal eighty percent of the steam vents and release all pressure." He ordered before turning back to the periscope.

As always the helmsman complied, and within moments a sharp whistle pierced the air. I held my hands to my ears as the noise intensified.

Eventually the whistle ceased, replaced immediately by an eerie silence.

"Good God, there's movement!" the Professor shouted. "The heat signatures seem to be leaving the buildings!"

I looked through the window, ready for anything. The Professor stood beside me and watched with the same level of apprehension. Eventually, the things the Crawler had detected emerged, and a cry of alarm emerged from both our mouths.

Creatures began to burst forth from various buildings. I couldn't tell what they were at first; maybe my mind was trying to make sense of what I saw. The closest I can come to rationalize them is that they were insanity made flesh. They were horrid things; loping, slithering, or crawling forth on misshapen limbs. Some seemed vaguely human, though only in that they possessed man-like frames. Others were more monstrous; their forms lacking any symmetry or biological logic. Even from our position, I could see their slavering jaws, unblinking eyes, and threatening claws.

"What are they?" I uttered in a hushed tone.

I turned to the Professor, and from the look on his face I thought he was speechless. I was wrong. "So this is the result of prolonged exposure on organic matter. My dear Dr. Freign, I do believe those abominations are the survivors of the cataclysm. The energy must have sustained them all this time, in a sense." He turned to me with a glare. "Shall we rescue them now?"

I wasn't sure how to respond. I don't think I was in my right mind at the time. All I knew was that those things were approaching us. "What do we do?"

To the Professor's credit he seemed very solemn, no doubt realizing the horror that had befallen those people. "Helmsman, please release the combat corpse-ervants. The entire regiment, if you would."

I was about to ask what he meant, but soon the Crawler started shaking. This was not the type of movement caused by the engine powering or of its pressure being released. This was something different. After a few moments something came, or rather marched, into view at the Crawler's sides.

They were soldiers, dressed in what looked like traditional Engarlian military uniforms. I recognized those uniforms well; my father had been buried in a similar one. I looked closer at these well-formed squads, quickly recognizing the bronze clockwork and greyed flesh of a corpse-ervant. They moved in perfect unison while hefting up large, bayoneted beam-rifles. Soon they stood before the tortured aberrations, forming a well-disciplined line in stark contrast to the approaching tide of flesh.

The battle, if it can be called that, was fierce but short-lived. The corpse-ervant soldiers opened fire on the abominations, filling the air with bright flashes of light. Their weapons puffed out clouds of steam as they cooled. As this occurred they knelt, allowing the line behind them to open fire as well. Many of the creatures perished before clashing into the soldiers' formation, but the damage they wrought afterwards was chilling. Many of the corpse-ervants were eviscerated or partially devoured, but eventually the combined weight of their fire and their bayonet attacks wiped the beasts out. Soon, after the last of them had been put down, the soldiers began marching back to us.

I felt sick when it was over. I never imagined I'd see such a thing, nor had I ever wanted to. Watching the dead fight tortured grotesqueries....

I turned to the Professor, unable to keep my hands from shaking. "Do you still think bringing the energy source back is wise?" I asked.

He didn't look at me at that moment; somehow I don't think he had the strength to. "This power is both great and terrible. The things that could be accomplished with it would raise our empire above all others or damn it to destruction. This incident is a warning to us, a sign that carelessness cannot be tolerated. I refuse to be deterred."

Soon we were back on the move, barreling towards the source of all this horror.

\* \* \*

"Now that's something of a surprise." The Professor declared, and for once I agreed with him.

Lying ahead of us was, for a lack of a better word, a towering castle. It was a bizarre structure, seemingly formed from some ethereal, multicolored stone. It didn't look like it was constructed by men; it looked as though it had been formed seamlessly out of the ground. The geometry its many towers and outcroppings formed didn't seem physically possible. Were it not for the unnatural energy of this place I doubt it could have continued to support itself.

"This is where the energy source lies?" I asked hesitantly.

"The Crawler's sensors seem to be working erratically." the Professor admitted, looking at one of the navigator stations. "But I believe it is. I'd heard that the original research team used a former military fort to house their experiments. This seems to be the effect of concentrated doses of the energy on that structure. Fascinating...."

I let out a breath I hadn't realized I was holding. "And you propose to enter that place?"

"We must," he declared, allowing no room for objection.

I was not yet fully resigned to this course of action, and I felt determined to at least make Professor Gunnery think somewhat objectively. "What about the risk of mutation?" I asked. "Aren't we at risk of being affected by these raw energies?"

"There is no evidence that short term exposure will cause any mutation. We may be disoriented, even made ill, but I have faith that we will be all right."

"Faith? I thought you put your beliefs in empirical facts."

"Are you coming or not, you infuriating little wretch?" the Professor snapped.

I glared at him for a moment. I still doubted this entire venture, but I wouldn't be left behind while the biggest scientific discovery of our time was made.

"Yes." I declared. "Let's get this over with."

\*   \*   \*

We brought thirty of the combat corpse-ervants with us as we made our way towards the castle, as well as a number of specialized variants that the Professor deemed necessary. Explosives were used to make an entry point into the structure, allowing access to its interior. The first chamber we came across was a long and cavernous tunnel. Lights seemed to play within the stones of the walls and ceiling.

Being so close to the energy source affected us sooner than I would have thought. Our sense of direction was completely ruined, and more than once we had to stop ourselves as we accidentally ran into the sides of the tunnel. An agonizing migraine built up behind my eyes, and it felt as though something was tearing its way out of my stomach. I pushed that thought out of my mind, too afraid that maybe it was literal rather than figurative. When we finally left the tunnel, entering into a large chamber that branched out into different directions, the Professor actually vomited.

"That's somewhat better...." He confessed as he rose from his mechanical knees. He looked around, noting the different pathways we could take. "As foolish as this may sound, I do believe we need to split up."

I sighed, realizing that it was the best way to cover ground quickly as well. "Fine. You go left, I go right?"

He smiled, wiping away the last of the bile on his mouth with his organic hand. "Agreed. This is the part people back home always talk about, the adventure. Far be it from me to go against my reputation as a lone, conquering hero." And with that bit of pompous prating we separated.

He slaved five of the corpse-ervants to my command before we parted, taking the rest with himself. I'd have been upset by that, but the less of them I had the less noise I would make as I made my way through those haunted halls. I also had a communications corpse-ervant, specially designed to give the Professor my location in the event that I located the energy source before him.

As Gunnery had said, this was an adventure. People tended to die in those. That thought kept running through my mind as I trudged forth, blissfully unaware of what I was about to stumble across.

What a fool I was....

*  *  *

After an hour of endless movement through yet another tunnel I broke down, feeling the full weight of the sickness the energy caused. I was on my knees, keeping myself from collapsing completely with one hand. I remembered what Professor Gunnery said after he'd wretched up his stomach contents and decided to stop holding back. After I'd relieved myself, so to speak, the nausea left for some time.

One of the corpse-ervants stood beside me, and I ordered it to help me up. I refused to look at the thing as it grabbed my hand, and rather than lean on it as we continued to move I placed a hand on the tunnel's wall. The material felt far softer than I thought it would be. I turned to look at where my hand was, and was shocked to see a girl standing beside me.

She was a pale figure, possessing dark hair bound in a ponytail and a dark brown coat. There was a small pair of spectacles on her clearly weary face, and she looked as surprised as I was. It took far too long for me to figure out I was looking at my own reflection.

I pulled my hand back. "Damn it. That nearly gave me a heart attack."

I continued looking at my unexplainable doppelganger, trying to figure out how the stone had changed qualities so radically. Suddenly things began to appear at the borders of the reflective portion, bizarre suggestions of transparent creatures. I can't really describe them as my eyes were incapable of focusing on them. They were coiling things rife with claws and fangs. They lunged at my doppelganger and tore her apart before my eyes. The carnage lacked any blood or viscera, but the agony on her face was real enough for me. When my reflection was completely consumed, the suggested aberrations squirmed out of the reflective vision, converting into lights once they reached the more typical stone. These lights flew down the tunnels in different directions and disappeared.

I was shaking after that, and my heart was pounding against my ribcage. I let out a few deep breaths, pushing what I had seen out of my mind, and ordered my followers to start moving again.

Eventually, though I can't say how long, time flowed strangely in that place, we came to a large set of doors made from slightly scarred wood. I ordered the corpse-ervants to batter them down, and once they had, the chamber ahead was revealed to me.

I was shocked at what I saw. It was a surgical amphitheater, similar to the ones held in the medical wing of the Royal University. As I entered, corpse-ervants ever at my heels, I saw the bones of hundreds of people scattered across the seats and piled in the center. I took out the portable scanner Professor Gunnery had given me. It seemed like I was getting close to the energy source, though I had noticed the readings spiking and dropping at random intervals throughout my time there. I looked around, seeing a doorway at the opposite side of the theater. Safe bet was probably on the energy source being beyond it, so I made my way towards it.

That is when it came, approaching with a sound similar to a human moan.

It emerged from the walls at the side of the amphitheater. I screamed when my eyes fell upon it, I couldn't help myself. It was similar to the horrors we'd encountered back at the ruined village, though its anatomy was far stranger. It was a disgusting, skinless thing, towering above me like a colossus of flesh. Its body seemed to be in a state of flux, but its limbs always seemed to remain unnaturally thin while its upper body was grossly thick. It had no neck, merely three human faces set deep into its center. Their eyes opened and turned towards our direction, and their mouths formed horrifying sneers.

"Spec… imens…" they wheezed. The creature hunched over, revealing a series of brass pipes protruding from its back. It let out a horrific roar, releasing burst of foul smelling red smoke from those fixtures.

"F-Fire!" I shouted, brandishing my ray-pistol. The corpse-ervants opened fire a fraction of a second later. The superheated energy from their weapons pierced the abomination, filling the air with the smell of burning flesh. I'd have thrown up once again if I hadn't been so busy using my own weapon.

The weapons were useless, and I bit my lip to hold back the terror this caused me. The creature didn't even seem to notice the injuries we inflicted upon it. It rose up, striding across the chamber in two long steps. It reached out its massive hand.

A chill ran through me when I noticed that at the end of each fingertip there was a wickedly sharp surgical tool. It almost got a hold of me, but I got out of the way with a quick, desperate leap. In my place one of the corpse-ervants was taken. The monster lifted the martial servant up, and I felt a strange admiration for it as it attempted to slash the creature's torso with its bayonet. It was a wasted effort though, and soon the creature set to work on it.

The abomination started by eviscerating its chest and abdomen, effectively gutting it. Then it proceeded to pull out what little intestines it still possessed. I gagged watching that, knowing full well that that could soon be me.

The creature worked quickly and grew bored with the corpse-ervant in moments. It tossed the body away, letting it land into a heap of bones. I looked at the broken construct, unnerved that its mechanical portions were still functioning despite its organic parts being torn to shreds. The creature wasn't satisfied with this kill for long, slowly turning towards me with a sneer.

I wasn't in my right mind at the time, all I can remember thinking was why the abomination didn't go after another corpse-ervant. Maybe it actually understood that the creatures firing at it were the same as the one it just vivisected, or maybe it could just smell my fear.

It reached out for me, and I backed away. I tripped on something beneath me, falling back and hitting the wall. I was trapped. The creature saw this, and its dark eyes filled with a malignant gleam. I screamed and raised my weapon, firing wildly in desperation.

To be perfectly honest, I hadn't consciously aimed at anything, it was more of a futile gesture to try and hinder the creature than anything else. Luck was on my side though, as a beam of white light lanced into the forehead of one of the creature's side faces. It reacted immediately, throwing its torso back and releasing a bone jarring howl that shook the room. More of the red smoke erupted from its back. My mind raced to figure out what the biological purpose of this was.

Thankfully, I quickly regained my senses. I finally realized what the creature's weakness was. While it was still reeling from the pain I'd caused, I leapt forward. I dodged its grasp and ran between its legs to return to the surviving corpse-ervants.

"Target its faces!" I ordered, firing my pistol at the center faces. Soon the expertly trained fire of the corpse-ervants hammered into their targets. The creature roared again, trying to shield itself with its hands. It was no use though; we'd done our work well. The beast collapsed, falling limply into the center of the amphitheater with a titanic thud. I wasn't satisfied with that, and I ordered the corpse-ervants to continue firing. Eventually the only thing left of the faces was some black and smoking craters in the beast's torso.

I took a moment, breathing heavily as I tried to regain my composure. After some time I felt well enough to continue moving, searching every darkened section of the chamber for any more surprises. When none were found I pointed ahead and gave my order.

"Take those doors down!"

The corpse-ervants performed the task with the same efficiency they displayed with any other, immune to the otherworldly horror that surrounded them. As the doors were torn open, my eyes widened in absolute shock and dread.

I'd found Professor Gunnery's prize.

\* \* \*

To both the Professor's and my surprise, the energy source appeared to be an organic creature, though the term organic may have been a bit generous. After I had opened the doors to the next chamber I found a massive cell, of a sort, and at its center, hovering high above the floor, was a ball of pale flesh and unblinking eyes. It couldn't have been more than half a meter in width, yet it still seemed to dominate the whole room.

I'd contacted the Professor immediately of course, and to his credit he came fairly quickly. Before his arrival however I observed this creature, and found it more unnerving than anything I had encountered previously on Antiquan. Its flesh, which could be described as taking the shape of a sphere, was loose and flowed like water across its own hide. The eyes, which were reminiscent of obsidian orbs, appeared glossy and reflective. I dared not look into them though; some part of my mind telling me to do so would be to risk damnation.

Damnation.

Such a strange term for me, a scientist, to use. It seemed apt at the time however, and it has not lost its appropriateness since.

The Professor's reaction to the creature, once his party arrived, was entirely unexpected. "Magnificent," he uttered in an awed whisper. He began stepping towards it, but I held him back by the shoulder.

"How do you plan on extracting this thing?" I asked.

He stared at me with a strange, distant expression, but within a few seconds recognition showed in his eyes. "Ah yes, A-Seventeen and R-six, please approach!" He called out, facing the collection of specialized corpse-ervants.

Two of the sepulchral things stepped forward. They were dressed in the garb of traditional servants, like the kind an Engarlian noble might possess. I noticed what made them distinct immediately. One of them was carrying a large glass dome whose dimensions could easily accommodate the creature. At the base of the dome was a short yet wide cylinder, clearly a device of some sort. The other servant had a harpoon gun built into its mechanical arm.

I looked at the Professor questioningly, and he began chuckling. "As I told you when we left the Land-Crawler, I made sure to be prepared for anything. Now then R-Six, fire at that creature!"

The harpoon servant obeyed, targeting the strange organism and firing within seconds. The harpoon flew, a thickly built rope trailing after it, and then pierced the lower portion of the creature. I was concerned that the harpoon might just slip through it, but it seemed to stick.

The energy creature released an ear rendering cry as it was slowly dragged forward. Concentrated energy formed visibly and dispersed from the beast like violet lightning bolts. Most of these discharges struck against the walls and ceiling of its chamber, warping them drastically. One managed to hit two of the militant corpse-ervants, tearing them in half. Rather than being burned I saw that grotesque mouths and tentacles had formed from the edges of these parts, stillborn horrors created from dead flesh.

Eventually the specialized servants managed to contain the creature within the glass dome. The device at the bottom of the dome released a burst of steam almost immediately after this.

I turned to the Professor, who had an unnerving grin on his face.

"The device was designed to convert any energy released within it into thermal energy. A liquid cooling system cancels this heat out and becomes steam, though it will only withstand so much. There's a specialized chamber meant to prolong the device's life in the Land-Crawler. That should buy us all the time we need as we rejoin the starship at the rendezvous point."

He left after that, not stopping to hear any objections I might have had. I would have said something, but I knew I would be ignored. He refused to be more than a few steps away from the creature, constantly staring at it and even rubbing the glass of its containment unit. This fact left me with an icy dread in my heart.

We eventually returned to the Land-Crawler, and once Gunnery had installed the creature into its intended chamber we were off. That, of course, was when everything went to hell.

\* \* \*

When it happened, it happened quickly. I'd chosen to remain in my quarters as we made the week long journey back to the rendezvous point. It didn't feel safe to be anywhere else. The atmosphere within the Crawler had changed considerably. There was an ever present tension, as though we were about to enter battle or something equally frightening. The corpse-ervants also seemed to act strangely. More than once I thought I saw them watching me.

So I isolated myself, just waiting for the whole horrid adventure to be over. I missed my home, the friends I had back at the University, and I even missed the egotistical ramblings of Professor Gunnery. Ever since we'd returned from the impossible castle he had been just as distant as me, locking himself away to "observe" the specimen we'd acquired. Little did I know evil was lurking within the Crawler, irrevocably corrupting it.

Truth be told I might have never known what was happening had my door not opened the day before we were to arrive at our destination. I'd been reading a book at the time, a bit of trashy fiction that I was trying to lose myself in to forget about the problems around me. I looked up from it to find a corpse-ervant in my doorway, one of the finely dressed servant variants. Its hands, both organic, were held at its sides and it simply stared blankly ahead.

I wasn't sure what was happening, so I stood up and approached it. "Is there something you ne—"

Suddenly, to my absolute horror, the corpse-ervant's mouth fell open and it let out a shriek that should never have come from a human throat, living or dead. The servant lunged for me, and the next thing I knew I was wrestling for my life as its hands wrapped around my throat. I tried to pull out my ray-pistol, but there was no way I could reach it. My mind raced as my vision began to darken.

I would have died there had my arm not bumped my desk, knocking a particularly sharp pen to the ground. With the last bit of strength I had, I grabbed the pen and thrust it into the corpse-ervant's eye, piercing it to the brain. Fortunately this was enough to kill it, making its body go limp.

I left my room after that, filled with terror despite having my ray-pistol out. What I found was not the Land-Crawler I thought I resided within. The place had become an asylum unleashed. Within every room the corpse-ervants were causing havoc, destroying sensitive equipment and mutilating themselves in ways I can't even describe.

More horrifying was the changes wrought on the Crawler's structure. Many of the halls, which had once been formed from unyielding iron, had begun to pulsate like throbbing flesh. I rested my hand on one portion of the wall, and my nails actually pierced into it, causing it to bleed a foul smelling ichor.

Somewhere along the way I found myself with a poker for a furnace. I'm not really sure where it came from; I think I was going mad at the time. The horrors I'd been through before were nothing compared to the Crawler. The only rational thought I had right then was that I needed to find the Professor, that perhaps he could fix what was happening.

Never have I been more wrong in my life.

\* \* \*

I found The Professor in the chamber he'd set aside for his specimen. As I approached the room its doors slid open, releasing a thick cloud of steam. The room was frightening, though it seemed unchanged. I looked ahead, finding the creature's containment unit built into the center of the far wall. Steam flowed constantly from various vents and pipes built around it, a testament to the power being bled from the horrid creature.

Staring up at this display was the Great Professor G. G.

Gunnery, the man who I begrudgingly saw as a mentor. I approached him slowly, both my pistol and the poker held at the ready despite myself.

"Professor, George, the Crawler is ruined!"

"Magnificent isn't it Lydia? Just think of how this power will benefit the Empire. I do believe even the Queen will pay homage to my greatness when I tap into this glorious being's power."

"No!" I cried. "That thing cannot go to Engarlia, the horror and madness it emits cannot be contained! Have you seen the rest of the Crawler George? It's been ruined, corrupted! You have to see that."

The Professor turned to me then, and when I saw what had become of him I almost died right there. He was an arrogant ass, but he had been the most present figure in my life for fifteen years. Now, the once wizened face I'd grown so familiar with was twisted into a tight sneer. His skin had burst at places along his skull, and perhaps the most horrifying part of all was the fact that his eyes had become glowing, violet orbs. His arm, his mechanical arm, was held up, and I could see his flesh had grown in vile tendrils along its length. The golden claws at the ends of his fingers had grown, resembling the talons of some terrible bird of prey.

He had become just as corrupted as the Crawler, and perhaps it was that realization that steeled my resolve. I cried out and lunged towards him, filled with what can only be called righteous fury. I managed to hit him across the head, a strike that would have killed him before his change. Now his response was to laugh the same mocking laugh he always made around me.

His claw lashed out and gripped my head. The next thing I knew I was being lifted off the ground.

"I knew it, I knew it! You're just like them, the fools at the University. You think I've gone too far, you think what I'm doing is wrong! Well, you're the one that's wrong! With this power, this energy, we can all transcend the limitations of what's natural.

Flesh, machine, and the immaterial can flow into one glorious being, to stand as something greater than its individual parts! I'm sorry you can't see that Lydia, I truly am." As he finished his rant, he threw me across the room.

I hit a wall with a thud, and I just barely managed to stay conscious. I looked up to see him stepping towards me leisurely, ever the arrogant bastard. That was his mistake. I lifted my ray pistol up and fired into his chest. He cried out in agony, but kept coming. My body raced quicker than my mind, and I shot him in the kneecaps, melting the metal of his artificial legs. He fell to the ground, continuing to crawl towards me with a sneer.

I jumped up, knowing that above all else the energy creature, the embodiment of chaos itself, had to die. I holstered my pistol quickly and grabbed the stoker in both arms. With all my might I threw it at the creature's containment unit, smashing the glass dome apart. The creature shrieked in fear, but I ignored it.

I trained my pistol on the abomination. A voice called out, and I recognized it as Gunnery's.

"Lydia no, please!"

I turned to him, seeing what he had become. Somehow seeing him like that affected me in a way I can't describe. "I'm sorry..." I whispered, pulling the trigger.

The lance of light struck the beast, causing a fair portion of it to burst. I knew that the wound was a mortal one. The creature began to release its own dirge, a horrible screeching that I could feel reverberate through every cell of my body.

Energy began to burst from the corpse in powerful arcs after that, and at its center I could see a growing orb forming. No doubt this would be its final release. I turned to run away, and as I did so I saw a stray arc strike Gunnery.

He burst into a gelatinous charnel creature, but I didn't stay to see what horrid anatomy it became. As I left the chamber it tried to follow me, but its bulk was too large to fit through the doorway. As I turned a corner I could see a golden arm reaching out for me, I pushed the image from my mind and kept moving. I fled as fast as my body would allow, and within minutes I found an escape hatch. I tore it open and leapt out of the Crawler.

The Land-Crawler continued to move after that, leaving me behind as the ethereal energy built up to the breaking point. I covered my eyes as everything around me was filled with a blinding light. The ground shook and my eardrums practically burst from the unholy cacophony that came.

Eventually, after I judged that it was safe, I looked up. Ahead of me was a horrid mess of twisted metal and flesh. Most of this organic material was clearly dead, but as I rose and began my journey to the rendezvous point I still avoided it.

I survived. The demon-thing the researchers had created or summoned was dead, and Gunnery right along with it. I let out a breath I hadn't known I was holding, and tried to make my mind focus on something other than the horrors I had seen. No doubt Gunnery's starship would have sensed the Crawler's destruction, and its crew would soon move to investigate. I would meet them with them at the rendezvous point, and I would tell them everything. With the ordeal behind me I began walking, the thought of home propelling me forward.

# UNDER A SHATTERED SKY

## Chris Wong Sick Hong

I T WAS always night. It would always be night, since the earth laid rent and the sky cracked. The void where the sun once was radiated an indifferent chill. Distant stars lay caged beyond reach, trapped by a web of jagged purple that spanned horizon to horizon, throbbing like exposed nerves. The pocked remains of two moons trudged through the darkness like smeared comets. Trails of debris sifted down upon the horizon mountains.

A city of gears and brick, accented with glints of glass and steel, lay broken in the plains next to a crystal lake. Great pumps suctioned clear water from the depths. The water rose through cracking pipes to be stored in great tanks over two hundred feet tall, and from there was distributed through smaller, overhead pipes to every point of need. These had once been arranged in a near perfect grid, cross braced such that they remained aloft with minimum support, but now they lay rent and ajar, mirroring the disruption of the city streets below. The earth had moved, and some streets ended abruptly at what seemed a cliff, only to carry on fifty, sixty, or even a hundred feet below. In those areas where the damage to the overhead pipes was especially severe, it rained a constant, freezing mist.

The engines at the heart of the city remained undisturbed, however. Monstrous devices buried miles underground, they combined the earth's heat with never-ending water siphoned from the lake. The resultant columns of steam powered the city above. The access ways and equipment tunnels, once triumphs of mining and engineering, had been mangled into an impossible catacomb, yet these chthonic leviathans lumbered onward in their eternal toil, only occasionally pausing to rumble as a great gear jammed or a turbine blade encountered resistance as it dug through the earth.

There was no one alive underground, nor anyone in the city above, but the keen of eye could observe hints of activity which belied the atmosphere of death. The hinges of the doors to the hydroponics factories were oiled, not rusted. Footsteps atop faded footsteps could be found in areas where the water from the leaking pipes had frozen into slush. The valves of several air compressors in the trade district had been polished smooth from use.

And in the power district, where raw materials from other cities were channeled in via pipes taller than a human being, there was an arrow, marked in chalk, pointing outward. Underneath the arrow was a date.

Following the raw material channels would lead one to another arrow, another date. Every two days, as measured at the pace of a strident walk, a cache of supplies would be hidden from the elements. Preserved food. A change of clothes. Spare tools. Brass canisters filled with air. And nearby, another chalk arrow on the pipes, pointing onward and possessing a date beneath.

There were no trees, no animals, and no insects out here, merely a coarse, mossy plant that covered the ground as far as one could see. And occasionally the hint of footsteps.

Further on, the ground grew rocky and even those disappeared.

\* \* \*

Standing on a promontory deep in the plains, Ellsbeth turned the rusty crankshaft handle furiously, ignoring the sweat pooling in her heavy leather gloves. The linen strips wrapped around her hands and wrists—a prophylactic against chafing—had already soaked through, but another steaming was due soon, and she had yet to make this place safe to stay the night.

The handle broke. Metal splinters lodged in the heavy overskirt she wore for prudence's sake. The brass helmet's viewing glass protected her eyes and Ellsbeth's clothes were as padded and thick as she could manage, for she could scarce afford injury. Not out here.

The sudden shift of balance threw her to her knees. It was a jarring impact, but her body did little more than protest as she gathered herself upright. It could have been much worse. Ellsbeth paused to assess the new situation.

Lacking a means of reattachment, the handle itself was now worthless. She tossed it aside in disgust and the truncated metal bar lodged itself in the rocks a few feet away. There was no other immediately apparent means of engaging the crankshaft, but Ellsbeth had spent the better part of two days hiking to this promontory with its promise of shelter, and as the steaming hadn't yet occurred, there was no need for frustration or panic.

The promontory had not always been so, and the ground sloped steeply downward. Three of the great channels that carried materials between cities converged a short distance away, and a control station had been built to oversee their operation. There had once been shacks for worker housing, but those lay broken at the bottom of an impassable ravine.

The control station itself—a mass of machinery once connected to switches in the channels below—was horseshoe shaped and flanked by metal tubes that had been vertical when the land was flat, but now surrounded Ellsbeth like a forest of drunken metal trees. She leaned against one of the panels and assessed the situation.

Several times a day, the channels would rattle and fumes would erupt around the large riveted bands holding them together. Occasionally the pressure would be great enough the rivets themselves would groan, inching slowly out of place. Ellsbeth shuddered to think of what would happen once they failed, but she did not have the means to reseat them.

At first, the steamings had just been steam, but a year and a half ago they turned blue and noxious, a clinging poison that burned the skin and was impossible to breathe. As a result, she could not use the channels themselves as shelter and kept them at a wary distance. The Shattering had turned the weather cold and icy, and the land had broken unevenly. Where the plains were still plains, suitable shelter was few and far between.

Ellsbeth could survive one night huddled in a small hollow where the wind was less, but always woke aching. After two consecutive nights exposed, it took hours of hiking to fully thaw. She was no outdoorsman and did not want to attempt three.

This control station was the only suitable shelter around. Like all control stations Ellsbeth had encountered, this one contained a sampling device connected to the channels. Originally, there were pressure seals to prevent it from being used when the channels were in operation, but the blue gas had proven itself capable of eating through steel given enough time, and Ellsbeth was certain the protective measures had been destroyed from within. Why should this control station be special? So unless she disconnected it entirely, it would channel the steaming directly up here, continuing to render this place unsuitable for shelter.

The architects of the control stations had not been foolhardy for men, and had devised a means of emergency disconnection. However, that required the compressor. They had also provided a means to operate the compressor under less-than-ideal circumstances, which is why after the last steaming had subsided,

Ellsbeth had rushed up the promontory to the crankshaft handle and turned it with as much speed as she could muster.

It had been hours of demanding labor, each turn more difficult than the turn before, until some predetermined threshold was reached and the compressor expelled its air deeper into the mechanism. Each time it did so, Ellsbeth had paused for a short, congratulatory break, then began her work again.

Now that the handle had broken, she needed another option.

She attempted to clean the face of the compressor's pressure gauge, and when her leather gloves only smudged the glass, Ellsbeth rummaged through her pack until she found a strip of cloth that hadn't been completely saturated with dust and dirt. This cleaned the gauge enough to show she was still many cycles away from generating sufficient pressure.

Other than her pack and tool belt, Ellsbeth carried two tall canisters of compressed air in a harness on her back. These connected to her brass helmet through flexible rubber tubes—insurance against getting caught in the steaming. Compressed air was compressed air, and if she could contrive a means of connecting a canister to the control station, she might not need the compressor itself. While Ellsbeth was a technician by neither training nor inclination, the necessities of the past few years had familiarized her enough with the compressors in the trade district that she identified no less than three promising valves, which was two too many.

Ignoring a growing sense of unease—the steaming arrived randomly, and the hair on her neck began to rise when more than several hours had gone by without one—Ellsbeth set to work.

One valve quickly proved to be a dead end, and she was tracing the path from another when the Voice announced itself.

"Did you think I would miss our daily chat?" it said.

The Voice emanated from a speaking tube near what had once been the head operator's chair. Each day, without fail, it would arrive to taunt her. The Voice was so warbled by the tube it was recognizable as neither male nor female. Indeed, it was barely intelligible. It may not even have been human, but instead a phonograph cylinder dutifully played in some far away city by machinery that still functioned properly.

Ellsbeth did not deign to reply and continued examining the compressor.

"This won't bring them back, you know," the Voice said, after a pause.

Again, Ellsbeth did not respond. She was close to confirming or eliminating the second valve, and if she chose wrong it would be a two-month trek back to the city for reprovisioning. Her supplies were low, which was another reason securing this station now was so important.

The Voice broke into her concentration, smug and snide. "It won't bring him back either."

This provoked a response.

"It doesn't have to!" Ellsbeth yelled, her breath fogging the helmet's viewing glass to where she could no longer see.

Her chest heaving, her ears ringing from the echo of her own voice, Ellsbeth lowered herself to the ground to calm down. Losing her composure now could jeopardize all her efforts prior.

*    *    *

It had been terrifying, waking to discover the sky had cracked, been transformed from a springtime blue to an endless, fractured night. The sun would not be seen again. In its place were the glowing purple scars that wove their way from horizon to horizon. Sometimes Ellsbeth thought it was a cage to keep her trapped. Sometimes she feared it was a fence to keep something unnameable out. The moons, limping through the sky like patients bleeding out on a surgery table, were impossible to watch.

The land had fractured as well, sudden heaves of earth jutting from previously flat ground. Mountains appeared where none had been before and sudden plateaus schismed upward, disrupting the carefully squared city streets. Some citizens had been found dead. Most, including Ellsbeth's fiancé, had simply vanished.

The few survivors, exchanging telegraphs with the other cities, had vowed to rebuild and triumph over adversity, but that was before they began to die.

The animals and trees began to die as well, and Ellsbeth still remembered the arguments as to the cause. The surgeon and scientist—she could no longer remember their names—had disagreed vociferously.

\* \* \*

The great hall had been unfinished. The steel frame that allowed such open expanses lay exposed like the ribcage of a mechanical goliath. In the center, occupying a modest fraction of the space, was a jumble of tables, stools and chairs arranged to face the hardwood double doors that served as the grand entrance. The doors were two stories tall, paneled, and polished to a dark red, yet so perfectly balanced they opened with but a light touch, swinging inward a fraction of an inch above the tiled floor.

This building had been intended as the city's civic center, capable of accommodating a full twentieth of the citizens in its chambers, theaters and wings, and lay mostly empty now.

Despite the reminders of what had once been, the survivors preferred to gather here, as evidenced by the sofas, chairs, beds and divans that clustered near the back wall. The Shattering had left an abundance of traditional slate-roofed brick houses unoccupied, but no one wanted to be alone.

"I must insist," the surgeon said once his meal was half completed. "This malady is clearly the result of some germ or miasma released during the recent…" he paused, "turn of events."

"But with all due respect," the scientist rejoindered, "how would such a contagion reach us, and why would it wait until now to strike? It follows the pattern of no known disease."

"On the contrary, I myself have experience with several such maladies. The pattern of affliction makes it clear that this poison needs to accumulate in the lungs, or possibly blood, before becoming fatal. Therefore, the prudent and obvious course of action is to bathe regularly to cleanse oneself."

"While I respect your learned opinion"—the scientist was careful always to emphasize the surgeon's opinion was just an opinion, and his tone of voice suggested it might not even be learned—"I can't disagree more. While your ruminations upon the source of the malady are undoubtedly correct, regular bathing is not the cure. This malady is the result of some fault in the lake water, which even now is being pumped into the reservoirs."

"Then what would your prescription be?"

"That is obvious. We should limit our contact with water to the bare necessities."

The surgeon nearly choked on his glass of water. He had been drinking at least ten per day and bathing twice.

"Surely you're not suggesting we die from thirst? Or that we descend barbarically into wretchedness from a total lack of bathing!" The umbrage, always present in the surgeon's voice, was especially apparent now.

The scientist stood, raising himself to his full height. "Perish the thought. But when drinking, be sure to add a trace of medicinal brandy for vigor. As for cleanliness, I grant it is not just a personal virtue, but a civic one, and cannot be avoided entirely—"

The surgeon stood as well. "Oh. Is it the distinguished scientist's opinion that we also bathe in brandy? Or perhaps my colleague would suggest whisky instead."

"Please evidence enough good breeding to let me finish. My professional recommendation is that one boils the water before bathing."

"And what of the water that nourishes our crops? Boiling that is, by virtue of impossibility, sheer madness."

"Madness?! I think not. It is well known to the educated that plants contain a natural filtering mechanism…"

The argument was circular, endless and the two participants had come close to fisticuffs on several nights. Nevertheless, it had reassured Ellsbeth. With two such learned gentlemen applying themselves to the issue, it doubtless would be expediently resolved. Then, they could turn their attentions to the missing, and once the missing were returned, she could get married and leave this nightmare behind.

These memories embarrassed Ellsbeth. She could not help but deem herself foolish and weak, but the memories were all that moored her to her life before, and she would not cast herself adrift in pride.

At the end of an evening's argument, the scientist and surgeon would resolve that half of the survivors would follow the scientist's hypothesis, and the other half the surgeon's prescription. This would irrefutably determine who was right while ensuring the greatest number of survivors continued to survive.

For their part, most of the survivors ignored the arguments in their daily habits, or chose sides without much enthusiasm. The only advice widely followed was diluting drinking water with spirits, and even the surgeon did so in ever increasing quantities. Ellsbeth herself, still awestruck by titles and learning, had attempted to follow both. She bathed once a day in boiled water. She filled her jugs only with water that had been filtered by machines in the industrial district, despite the forty-minute walk, and only drank the water after a carefully measured shot of brandy had been fully dissolved therein.

In due time, all but Ellsbeth fell into a sallow sleep, then died. She could not bear to bury the last on her own, and had avoided that part of the city from then on.

The great hydroponic factories at the heart of the city had

lumbered onward. A few of the plants proved themselves immune to the mysterious malady killing everything else, and while these numbered at most one out of every thousand, the factories were vast enough that even this was enough to produce and preserve more food than she could hope to eat in a lifetime. Supplementing her diet with a strict rationing of meat dried before the Shattering—meat kept in a dark, subterranean room, carefully away from as much lake water and outside contamination as possible—Ellsbeth could eat like a queen until the end of her days.

The telegraphs had stopped when the sickness struck, and at first Ellsbeth decided to wait for help from the other cities. None came, and she resigned herself to her fate. But when the steaming turned poison, she summoned the courage to act.

\* \* \*

"Do you even remember their names?" the Voice taunted, tinny and obscure.

Ellsbeth could damage the speaking tube—it was rusted enough that a few good hits from the wrench at her belt should break it in half—but the years of isolation had ground her down. She was not so prideful as to deny she was lonely. Furthermore, time spent on vandalism was time not spent towards securing the control station.

Her helmet's viewing glass was still fogged and did not seem like it would clear any time soon. With both hands, she eased its weight off her head, careful not to damage the tubes that led to the air canisters. In the days of her first expeditions, her hair would catch on the helmet's rough edges and be pulled out, so she'd shaved it off. When that proved chafing, she'd begun wrapping her head in linens. In deference to the near freezing temperatures outside, the wrap extended around her face as well, leaving only her eyes, nose and mouth free.

Still, the shock of wintry air burned her lungs as the helmet came free. For all its cumbersome annoyance, the helmet not only protected her from detritus and debris, but also trapped a thin layer of heat. Without it, it seemed she inhaled the night itself, an infinite chill filtered through the purple cage that partitioned the sky.

Ellsbeth coughed sharply and her eyes teared. When the fit passed, she returned her attention to the compressor. Her examination had left her still unsure as to which of the two remaining valves was correct and there could not be much time left before the next steaming. If she didn't choose now, she would have to retreat anyway and, upon her return, she'd be no wiser. Picking the closest one, she set to work attaching a canister of air.

Her improvised connection between canister and compressor valve hissed mightily as the air emptied within. Ellsbeth did not know how much would be required, but did not want to fail due to timidity, so she emptied it all. When the hissing subsided, she returned the canister to its harness and checked the pressure gauge once more.

"Do you even remember *his* name?" the Voice said.

Ellsbeth tensed. The Voice was a distraction, nothing more, she kept repeating to herself. An obstruction to the work at hand.

"You don't, do you?"

That was true, but she would not admit that to anyone.

Before Ellsbeth had a chance to engage the emergency disconnect, a whistling keen filled the air from the great channels below. The steaming had begun. Ignoring the Voice, Ellsbeth made haste to don her helmet once more.

Faster than she would have thought possible, plumes of blue gas erupted from not just the sampling device, but all the panels of the control station. The poison must have eaten its way through entirely, leaving little more than a leaky metal shell. The gas expanded into a crystalline smoke upon hitting the cold air, a smoke which shattered against any exposed surface into a choking mist.

Ellsbeth had not yet firmly seated her helmet, but there was no time now. She grabbed her pack (which held her only hand-drawn map) and raced down the slope of the promontory, but the choking mist was faster. Ellsbeth reached to her back and flipped the switch to engage the air canister. Nothing happened. Realizing she'd flipped it the wrong way—toward the canister she'd just emptied—Ellsbeth was rectifying the error when a soft patch of ground caught her foot, tumbling her.

There was a gap between her helmet and shoulders even in ideal circumstances and now, with the helmet knocked partway around her head, it did nothing to impede the mist as it engulfed her. A searing pain ravaged her lungs as the helmet filled with the noxious blue gas.

Even in this calamitous state Ellsbeth knew she must get clear before taking off the helmet once more. She managed to find the air switch and a blast of stale air cleared the helmet slightly, enough to diminish the pain from egregious to overwhelming. The further away from the station that she got, the more the gas would have dispersed, and the mist was heavier than air so if she could struggle to stand and take a few more steps...

The clack of the helmet's clapper valves, which would normally regulate the air flow, was a metronome marking time with her labored breath. She could barely think, could hardly see, and more than once wondered if this was the last sound she would ever hear.

When her lungs could no longer bear it, she ripped off the helmet and took a desperate gulp of freezing air before collapsing to the ground. Nearly unconscious, she nevertheless instinctively reacted to the tingling and burning of the poison mist enveloping her yet again by desperately crawling forward. Forcing herself to her feet, she ripped the air hose free from her helmet and breathed directly from it. The pressure distended her lungs to near bursting.

Certain she was going to die, Ellsbeth staggered forward, then collapsed.

\* \* \*

Ellsbeth awoke. She was lying on her back. The endless night was colder than ever, and all of her ached with a pain she could not describe. The stars above struggled to be free from the glowing purple web which caged them all. For a moment Ellsbeth felt like the blasted moons, with their remains smeared across the sky.

She must have stumbled free from the noxious cloud and that last blast of air must have cleared the poison gas from her lungs, but at what cost? She did not know if she could move, and some part of her wished she had been bested by this tortured world, that giving up and letting go would not be a failure of her resolve.

But as had happened so many times before, she found she could move. And when the dizziness and nausea subsided to where she could stand, she stood.

The supply caches on her path back to the city would be clear of any further steamings, so she left the air canisters behind. Her helmet contained only a trace of gaseous residue and the endless night would quickly turn frigid, so she swallowed her lungs' aching panic and donned it anyway. She found her pack and dumped all but the map and the enough food necessary to reach the previous cache. The tools would only slow her down, and while she hated to deplete the caches of food because she'd need to make a trip specifically to restock them, once she returned to the city she'd be able to scrounge for more.

With a strangled cry that was half pain and half desperation, she began the journey.

"*If* there are any other survivors," the Voice said, "this is not the way to impress them."

Part of Ellsbeth marveled at the mechanical ingenuity

necessary to project the Voice from the speaking tube to her current location. This was the part she allowed to lie, for admitting the truth would be perilously close to losing all hope, and she could not be the only one left alive. There were others, and she would find them.

# AYELEN

## Igor Rendić

STEAM didn't curl in the stiff breeze; nothing moved on the deck or behind the bridge's windows; the large ship was dark and at the mercy of the currents. Letters on the weathered hull named it *Zodia*.

*Cora* was slowing down now, preparing to dock with the massive ship; a docking platform was sticking out from *Zodia's* port side. As *Cora* was pulling closer, the cutter seemed like a young and agile hound approaching an old, sleeping bull.

Ayelen Itzel, captain of the Avella Security Fleet cutter *Cora*, finally gave up on picking out any sign of life through her binoculars.

"Still nothing?" said the ship's pilot at her left.

"Nothing. We've flashed them, radioed them, shot a flare. Nobody's home," Ayelen said as she glanced left at the speedometer on the pilot's console. Her pilot was a redhead Nihoni who only ever gave her name as Hashi—which Ayelen found hilarious when they first met. Still, it was no wonder that nobody picked up on the obviously fake name: Nihon was an isolationist culture and few non-Nihoni on *Earth* knew the language, let alone in the Colonies. The clerks of ASF certainly didn't know it or they wouldn't have allowed Ayelen's pilot to sign up as 'Chopsticks'.

Hashi kept her eyes firmly on *Zodia's* docking platform while her hands deftly led *Cora* through the docking maneuver.

Ayelen surveyed the dull grey hull. Pirates were uncommon in these waters but not unheard of—the reason *Cora* was here—but there was no trace of *Zodia* having been fired upon.

The shadow of the docking platform crept over the cutter's bridge. With a pull of a lever, Hashi killed the engines and then flipped a switch on the microphone built into her console and said, "Pavel, go."

Behind and above the bridge, Pavel Kekelin operated a large crane-like metal arm that grabbed upwards at *Zodia's* docking platform's clamps and locked with them.

Ayelen looked at Hashi. "Well, let's go take a look."

On *Cora's* deck, the boarding party was already assembled. Pavel climbed down from the docking arm control seat as Ayelen and Hashi approached the group of waiting crewmen. Pavel nodded at Ayelen as Shimi Cormani, *Cora's* machinist, handed him a backpack and equipment belt and then stood in line between her and the ship's surgeon, Henry Carville. They were good crew. All of them adamantly refused the offer to change ships when Ayelen and *Cora* got on admiral Pel's black list and were exiled to this godsforsaken section of Avella's oceans.

"Alright," said Ayelen as her crew stood to attention, "the ship is *Zodia*. According to our register, a cargo hauler repurposed as a scientific research vessel for an Earth institute. As you've probably noticed, it's apparently abandoned. Cormani's team; the engine room. Kekelin's team; search the ship for survivors. Take the Doc with you. The rest are going to the bridge with me and Hashi. Understood?"

There was a round of "Aye, aye, Skipper" and then they were off, climbing the docking arm's ladder up to the *Zodia's* platform.

Ayelen was the third on the platform, after two marines from her team, both with drawn revolvers. The platform was deserted, and the large loading bay it lead into seemed likewise. There were no lights inside, so electric torches would be needed.

Crossing the platform, Ayelen took note of various pieces of equipment strewn across it: tools, lengths of rope, small containers, folded tarpaulins. Left there by a particularly careless crew, dumped in an emergency, or rolled out of the docking bay during bad weather? She crossed off the last option when she noticed the items were scattered around a large empty area. There was also the loading crane, poking out of the loading bay, its hooks hanging over the edge of platform, swaying with the motion of the ship.

The wind picked up and filled her nostrils with the strong scent of Avellan sea: brine and that other thing that faintly reminded her of cinnamon. Meters below the loading dock, the dark blue waters, darker than any Earth ocean, sometimes almost indigo, lapped against the hull. Ayelen looked to the horizon, a line of dark clouds against mostly clear sky, its almost familiar blue hue tinged with a pale green. Hopefully there wouldn't be a storm tonight.

"Hello!" Kekelin shouted into the loading bay, and Ayelen turned around. No answer came.

The loading bay was dimly lit by the waning daylight, and their electric torches stabbed at the shadows, illuminating bulkheads, crates and containers. All was dead quiet, bar the footsteps of the boarding party.

A ship this large and slow would be of no use to pirates, and if *Zodia* had been raided, then it was for supplies and crew. Slavery was illegal on Avella, but there were vast swathes of land on continents and islands not under ASF scrutiny, rich with resources and hungry for cheap labour.

A quick search of the loading bay revealed no traces of the crew and no evidence of violence. The passageway on the other side of the bay's main door was pitch black, and the switch beside the door failed to turn on the electric lights. There was also a comms console, built into the bulkhead. The lights on it flickered when Ayelen tried it and there came the crackle of static from the speaker. Main power was obviously off, but it seemed that at least the comms now worked on emergency batteries. She flipped the 'Bridge' switch, spoke into the fixed microphone. "Hello? This is Captain Itzel of the Avella Security Fleet cutter *Cora*. Can anyone hear me?" She flipped the 'Engineering', 'Crew Quarters', 'Medical' switches one after the other, repeating the message but the only answer was the crackling and the faint echo of her own voice from the dark passageway.

*   *   *

"Anything?" Ayelen asked Hashi while they walked. Two pairs of marines escorted them.

"Just the general creepiness of the place, Skip" Hashi said.

One flight of stairs before the bridge, they found open doors to a small room. The sign on the bulkhead said 'Emergency beacon'. The device was inside the room, on the far bulkhead: a powerful radio with its own antenna—and without a power source. There should have been a small steam powered generator, and its outline was clearly visible as a discoloration of deck and bulkhead, but the generator itself was missing.

The bridge was a large, square room atop a short tower, as empty as the rest of the ship they'd passed through. There were signs of life here, empty cups, bottles, charts spread out on a navigator's table, a raincoat over the back of the pilot's chair—but still no clue to what happened to the crew or the ship.

From the large windows of the bridge, the entirety of the foredeck could be seen: hatches opened or closed, crates, tarpaulins flapping in the breeze.

Hashi leaned over the pilot's console. "No course preplotted and locked into the autopilot, Skip."

Ayelen's attention was given to the large, leatherbound volume on a stand in the corner. The ship's log: thick, its pages filled with entries. In German. Ayelen sighed. "Of course," she murmured.

"Skip?" Hashi asked.

"Ensign, take the ship's log and put it in your backpack," Ayelen said to one of the marines and then grinned at Hashi. "The language of my forefathers, which I of course never bothered to learn properly."

"Oh, Spanish," Hashi said with a grin.

There was a brief embarrasing pause for Ayelen before she said, "Er, no, German."

Hashi's eyes gleamed. "And yet you speak and read Nihoni." The pilot never passed up an opportunity to point out that while her captain was of Albion, German and Spanish descent, she'd grown up speaking only English—and then learned Nihoni, which not many people outside the Empire of the Sun spoke. Ayelen usually defended herself by pointing out that it was because of a girl and then defended *that* by pointing out that she had been fifteen.

"Anyways," Ayelen said promptly. She approached the comms console and flipped a switch that would allow her to speak to the entire ship. "*Cora's* crew, this is your captain speaking. If anyone found anything useful, report in, please."

Lights blinked. Ayelen flipped the first switch. "Shimi."

"Not good, Skip," said a crackly voice. "Somebody did a real number on her. Some of it seems intentional, some collateral. The engines themselves seem fine. It's dead cold down here, there's been no heat for days. Also, the main valve's shot—literally, I think somebody took a blunderbuss to it. The entire left intake's busted, needs to be torn out before I can even start to think about rerouting. Somebody used explosives on it. Secondary valves on the right intake are corroded—swear to gods, I find this ship's mechanic, gonna give him an earful, no way to treat a ship like—"

"Shimi, focus."

"Sorry, Skip. Look, long story short, it's dead in water and it's going to stay like that for at least a few days."

"How many is few?"

"Four. And that's the bare minimum to get her limping back to the nearest port. I'm not keen on floating out here, but that's the way it is."

"What about electricity?"

"Well, parts of ship are powered by the batteries, the comms for instance. But the lights, well, somebody tore out all wires straight from the main transformer. I need to patch that and then restart the generator, which also seems to have taken some beating. I'll make that my priority, don't worry. Nobody likes walking a deserted ship in the dark."

"Do what you do best, Shimi. There'll be someone on the bridge at all times to take reports."

"Aye, aye, Skip. Send us lunch later, please."

Another flip of the switch and Pavel's voice said, "Skip, we've found bodies in one of the passageways on the lower decks. Three male, one female. I'd say crewmen, from their clothes, what's left of them." There was a pregnant pause. "It's, uh, it's bad, Skip. They're covered in blood and bruises. There's broken limbs and—uh, look, we'll take them to the infirmary so Doc can have a proper look."

"I'll be down there shortly," Ayelen said and turned off the comms. "You hope this time it won't be..." she said, looking at Hashi. The marines were calm as usual but Ayelen knew her crew too well not to notice the tension.

"But it always is," the pilot said resignedly.

"I'll go see what the Doc has to say," Ayelen said while motioning to two of the marines. "You take a look at their charts."

Hashi nodded, and Ayelen descended the stairs, back into the dark passageways.

\* \* \*

"Captain," Doctor Carville said when Ayelen entered the infirmary. Every bed had a body on it and all bodies were covered with sheets but one. Carville was leaning over it, examining the bruised flesh.

"Beaten to death, all four of them. There was a lot of bleeding, torn skin and flesh, but all four share the same cause of death." His voice had the usual calm, professorial tone. Carville had an almost permanent aura of a university lecturer, which is one of the reasons Ayelen always thought of him as Carville, even when she called him Doc.

"Yes?"

He raised his head and looked at her over the rims of his glasses. "Their skulls were bashed in."

"Ugh," was all Ayelen could say.

Carville motioned for her to come closer.

"I'm not going to like this, I can tell," she said as she approached the bed.

"All of them have bite marks. Multiple bite marks, on various parts of torso, limbs, neck and head. Judging from size and shape of the bites, they were made by human mouths."

"Mouths. Plural." Her voice was that peculiar kind of flat caused solely by things that cannot even be deemed 'unexpected'.

"I'm afraid so," Carville said.

One of the marines in the infirmary spoke up, "Ma'am, there were also traces of firefight in several locations. And blood trails, I'd say from bodies being dragged."

\* \* \*

She pulled everyone but the skeleton crew from *Cora* and sent them searching deck to deck. The search parties kept reporting in every few minutes: pools and trails of blood, marks on the bulkheads, floor and several doors that could have only come from somebody's head or fist being smashed into it. They were also finding bodies, in groups. Some had wounds identical to the bodies in the infirmary; others had numerous stab and/or bullet wounds. A good percentage had bloody mouths; several held pieces of human flesh in tightly clenched jaws.

The bodies would be later transported to a single location on the ship. They had already found the ship's crew roster, with photographs of each member.

While they were back on the bridge waiting for reports, Ayelen gave the ship's log to Carville. He opened it up at the last few filled out pages and scrutinized the minute script for a few minutes.

"Well, they were on an expedition to the south pole, collecting samples of ice. Six days in, they encountered bad weather, decided to turn back. Two days later they saw signals off their port side. It was a makeshift raft, one man aboard. Claimed to be the sole survivor of a trader sunk by pirates. They took him onboard, set course for Kellenport. Two days after that, they encountered another storm. That's the last entry. Three days ago."

Hashi hummed. Ayelen saw her lips move wordlessly, the pilot's eyes focused on nothing in particular somewhere on the floor. She was doing calculations in her head, taking into account myriad factors. Moments later Hashi said, "Yes, that's it. I've seen the course they plotted for Kellenport; taking into account their average speed and the storm, three days ago the ship would have been close enough to Pallani current to get swept up by it, end up here."

The comms buzzed. It was Pavel. "Skip, I just found the mess hall. The doors are sealed. From the inside."

"Did you knock?"

"Yep, banged on it, first with my fist then with the wrench. Not a peep from inside. I'll report as soon as we're in."

Ayelen turned towards Carville. He just nodded and picked

up his bag.

\* \* \*

Whoever was on the other side of the mess hall doors did their best to keep everyone else out of it. In the end, there was no other way than explosives. Just as doctor Carville arrived, Pavel's team was ready to blow the charges. There was a roar and then a dull *thunk* as the doors fell into the room.

Inside, chairs and tables were overturned and stacked into a barricade at the far end of the room. Pavel and three marines stepped into the mess hall slowly, their eyes surveying the room.

"We mean you no harm," Pavel said in a loud, steady voice. "Nous vous voulon pas de mal," he added in French, just in case. English *was* still the lingua franca of mariners across Earth and Colonies but there was no need to presume.

There was a rattle behind the barricade and a disheveled man emerged. "You've come!" he cried and charged at Pavel. The marines were faster and immediately wrestled him to the floor. But the man didn't fight them: to Pavel it seemed he cried out from joy and relief. Pavel was about to tell him to calm down but the man suddenly went limp in the marines' hands. Doctor Carville passed Pavel and put his hands on the man's throat, opened his eyes, checked his breathing.

"He's unconscious," the Doc said to Pavel. "Also lightly dehydrated. We need to take him to the infirmary immediately. Oh, and it would appear he's the captain." Carville pointed at a small golden patch on the man's right breast.

"What about his head?" Pavel asked. Carville ran his fingers through the man's matted hair. "Blood, but not his."

"It's his," said one of Pavel's team members. She was pointing at something behind the barricade. "There's a body here."

"I'd recommend you strap him to a bed once you get him into one," Pavel murmured to the Doc. The physician just let out a small "Hmm."

\*　\*　\*

It *was* the ship's captain, Henning Werner. They confirmed his identity using the photograph in the crew roster. It had been taken when he was a few years younger and a lot less haggard but he was still recognizable.

Captain Werner was now strapped down and still unconscious as doctor Carville was finishing up with the examination.

They had also found the cabin where the castaway slept, but a search discovered nothing useful, just a cloth bag shoved under a bed with a few pieces of tattered clothing inside. The smell of Avellan ocean was strong on them, as well as an overpowering stench of body sweat and another, very faint smell that Ayelen couldn't quite place.

"Bruises and cuts, but nothing life threatening. Marks on his neck, someone had tried to asphyxiate him. He, most likely," Carville said and pointed towards the body they'd recovered from the mess hall.

Ayelen glanced at that body again. It could not be identified from the crew roster—the face was caved in from, as Carville put it succinctly, 'repeated blunt force trauma'.

"Can you wake him up? I'll call Hashi down here" Ayelen said.

Carville frowned, thinking. "He has been through a severe trauma. Be gentle."

\*　\*　\*

Shimi had seen all kinds of damage done to ships and parts of ships but *Zodia's* was just so damned peculiar. Dozens of places with evidence of explosions or gunfights or small fires were par for the course—she had served for years on several ASF cutters and had seen her share of ship and outpost raids and full-on battles' aftermaths. But there was some damage here that just made no sense.

"There's damage to the steam pipes all over the ship. The heating pipes specifically," she had reported to Captain Itzel earlier.

"Cause?" the skipper had asked over the comms.

"Well, seems to be ruptures caused by too much pressure. Recent damage. Just giving a heads up, if anyone gets cold, button up, I won't be turning on the heating anytime soon."

Now Shimi was back working on the electricity generator, but in the back of her mind those damaged heating pipes niggled at her. The generator itself was also damaged, by what she concluded was an improvised incendiary bomb.

There was a strong scent of alcohol and chemicals all over the damaged components of the large steam-powered device. But the damage was repairable. Most important, the heatstone was still in the boiler, still active. She had tested it by the tried and true method of spitting on it while holding it in gloved hands; the peculiar slender stone hissed and her spittle bubbled and steamed on its surface. Well, at least there's that, she thought as she replaced the heatstone into its holder, ready to be lowered into the boiler's water tank once the generator was to be activated.

By appearance the heatstone was somewhere between a crystal shard and a piece of coral, by nature still, after decades in use, a mystery to all but the few men and women in the employ of Angus MacMillan, nicknamed Lord of Steam and by that implicitly King of the Worlds, because the modern civilization depended completely on his patented steam engines.

Collins, her right-hand man was ready. She moved into the next chamber, with the console that gave control over all the steam-powered devices on the deck: the electricity generator and the two engines that powered the ship's propulsion system.

"Ready?" Shimi shouted.

"Ready, ma'am!" came Collins voice.

\* \* \*

Captain Werner slowly opened his eyes and noticed Ayelen and Hashi standing beside the cot.

"ASF?" he asked, squinting at their uniforms.

"Yes. Captain Itzel, of the cutter *Cora*. What happened to you?"

He closed his eyes. "Picked up a castaway. Steinwall. He did this. He did all of this."

"What exactly did he do, Captain Werner?" Ayelen asked in a level voice, trying to keep Werner calm and coherent. It would help him talk, and it would help Hashi read him.

"He said he was just a civilian," Werner said, almost pleadingly. "Wanted to help out, repay our kindness in some way. When it..."

There were tears in his eyes as he stared at the ceiling.

Ayelen cast a quick glance at Hashi, who'd moved a step back and out of Werner's field of view. The redhead Nihoni's eyes were closed, her lips lightly pursed in concentration.

"What happened, Captain Werner?" Ayelen asked again, touching his hand and smiling gently.

His face was despair and sorrow and fear. "He's a monster."

Ayelen noticed Hashi twitch at the words, which meant that the mental images she "read" from Werner's mind were strong, very strong.

"He snuck into the engine room, he—he killed poor Albert, slit his throat.... We tried to get to him but the doors were barred and then—it was too late, he'd already gotten to the boilers.... It spread through the ship, so fast—we fought them but I couldn't, I couldn't. Told them we need to barricade ourselves in, they wouldn't listen...."

Hashi's eyes snapped open and she looked at Ayelen with horror. "Skip, there was something in the steam. All those breaches in the heating pipes, that was intentional. Something in the steam made some of the crew go berserk, start beating and biting the others."

Ayelen ran to the wall, grabbed the comms microphone, and started shouting into it, praying to gods it wasn't too late.

\* \* \*

Shimi watched the dials move steadily towards green. She shouted through the rising din of a resurrected steam engine. "Collins, how does it look?"

"A-bleedin' okay, ma'am!" came a happy reply from the next chamber accompanied by several puffs of steam. The lights on the engine deck flickered on.

The thermometers showed the boiler heating up nicely—and then Shimi heard her captain's voice bellow something from the comms console on the far wall. She hustled towards it and was half way there when she made out the shouts of "Don't activate the boilers, Shimi! Don't activate the boilers!"

Shimi felt something twist her insides as she turned towards main control console. In the flickering lights she could swear there was something off with the color of the steam coming from the chamber next door—and from the chamber Collins burst out, shrieking, all bulging eyes and flailing arms and a terrible rictus grin. His eyes focused on Shimi, and he ran towards her, staggering over his own feet, wailing and gibbering.

Shimi had experienced violence, fear, myriad kinds of threats, some which women faced more than men. She had fought, been stabbed and shot. She had seen violent men before, their blood up from drink, drugs, despair or wanton desire. She had also known her crew, known them for years and known them well.

This was not Collins. The distorted features resembled him but there was nothing of Collins in those horrible manic eyes as Shimi was tackled to the floor and hands began to beat at her torso. Teeth clicked, missing her nose by a hair's breadth. She slammed her fist into his chin, grabbed his face and pushed it away. His fists kept pummeling, hitting blindly but connecting every time. She felt her ribs crack. She grabbed at her utility belt with her right hand, fighting the rising panic. She felt something round and thin under her fingertips, pulled it from the belt and shoved it deep into Collins' neck, pulled out and shoved again, all the while screaming violently.

Collins slid off her, and she lay there, trying to catch her breath, shaking from the adrenaline and fighting back the sobs that suddenly tried to overcome her. She rose, staggering. Collins lay in a pool of spreading blood, dark under the dim lights, his face still contorted. She let the bloody screwdriver fall to the floor.

Shimi reached the controls and turned the boiler off. Her sides burned and stung as she approached the comms unit, the chamber once again lit only by the lanterns they'd set up before.

"Skip," she spoke with heavy breath, "Collins is dead."

"Shimi!" The voice was Hashi's. "The Skip is on her way with marines and the Doc. What is going on? Are you okay?"

"Yes, I'm—" she looked at the body of a good machinist and a good man. "I'm okay."

*   *   *

"How the hell is this even possible?" Ayelen demanded as they stood over Collins' corpse. Carville was tending to Shimi, who insisted she was okay. Collins was a good man, a good machinist, and a good crewman. Ayelen had lost crewmen before, to violence and accident, yet every new one hurt as if he or she was the first.

"I have no idea," Carville said. "There are compounds that can make a man lose his wits, the ancient Norsemen had berserkir, warriors that would use a concoction to drive themselves into a killing frenzy. But I've never seen anything like this."

"This is wrong," Shimi murmured, looking at the dead man.

"Drink this," Carville said, handing Shimi a small bottle from his satchel, "and sit down for a few minutes. Now."

Shimi did so, glaring at the Doc. Ayelen turned to Carville, who continued, "Peculiar way of delivering the toxin. Perhaps its presence couldn't be masked in food or drink and that is why he…"

Ayelen's mind switched into investigative mode. "Could it be that something causes … this … only when exposed to high temperatures?"

Carville shrugged. "Possible."

Ayelen made a decision. "We're abandoning this ship." She turned to Shimi, who kept looking at Collins. "Shimi," Ayelen said curtly, and Shimi raised her eyes. "Get a portable generator, have a team set it up to power the emergency beacon. We'll need to be able to find *Zodia* again when we get back with more ships. Understood?"

"Aye, aye, Skip," Shimi said, gave one last look at Collins and moved out.

\* \* \*

Hashi was psychic. The ASF employed psychics, but Hashi was not one of them. Aside from the crew of *Cora*, no one in the entire ASF knew of Hashi's ability. This was of course very, very illegal. The ASF demanded all psychics on active duty be registered, tested and assigned a rating according to their abilities and their potential use. Hashi wouldn't do it. Nihoni were still a mostly isolationist culture, and few crewed international ships on Earth, let alone the Colonies. Hashi wanted to sail so much she wasn't willing to lose her options because of a fluke of nature that gave her psychic abilities.

Ayelen had found out soon after Hashi was assigned to *Cora*. She kept her pilot's secret. She'd said she understood why Hashi hid her ability, understood the call of the sea she'd felt all her life.

She'd said Hashi's real talents were on display behind a pilot's console and the fact that she could read or sense minds was to Ayelen a completely secondary talent. Hashi loved her for that, treating her sailor first, psychic distant second. Because of that she didn't mind using her ability to help out if it was needed.

Captain Werner had to be sedated before Doc and the skipper ran to Shimi's aid because he had started screaming incoherently. Hashi had to take deep breaths, concentrate on clearly seeing the images that had occupied her mind when she 'read' Werner. Acknowledging them fully was the only way of making them eventually go away.

Among the images was the body in the mess hall. Werner had come to blows with the man a day into their self-imposed captivity. The cause was just a bar of chocolate, but they were both cold and terrified and it escalated quickly and ended savagely.

And then she saw something that made her run for her captain.

* * *

"A psychic?" Ayelen said. They were back on *Cora*, on the bridge.

"Yes. The castaway, Steinwall, took a hostage with him after murdering the chief machinist and the two men who were on shift and sealing himself on the engine deck. Sara Ellinson, a biologist.

She was alive when the crew tried to break in, they heard her scream for help. But that's not all. Werner heard her later, after locking himself in the mess hall. Steinwall and Ellinson passed by the door, Steinwall even knocked, taunted him. Werner heard Ellinson shout that Steinwall was taking her away."

"On what?" Pavel interjected. "All the boats are accounted for. And the Doc said that, according to the ship's log, Steinwall's raft was left behind when they picked him up."

Ayelen's mind was racing over the various discoveries made in the past few hours, from docking to now. The loading bay, the tools and materials and tarpaulins on the docking platform, around a large empty area. The loading crane. The emergency beacon's missing generator. And then, like a knife slowly twisting in her gut, the memory of the strange smell of the castaway's clothes finally opened the right door in her mind, a door she preferred firmly closed.

"He built another raft," Ayelen said. "That's the stuff that was on the docking platform. He built another raft, lowered it using the loading crane."

"Okay. Where do we search for him?" Pavel said. "The nearest landmass is the south part of Addison's Hand and that's just an unexplored wilderness. He must have a ship or airship waiting for him."

"No," Ayelen said. "Hashi. Head for the south pole, full speed."

Hashi turned and started executing the command, letting Pavel ask the question. "Skip?"

"Took me a little to connect the dots. Steinwall claimed he was a passenger on a trading ship. While it's possible a trader was this far south, it wouldn't have been so far south as to make ice and frostbites likely. The captain's log said some of the raft's provisions were in a box filled with ice. And the ship's surgeon wrote down in his log how he found evidence of frostbite on Steinwall. Yes, could have been from exposure and he could have encountered an ice floe and used it for water and keeping his food fresh but then there's his clothes. I wouldn't blame you for not recognizing one of the smells on it. The situation I was in was … memorable."

"Skipper, I have no idea what you're on about," Pavel said.

"Aetherships are plated in aluminium not just because it's good insulation from long term Aether exposure. It's also handy because aluminium does not take on the smell of Aether. Wood does—and cloth does. Skin and hair too, I can attest to that personally, but that fades away relatively quickly."

"Oh," Hashi said, finally realizing. "The *Pirinee*."

"Yes," said Ayelen, "the *Pirinee*. It was a long time ago and the smell on the shirt is very faint and mixed with sweat and other smells but, well, nothing jolts a memory quite like a scent, even if it is with a delay."

"You think our man was exposed to Aether?" Doctor Carville interjected.

"Yes."

"But the Tear is … *north*." Pavel's voice was as confused as the look on his face.

"The one we know of, yes," Ayelen said.

"Captain, surely," Carville started, "They've performed extensive surveys in the first several years of the colonization, a Tear—"

"Is relatively easily spotted, yes, I know. If it's a large one, like the one we used to reach Avella and other Colonies. But just because all the Tears we've encountered so far have been large, does not mean all of them have to be. Nor that a world cannot have more than one."

"I'd say this was pure speculation," Carville said, "were it not for the fact that the northern Tear is several weeks away by air or sea and I have it on good authority the smell of Aether fades from clothes completely within a week."

Ayelen smiled. "You remember."

Carville nodded with a polite smile. "As a man of science, I make a point of always memorizing information on interesting occurrences. Even if I am half-blind drunk."

That was the first time Ayelen had spoken to anyone about what happened aboard the *Pirinee* and even then it took her several jugs of 'machinist's milk', that classic 'hooch' of mariners which received its name from the fact that the ship's machinists traditionally made it and from the peculiar effect the heatstone had on any alcoholic beverage it was dipped in, that is, turning said beverage milky white. She told Carville and Hashi, because she needed to tell someone and they offered an ear and a jug and she had been thankful for both.

\* \* \*

As her ship sped southward, Ayelen's thoughts were once again filled with that voyage on the *Pirinee*. The Tear, so named because it literally resembled a giant rupture in the air above the icy waters of the Arctic, allowed the various nations of Earth to access the vast interdimensional medium, the Aether, and through it, other worlds—all you needed was to go into the Aether and find another Tear. The *Pirinee* was a cargo/personnel transporter, a massive airship powered by steam and covered in aluminium plates. When its engines were sabotaged and a terrifying explosion almost tore the aethership in two and exposed dozens of compartments to Aether, Ayelen was one of the exposed passengers. Aethership crews called the Aether the Emerald Sea (even though it was more similar to gas), and for a year after the incident Ayelen had had violent nightmares about green all around her, pressing and suffocating her as she sank deeper and deeper.

The knots in her stomach weren't from the memories of past but the anxiety of imminent future. What was Steinwall doing? And would they be fast enough to save Sara Ellinson?

They'd passed the location where *Zodia* had picked up Steinwall, and since the ship's log didn't mention any sort of propulsion on Steinwall's raft except makeshift paddles, Hashi had done some calculations and mapped out an area for them to search for Steinwall's point of origin. The area was large. But it helped that they were scanning the horizon for a flash of green.

They had buried Collins at sea a day ago. He'd had a wife, no children. Ayelen would visit her when they returned to New Cordoba, give her the terrible news in person. The mood of the crew was quiet. One of their own had died, and they were in pursuit of the man responsible so of course, everyone was giving their best, but there was also the fact that they were pursuing a man who had killed an entire ship's crew by turning half of them into mindless brutes.

And also, there was the Aether to consider. Tears were stable—most of the time. Sometimes they'd fluctuate in size and shape, expanding or contracting in the blink of an eye. All the known Tears had been carefully studied and their *moods*, the Aethership crews called them, such a wonderful euphemism, could be predicted, but if Steinwall had really been in contact with a Tear here in the southern polar region, it was a Tear whose mood was unknown. She didn't want some of her crew or her entire ship to suddenly be engulfed by the Aether.

A buzzing comms snapped her from her thoughts.

"Skip, I think I see it," Pavel said.

*   *   *

The Tear glimmered in the polar dusk, a grin dozens of meters across. It was tiny compared to the ones the Aetherships usually traveled through but it was still a rent in the fabric of space-time bleeding dim emerald light and wisps of Aether. It loomed over a large ice formation, and directly beneath it Ayelen could see the remains of some type of outpost: shacks, tents and a large, tall wooden structure.

She noticed the flickering of an open fire by one of the shacks. Her binoculars revealed more: a figure hauling a large sack. Steinwall, she guessed. And there was also the vessel he'd used to reach this place. Ayelen let out a quiet 'What the..." when she discerned its nature: it was some sort of aircraft. The tarpaulins were not being used as sails but wings, and there was a makeshift propeller at the aft.

On the deck, Pavel, Hashi and Ayelen's marines were ready.

Ayelen checked her gear again, the padded body armor under

a coat, a revolver and cutlass, then pulled the goggles over her eyes and stepped out onto the deck. The cold air rushed at her and a million icy needles carried by the wind stabbed at her face and the glass of the goggles.

She put the megaphone to her lips.

"Steinwall! This is the cutter *Cora* of the Avellan Security Fleet! Cease all actions and surrender! I repeat, cease all actions and surrender!"

Pavel put his binoculars down and shook his head. "He ran when you called out to him. He's doing something in the aircraft."

"Hashi?" Ayelen asked. Her pilot looked anxious while she answered, "I can feel her, Skip. It's hard not to, she's so terrified it's like a beacon."

The deck shook as *Cora* made contact with the ice. The planks were lowered and boots thumped over them as the marines charged, led by Ayelen. They were closing the distance as the wind was slowly picking up.

Here, closer to the Tear everything was bathed in the emerald glow. Steinwall was a dark shape running from his aircraft towards the tall structure. The structure was so tall, Ayelen was now sure, that you could probably stand on the platform at its top and reach for the Tear.

She heard shouts from the aircraft.

"Pavel, Shimi, aircraft. Squad two, with them! Squad three, check the buildings! Squad one, with me!" Ayelen shouted.

Steinwall was fast, so fast. Ayelen had at least two marksmen who could take him down, moving target and strengthening wind notwithstanding. But she needed him alive. *Zodia's* crew and Collins deserved him on a trial and sentenced to the harshest punishment in the Colonies: hard labor for life. The Colonies didn't waste resources.

They reached the structure a good half a minute or more after Steinwall had ran into it. The wooden door was barred from the inside. She nodded to her marines, and two of them pulled axes from the holsters on their backs and smashed their way inside in a matter of seconds.

It was dark and silent inside. They lit their electric torches and found a staircase that led to the next floor. Muffled noise of footsteps came from above. First floor, second floor, and third floor were just large spaces with some equipment and crates. Several times Ayelen noticed traces of small explosions and large stains and frozen pools of what could only be blood.

And then, they reached the topmost floor, with an inclined platform leading from the floor to an opening in the ceiling. The Tear's glow spilled through it. The smell of Aether was heavy in the air. Ayelen's guts twisted into a knot. She motioned to the marines. Ten steps, up and out.

The wind was hissing at her, pinpricking her cheeks and lips. The Tear was directly above, stretching left and right. The not-quite-gas slowly moved in tendrils and swirls. Darker and lighter patches of emerald green stretched towards infinity just beyond the lips of the spatial rift. The Tear loomed over her, vast and unknowable.

Ayelen's breath caught. The *Pirinee* started crawling back into her mind, the screech of tearing metal—she slammed the door on the memory with all her mental might.

At the edge of the roof was a large metal crane, stretched out to its full length *into* the Tear.

A dark shape was clambering across it.

"Steinwall!" Ayelen bellowed and fired off a warning shot from her rifle. He stopped and she saw his head turn. A hood was covering his head; the light of the Tear glinted on his tinted goggles.

The marines had spread out around her, rifles aimed at Steinwall.

"I am Captain Ayelen Itzel, Avellan Security Fleet. You will descend the crane and surrender."

His voice was hoarse. "The world needs this, Captain!"

His hand moved, and Ayelen saw it drop something. A flare; its red glow mixed with the Tear's light. The flare hit the metal base of the crane and caused a small flash of white light. Ayelen knew that flash. Everyone in her squad knew it. Her eyes surveyed the snow covered roof. She had seconds, if that.

There: two small mounds, no bigger than if a shoebox was buried under them. Two hissing sounds moved rapidly from the crane towards them through the snow, trailing white smoke. One of the mounds was several meters away, but the other just a few footsteps. Ayelen moved.

"Incendiary!" she shouted as the marines ran back towards the platform.

She reached the mound, dropped her rifle and shoved both hands into the snow. There, a wooden box. She grabbed it and hoped that it was not bolted to the roof. It rose from the snow as she pulled, trailing a thin detonator wire. Ayelen threw it.

The incendiary sailed over the edge of the roof as Ayelen lay down into snow. Two blasts and the zipping sound of shrapnel. Had it been warmer the wire would have burned faster. Gods look out for their fools, Ayelen thought. She rose, saw her marines rising—or in the case of two marines, running up the platform back onto the roof, visibly hurting from the jump they'd executed moments earlier.

Steinwall was not on the crane. She noticed a shape behind the crane's base. She ran, her marines following.

When they reached him, Steinwall was kneeling over the opened boiler of the small steam engine that powered the crane. His coat and shirt were torn to pieces; there were several gashes across his chest and arms from stray shrapnel. The blood was dripping into the boiler's water as Steinwall's face lifted towards Ayelen. His right goggle glass was cracked and she could see a green, bewildered eye.

Ayelen wanted to say so much now that they finally had him. But looking at Steinwall, bleeding from the chest and arms, what came out of her mouth was "You fucking idiot."

Two of the marines stepped forward, grabbed him under each arm.

Steinwall grinned and from the fingers of his left hand a heatstone fell into the water. There was a hiss and a small cloud of steam burst from the opened boiler.

Realization and despair took hold of Ayelen's mind as she watched the two marines recoil from the steam.

Their eyes bulged, veins popping in their necks as they shrieked and charged. Other marines snapped into action, grappling with their maddened comrades.

Steinwall was hobbling away from the steam engine. Ayelen saw a marine run up to the steaming boiler and kick at the cover, dropping it down over the opening and then scramble for the water release vent.

She charged after Steinwall, ramming into him just a meter before he reached the edge of the roof. It seemed he was ready to jump in an attempt to escape. Ayelen slammed her fist into his face once, twice as she kneeled atop him. All the while he was grinning. He reeked of Aether.

She pulled out a set of heavy handcuffs from her coat, slammed her elbow into Steinwall's face, and then cuffed him with ease.

"Fucking monster!" she screamed at him as she drove a fist into his plexus. "What the fuck did you do to my men?!"

Through broken teeth and blood he said, gasping for breath, "I was in there. We all were, that's what we came here for. But only I was good enough."

"What?"

"Only I realized you had to be naked to honor its magnificence. And in turn only I was myself honored by it."

She turned at the sound of two gunshots. Her marines were silent, heads down. One of them was getting up from the roof, holding a bloodied hand to his neck. There were two bodies in the snow. I'm so sorry, Ayelen thought, her throat tightening.

She turned back to Steinwall.

He smiled. "I saw it for what it is. I dove deep—and was remade. My blood is now poison to common minds. My mind expanded beyond mortal limits. But they couldn't abide that. Wanted to take me away, take it from me. *Cure* me, they said. I wouldn't let them take it from me."

"You killed them."

"Some. Others escaped on our ship, believed they'd marooned me here."

"So you made a raft and then *Zodia* found you. But why did you kill *them*?"

"Because I needed to come back, once I realized what Sara was," he said. "You wouldn't understand," he added softly.

She forced him to his feet. The marines were carrying their dead comrades back towards the platform. The boiler was cold. The Tear glowed above.

"How did you find me?" Steinwall asked, as if the thought just now occurred to him.

"I used my limited mortal mind," she said as she shoved him forward.

In front of the structure, several marines waited, with Pavel and Hashi.

"We found bodies, Skip," one of the marines said. "He'd piled them."

"Ellinson?" Ayelen asked.

Pavel nodded. "She was in the aircraft, tied up. He'd turned the steam engine to full power, tried to overload and explode it. Got there just in time. I guess he didn't want us to have her."

"She has the sight. I just wanted to expand it," Steinwall said.

Ayelen saw Hashi flinch slightly. The Nihoni's fingers moved towards her revolver, then stopped.

"Take him to the brig," Ayelen said as she handed Steinwall off to the marines. "Have Doc bandage his wounds and then keep him chained up. No sharp instruments of any kind. It's hard to believe it, but it seems his blood in the water was responsible for what happened to Collins and two of the marines."

"I don't think there is a man or woman aboard who'd hold it against you if we hanged him right now," Hashi said quietly as they watched Pavel and the marines lead Steinwall away.

"He killed three of our own; I want him to pay for those deaths with every strike of the pickaxe for years to come. No easy way out for him."

"You really think his blood is what did it?"

"I'm not taking any chances. We'll let the Admiralty deal with him. If he really exposed himself to Aether, if it changed him— well, what they do to him when they start testing might just be worse than forced labor," Ayelen said grimly.

Hashi nodded slowly as they walked towards *Cora*. "Are *you* okay, Skip?"

Behind Ayelen was the outpost, filled with dead; the Tear was glowing implacably above it. In the distance the sun was setting and the wind picked up again, carrying with it the smell of the sea; brine and that thing that reminded her of cinnamon. Her ship was waiting ahead, bobbing lightly on the waves. Figures moved on the deck, under the lights of lanterns.

Her ship. Her crew. They'd been through a lot in the past years, victories and losses. Today they lost two more but they'd bring a madman and murderer to justice. They'd done their duty.

"I'll manage," Ayelen said. "Just like we always do."

# THE INTUITION OF FUTURE TRUTHS

*"When a scientist is ahead of [their] times, it is often through misunderstanding of current, rather than intuition of future, truth. In science there is never any error so gross that it won't one day, from some perspective, appear prophetic."*

Jean Rostand

### David Boop

JALEASA ROUNDTREE marched over the sodden earth to the emitters. She carried the requisite two buckets of water to turn them on. The sun hadn't yet crested the trees, but the dark relented enough for her to aim at the water funnel. Boiler full, she pressed the ignition button until the dried peat in the boiler's furnace caught fire.

While waiting for the water to boil, Jaleasa cut new blocks of peat to place in the furnace once the job was done. She finished just as the engine kicked in. Steam slowly lifted the lid of the exhaust, building until a full gust kept it flipped open entirely. Jaleasa cranked the release and steam funneled from the reserve into the pipes. A dial indicated that, indeed, the machine emitted a low frequency pulse. Humans couldn't hear tone, but the worm-like *marshers* could. In a matter of an hour, the pasture would contain about a dozen of the earth-dwelling creatures, as they burrowed up to the surface to see what all the commotion was. By then, Jaleasa's farmhands would be ready to bind their bisected legs and flip them over for milking. Jaleasa gathered up her buckets and returned to the barn. She'd milked enough *marshers* in the early days.

No word had come back on the blueprints Jaleasa submitted for a *marshers* milking machine six months ago, but then, the resources dedicated to building new tech was limited to transportation and defense.

All part of being a farm owner on the colony world of Eurynome.

"Momma? Where are you?"

"In the barn by the irrigation vats!" Jaleasa yelled back to Karlus, annoyed. He was still up by the house. Why the good lord hadn't put enough sense in him to look in the barn first instead of screaming his head off all over creation she'd never know.

Karlus walked in, and though she'd told him right where she'd be, he still looked around the barn for a bit before stumbling upon her in the back room. "Oh, there you are."

He was her youngest, only fourteen by Earth standards, and though Jaleasa loved him as much as her other children, she often wished he'd stayed in her womb longer to cook. She tried to be as patient with the boy as possible, but he could be taxing.

"Yes, right where I said I'd be."

Karlus knelt by the clear vat where tens of thousands of irrigation beetles swarmed in sawdust. He tapped on the Plexiglas and a large group responded by massing at the spot. It was a good thing the vat was made from the same materials as a starship portal, otherwise the bugs would burrow through it with pinchers twice the size of their bodies. He stared at them, oblivious to his mother hovering over him.

"What's up, son? You were looking for me?"

Not looking away from the bugs, Karlus said, "There's some men comin' up the road. They look all official and what not."

Officials never meant anything good.

Jaleasa returned the scoop of irrigation beetles back to the breeder vat, annoyed that seeding the north field would have to wait until the next day. She dusted down the length of her overalls and clapped her hands free of any dirt.

"Let's go see what those officials want, eh?"

Karlus grinned widely in a way that left no doubt that he expected the representatives of the colonial government to bring him a gift.

"Oh, don't get excited. People like that only bring trouble."

\* \* \*

"We think we've found oil."

They could've knocked Jaleasa over with a *squegret* feather. Since Eurynome was first surveyed some fifty years ago, the search for oil, or a gasoline-like equivalent had been the number one priority. Many other planets produced it, but not this one. Something about the soil caused all decay to just filter back into the soil, regardless of time and pressure. That was why their technology reverted back to steam. And while that was fine for farming, it created problems for higher power instruments such as computers, weaponry, and others.

"Well, that's good. But why tell me?"

Jaleasa had invited the three representatives of the government into her house. They accepted the *rumbard* tea and *tika-nut* biscotti she'd offered in the living room. Karlus spied in from the doorway, and despite repeated attempts to shoo him away, he just kept coming back.

A lady with gray hair wrapped tight in a bun answered. She

wore the insignia of being a Terran liaison. "You've got quite a reputation around the colony, Ms. Roundtree. Your farm is the best producing with the lowest record for health issues. Even those back on Earth have noticed how successful you've been in such a short time. Especially with so few hands. Other colony worlds want to know your secrets."

"It's because I don't hire a bunch of idiots that I don't have mistakes. Sure, we work harder than some, but I'd rather keep my good name."

"Well, it's that type of pluck we need!" An overly positive man said. Jaleasa knew him all too well. Hector Gallegos traveled to this world on the same colony ship she had, the first. Primed since birth to be a leader, Hector knew how to get people to rally around a cause, even while sticking a knife in their backs. "See, this recently discovered oil doesn't come from the ground, the same way it does on most planets..."

Hector left the end hanging as cue for the last visitor to speak and while Jaleasa didn't know the boy's name, she knew what he was; a savant. Genetically manipulated in the womb, savants were hyper-intelligent in certain areas.

"It comes from a certain plant, the most unusual genius of eukaryote that we've discovered on any planetary structure. It draws nutrients from the deep within the crust, where we'd normally look for oil, and produces a fruit with juices that have ignition properties normally found in petroleum." The excitement in his dark green eyes betrayed the child beneath the adult-sounding voice.

Jaleasa may not have been born a savant or anything, but she certain could piece together why they'd come to her.

"You want me to find a way to harvest these fruits and turn them into fuel, am I right?"

Hector nodded. "If anyone can do it, you can."

The liaison agreed. "We wish to put you in charge of all farming operations. We'll supply you with extra hands to keep your place running while you're gone. Plus, you'll be backed by a full contingent of our finest from our engineering division, agricultural department and the defense force."

"Defense force? Why do we need guns to farm some fruit?"

The three representatives looked to each other, a nod choosing Hector to answer.

"There are some... complications."

Jaleasa looked over to where Karlus hid poorly behind the doorframe. His mouth was over his hand to stifle a giggle.

"See what I told you? Trouble. That's all they bring."

\* \* \*

Lieutenant-Commander Trevion Roundtree of the Eurynome Defense Force wished his younger brother, Dacquon, was there. Growing up, Dacq had been the peacekeeper on the farm. He could use some of the geneticist's rational thinking.

"I'm not going to tell you again, Mrs. Roundtree. We're not approaching the *vorarous* without a plan."

"Don't you 'Mizz Roundtree' me," his mother, Jaleasa, said, "just because you run off and join the military doesn't mean you can't call me mom anymore."

Things had been tense between the two of them since he landed the dirigible at the farm in the middle of *marshers* milking time. They scattered everywhere as the rotating props tilted to provide the ship a soft landing. Tasked with things more important than milk, he hadn't even considered the timing. The look his mother gave him as he walked down the gangplank indicated she had. It became quickly apparent in the ensuing fight that she hadn't forgiven him for leaving the farm to join up with the military. This atmosphere of discontent lasted the whole way to the rendezvous point. She either undermined his authority or embarrassed him every chance she got.

"As long as you're under my protection, *Mom*, you'll do as I say. This… thing, has taken the lives of dozens of good men. If we're going to make this work, you're going to have to trust me."

Trust was in short supply. When her and Dacquon's names came up as members of his team, Trevion knew his recent promotion was not as earned as he'd hoped. The twenty-five-year-old had risen quickly through the ranks, but had stalled out. Thirty-years since the EDF's creation and there just wasn't anything to defend against. Though a large portion of the planet had yet to be explored, there were no signs of any sentient species or local wildlife that couldn't easily be confined or controlled.

Until the *vorarous*.

"I read the reports, Trev. I know how dangerous it is. But I can't start devising a plan until I see it with my own two eyes. Dacquon's seen it."

"Yes, and barely survived the experience."

That'd been hard on them both, reading the report from Dacquon's exploration team. The twenty-year-old was in the final years of his doctorate in xenobiology and that meant field work. Only five out of ten people made it back from their initial discovery of the carnivorous plant. Dacquon's face took a hit from one of the creature's thousand thorny vines and he'd been laid up for weeks. Cosmetic surgery was not available on Eurynome yet, so he would have to live with the scars.

"Trevion, that wasn't his fault, nor none of those good people. There just so much we don't know about this planet yet, but we do know how this thing feeds now. We'll be careful, I swear."

Trevion sighed. They were both right. She knew the risks and he had the weaponry to keep them safe. They walked a fine line with the beast, and if its fruit didn't hold the future of the colony within its pulp, they would have just bombed the thing from above and be done with it.

"Fine, I'll set up a viewing trip, but no samples, okay? Dacquon's team is collecting those from below."

"Agreed." Jaleasa turned to Trevion's youngest brother,

Karlus. "Honey, Momma's going to go on a short trip for just a couple hours, not long. You stay here at the camp and keep working on your homework."

The decision to bring Karlus on the expedition was the result of a huge Karlus meltdown before they'd even left the farm. The thought of their mother going away for an indefinite amount of time caused too much stress on the simple boy. Early aptitude tests hadn't shown any sign of retardation, autism or other neuro-eccentric condition in Karlus. He just contained too many emotions and too few smarts to be left in anyone else's care.

Trevion considered his mother selfish to have had a third child. It was only her standing within the colony that had gotten her permission. She did it, he felt, to have another hand on the growing farm. She swore it was because her first two had come out so good, tops in their classes, well on their way to greatness, that she owed it to the colony to have another.

Karlus nodded and went back to his tablet where he worked at getting through the third-grade.

Jaleasa slapped Trevion on the shoulder and commanded, "Let's go meet my opponent."

He wondered, as they prepared to depart, if the plant knew what it would be going up against.

\* \* \*

Of the many of the steam-powered vehicles the colony engineers had created to get around Eurynome, Trevion loved the MACs best. Half-all terrain hover-cycle, half mini-tank, they moved like a *lazerblade* through over any landscape. It also came armed for just about any creature they encountered with side mounted missiles that could be activated remotely, if need be.

He should've been riding in the APCs with his mother and her support staff, but he'd had enough tension and longed for the independence of the micro-assault craft.

Eurynome's surface was as varied as Earth's, which made it a perfect planet to colonize. The area where the *vorarous* grew felt much like the Rockies of Earth. Foothills, wide gorges and snowcapped peaks made the region beautiful and dangerous. Between two mountains, a tear in the ground had produced a ravine a kilometer wide.

As Trevion approached the hot zone, he slowed his expedition down. The majority of the plants trigger vines lay close to the lip, but as one unfortunate soldier discovered, a few shoots extended farther into the trees.

"We'll walk from here," Trevion spoke into the headset.

Oil was the colony's most expensive import; it was reserved for only keeping machinery moving smoothly and not for burning. Trevion knew all eyes were on the success of this mission.

Trevion's team spread out along the recently blazed trail, testing every root, every shoot with a pike in case it should come to life. The trees thinned closer the rim and the *vorarous* vines became easy to identify. Thick and sickly-green with orange striations like veins, the tentacles of the monster had rows of thorns that locked onto any object that touched them. One soldier, who stepped on a vine when he sneezed, chose to have his leg shot off at the knee as opposed to being dragged into the *vorarous's* massive maw.

Jaleasa came up alongside him. "We're not even to the rim and they extend this far? I wonder how old it is."

"That's part of what Dacquon's team hopes to find out."

"Are they safe down in those caves?"

No one had informed either them of Dacquon's near death by his own request.

When the expedition had stopped at the University to pick him up, Trevion became concerned at the changes in his brother. It wasn't the scars on his face, or the notion he didn't smile upon seeing his family for the first time in years. Dacquon had become hard. At his core, Trevion felt, was stone. Like the creature had taken his soul, not just his looks from him. The whole flight to the rendezvous point, Dacquon barely said a word to him, Karlus or their mom. When he did, he spoke only in relation to the biology of the *vorarous*. The second they touched down, Dacquon took his team and headed off to a series of caves they believed would run under the plant creature, allowing them to take samples from its roots in case the precious petroleum-like fluids could be harvested that way.

"They believe the roots are not prehensile like the vines, but yes, some of my best soldiers went with them. They'll be fine."

His mom looked like she wasn't buying what he was selling, but chose not to argue about it. They had a task at hand.

On his orders, soldiers moved forward with a small generator. Using peat pellets, they lit up the furnace and waited for the engine to crank over. The noise was deafening when it came to life, but the technique was the only sure way to get to the rim. A score of pikes were connected to the generator by wires. Carefully, each soldier planted a pike in the ground close enough to a vine to trigger its defenses. In the blink of an eye, the tendril would wrap around the pike and attempt to yank it from the ground. Once they had several vines "caught" the generator was flipped on, allowing electricity to flow through the wires and fry the vines. The creature released the pikes and the burnt members were drawn away. This process was repeated until they could get to the lip and look over.

Jaleasa began, "Why can't we just do that until…" but her words trailed off. A three hundred meter drop lay before her. Along the sides of the ravine were millions of vines like a carpet. She didn't have to be a biologist to know, the amount of electricity needed to clear a path to the stalk would kill the creature and rob them of any chance of harvesting its fruit.

At the epicenter of the plant, about thirty meters below the rim, grew a thick, bulbous stalk the same color as the vines. Like a thousand potato eyes, globular dark purple fruits lay embedded within it. One spot on the stalk was charred where a fruit had been ignited accidentally when an unfortunate victim, one of Dacquon's original team, had tried flaming it with a torch before being sucked in to the currently invisible maw.

"It only opens when food is being delivered. If that victim hadn't discovered the fruit was combustible, we would have killed this thing and moved on."

"And we've discovered no others like it in the area?"

"We're not even sure how it reproduces yet. We can't get the fruit off of it intact. We've tried grapplers, but the fruit bursts apart. We tried lowering a person down from an airship, but as soon as they touched the fruit, vines wrapped around them and nearly brought the airship down with them."

"I'm sorry to ask, but I need to see it feed."

Trevion nodded. It'd been part of the plan. He signaled for the livestock to be brought from one of the trucks back at the debarkation point. Fifteen minutes later three *goatigs* arrived at Trevion's location along with one small stow-a-way.

"Hi, Momma. Hi, Trev. I made some friends."

Karlus grinned at them like he hadn't a care in the world.

\*   \*   \*

"KARLUS!" Jaleasa barked. "What in the five colonies are you doing here?"

The boy tucked his head down shamefully. "Well, I was on my way back to the tent and well, there was this noise I hadn't heard before and well, I looked into the back of this truck and there were these cute animals and well, I wanted to pet one, cause they looked kinda soft and well, someone closed the back of the truck and it started moving and well, the animals were scared so I told them I'd stay with them and keep them safe and well…"

Jaleasa had heard enough. She spun on her eldest. "How could you let this happen? He's not that small a kid to be missed by your people!" Trevion then turned on his subordinates, none who had a decent answer.

As she watched this trickle down accountability, the realization started hitting her. Her actions brought this. Her arrogance. She'd been taking care of herself for so long, ever since she left Earth for the colony, that there wasn't anything she couldn't handle. Even her boys. Trevion's command of her team and the discovery of Dacquon's near death had thrown her off her game. She knew Karlus didn't have enough sense to know that *goatigs*, when scared, can bite... hard.

"Did they nip at you any?" Jaleasa spun the boy around looking for marks.

"No, Momma. They just licked me. They are real nice!" To demonstrate, he knelt down by the closest *goatig*, who licked his face as if he had food on it. Karlus giggled and laughed like he was being tickled.

"Remarkable," Trevion said as he returned. "I've got a soldier who lost the tips of two fingers getting them into the back of the truck."

"He's got a knack with the local wildlife. *Squegrets* eat right out of his hand. Even the *marshers* calm down when he's with me. He still takes too many damn fool chances, though. Sometimes, I'm picking his cryin' ass off the ground. Sometimes, though, they just work out. You left too soon to see that."

Jaleasa realized after she'd spoke that she'd treaded on a difficult subject. She looked her son in the eyes and sincerely tried to apologize. "I'm sorry. I didn't mean to imply..."

Trevion put a hand on her shoulder in a comforting way. "I know. I'm sorry I didn't talk to you before I enlisted. I figured you couldn't talk me out of it if I'd already signed the form."

"I wouldn't have. No, that's not right. I still would have been fit to be tied. I needed you. Trying to get the farm stable, that was a lot of work by myself."

"You had Dacquon. I figured you'd be okay."

"Ha!" Jaleasa laughed. "Your brother spent way more time in books than he did in the fields. I was just lucky that the money I saved from not feeding you allowed me to hire on an extra hand." Jaleasa patted her son's stomach to strike the point home. "More food made it to market, too."

She was struck by how hard Trevion's stomach was. There were other changes. Maturity, she guessed. He'd grown to be a fine leader, well-respected by his men. "I've never said this out loud, but I'm proud of all you've done, son. I'm sorry I'm such a bitch sometimes."

Trevion pulled her in for a hug. Karlus came up behind them. "Me, too!" And wrapped his arms around them both.

After a moment, she noticed the assembled team waiting on them to finish. She stepped back, wiping a small tear from her cheek. "Okay, let's get this show going."

*　　*　　*

Trevion ordered his team to position a *goatig* near the lip of the ravine. They staked it to the ground with a small pile of feed to keep it distracted. The furry quadruped happily munched away while everyone retreated to safety.

"What's he doing, Momma?" Karlus asked.

"You just watch," his mother replied.

"It won't be long," Trevion seconded.

Slowly vines slid back into place where the soldiers had made a clearing. The tendrils were hesitant, at first, pain still within monster's limited memory. The clearing shrunk and the *goatig* grew nervous.

"He's scared."

"Yes, but it'll be over soon."

"What'll be over?"

"Dinner time."

Trevion knew his brother was slow, but he didn't consider

him naive. He lived on a farm where creatures often were fed to other animals. The boy must know what's coming, right?

The first vine touched the leg of the *goatig* and it jumped back, belting in fear. A second vine ran across a hind leg and it darted again, but the sacrifice couldn't get free from its tether.

As the *goatig* grew more afraid, so did his brother. "Momma! Momma!"

Jaleasa held tighter to Karlus, but he shook and twisted as if the vines were crawling towards him. "Shhh. It's okay," she comforted, but Karlus wouldn't settle down.

Trevion bent to his sibling. "Sorry, little man. But sometimes big things eat little things. It's part of life. You'll understand more when you get older."

"No." Karlus said in a hushed breath and broke free of their mother's grip. He moved faster than Trevion expected, escaping from his attempts to snatch him.

"KARLUS!" Jaleasa screamed. She moved to chase him, but three soldiers held her firm. Karlus ran down toward the sacrifice like the wind and Trevion knew he'd never catch him in time. He jumped on his MAC and fired it to life.

By the time he arrived, the *goatig* had already been lifted into the air by its front legs, bleating loud enough to be heard over the roar of the MAC. Karlus dangled by the animal's hind legs. His grip tenuous as the sacrifice emptied its bladder on him. Trevion watched as his brother slipped farther down the animal's legs.

Gunning the MAC, Trevion drove over the slithering tendrils causing them to launch up at him. He kept his focus on Karlus. With an extra punch of speed, Trevion shot out over the ravine, toward the dangling boy. Trevion's arc placed him directly under Karlus as his grip finally failed. Trevion let go the MAC's handles and caught his brother. The MAC didn't have enough force to keep them aloft at that height, and they started a decent that would land them dead center of the deadly carpet of *vorarous* vines.

Timing would be everything. Trevion kicked off from the

MAC, aiming the front end straight down and pushing him and Karlus into a freefall behind it.

Thirty meters to impact.

Trevion swung Karlus onto his back.

Twenty meters to impact.

He took the remote launcher from his belt.

Ten meters to impact.

He fired the payload from the MAC's side rockets. They hit the ground creating a blossom of fire, debris and *vorarous* parts. Other tendrils scatter wildly from the flames.

Five meters to impact.

The MAC punches through the smoke, hitting the crater created by the explosion. A secondary eruption happens when the peat reserves ignite, blasting a hole in the earth as a consequence.

One meter.

The cave below deep and dark, but Trevion believes that if he lands right, Karlus will survive. Maybe Dacquon will find them before the *vorarous's* vines do. Even death this way has to be better than the slow, suffocating death in the *vorarous's* stomach. He holds that slim hope as the black envelopes them.

\*   \*   \*

Dacquon Roundtree was enjoying the quiet of the caves. The rocks didn't ask him if he was okay. The roots didn't care about his scar. And there were no psychologists wanting to check his emotional state since the "failed" expedition. Everyone's repeated attempts at comfort or pity dragged his mind from the tasks laid out before him. He didn't go home, nor tell his family what had happened for that very reason. He'd be all right once he solved the *vorarous's* make-up.

How did it produce oil in its fruit? How did it reproduce? So many mysteries and only one lifetime to explore them.

It didn't take long to find its root system. Unlike the surface vines, these roots only drew water from the soil. The plant-like creation seemed to not use any form of photosynthesis to produce food. More like an animal, it took in food and water separately. If only they could dissect it. He'd build his entire career around its origins.

The closer he and his team moved toward the coordinates of the stalk, the thicker the roots became in both size and frequency. Water dripped from the rocks in volume and they took readings as the tiny shoots sucked up the moisture.

"Professor? You've got to see this?"

One of the scientists peeked around a corner. As Dacquon approached, the sound of rushing water could be heard. There, directly under the *vorarous's* trunk was an underground river. Roots hung from the ceiling, dangling the ends like toes in a lake. Behind the mass of vines, something big was concealed. Whatever it was would have to wait, for at that moment, the sound of a large explosion rocked the cave.

Crumbling rocks showered down on the team and Dacquon told everyone to get back. Seconds later, another eruption blew the ceiling part and the remains of a MAC crashed into the river.

It was followed by the form of a man with a large backpack.

He hit the water hard and Dacquon wasn't sure if the man would surface again. But soon a hand reached up and grabbed a nearby root. The man pulled at the water in a half-swim, hand over hand, until he made his way to the river's edge.

"You fool! You risked everything I've carefully planned!"

Dacquon wanted to throttle the intruder only to discover it was none other than his older brother, Trevion. And while that didn't surprise him as much as it should have, the discovery that the backpack was actually his younger brother, Karlus, left him speechless.

"Sorry to drop in on your party, Dacq."

The team helped both water-logged brothers to the cave floor. Trevion breathed hard, adrenalin clearly still coursing through his veins. Karlus smiled his unconcerned smile, as he always did, looked at his brothers and said, "Again!"

Trevion's laugh started as a choke but grew into a riotous infectious gut-buster. Karlus broke into giggles next, clueless about what was so funny, Dacquon was sure. Soon, before he could stop himself, Dacquon started laughing along with them.

\* \* \*

It didn't take long for both Trevion's and Dacquon's communicators to buzz. After assuring their mother that all three of them were fine, the new arrivals took in their surroundings. The light that had been let in by the sudden hole dimmed. The *vorarous* vines slithered over the opening, slowly sealing the cave from the surface world.

"Why aren't they coming down here," Trevion asked.

"This organism seems to have very specific roles for its appendages. The ones above gather food, the ones here, water. It's like it can't break its own rules."

They re-lit peat lanterns that'd been doused when the ceiling collapsed.

"Speaking of breaking rules," Dacquon chastised, "you nearly destroyed the whole operation."

"Whoa, little brother. Wasn't like I had a choice." Trevion knowing this pattern from youth, extended himself to his full height, brawn to his brother's brains. "Did you want Karlus here to get eaten by that thing?"

Karlus, who'd been looking at the roots turned at the sound of his name.

"Maybe." Then Dacquon recanted. "No. That would destroy mother. But still, everything depends on the success of the mission. Our world can't keep relying on off-world oil. It's too expensive. We need to find a local equivalent. And yes, that sometimes means sacrifice. If your actions just now had killed the *vorarous...*"

"Like it almost killed you?"

Dacquon got up in his brother's face. "I knew the risks. Exploring a new world is going to have them. I didn't sign up for something easy like the defense force."

"Easy! Do you have any idea the things I've had to do since signing up?"

"No. I don't. How could I? When you left, you didn't just leave Mom, you know. You bailed on us all!"

"What's oil?"

The two older siblings turned to address their little brother, the heat from their argument almost spilling onto his innocent question. His face, unnerved by the fight, calmed them and put them back in control of their emotions.

Trevion whispered to Dacquon, "We *both* know the risks, but he doesn't." To Karlus, he answered, "It's a liquid that burns like the peat moss, but it burns hotter and wouldn't require all the hard work that goes into designing machines to run on peat."

The middle brother continued, "The plant up there has the ability to produce something like oil. Remember those purple fruits on its trunk? Well, if they can be harvested, then the whole colony will do better."

"Only, the creature won't let us get close enough to pick them. It hurts anyone that gets close."

"Like my *goatig*?"

Trevion smiles, "Yes, like your *goatig*." He rustled Karlus's curly hair. "Sorry about that little man. Didn't mean to make you upset."

Karlus grinned. "Is okay, Trev. Have you asked the plant to give you the fruit?"

Dacquon squatted down to address his brother man to man. "The *vorarous* doesn't speak. We don't know how to communicate with it."

Placing his hand on his chin, Karlus looks confused. "But,

Dacq, we talk to the *marshers* and they let us milk them."

"We don't actually talk to them. We've trained them to do what we want."

But that just deepened the boy's agitation. "But I talk with them all the time. They're happy to help us. It hurts them when they get too full of milk."

Dacquon stood and looked at Trevion, checking to see if it was all some sort of joke. "Are you saying you *actually* talk to them, Karlus?"

Karlus backed away, worry on his face. Trevion quickly comforted him. "Nobody's mad at you, little man. How long have you been talking to the *marshers?*"

"Not just them. Irrigation beetles. *Squegrets. Jarbits.* All my life. I could understand them before I understood Momma."

You could've knocked the older Roundtree brothers over with a *squegret* feather. Dacquon asked the question they were both thinking.

"Can you talk to the *vorarous*, tell it we don't want to hurt it, but that we're friends?"

"You can tell it yourself."

Karlus turned and pointed to where the thickest mass of roots hid something. Parted, they revealed a gelatinous brain-like organ with a single eye. It stared at them.

Dacquon inhaled sharply. It was more animal than plant. A hybrid of some sort. Nothing he believed to be true was anymore.

Trevion drew his sidearm, but Karlus put his hand on it. "Don't. It's scared enough. You've been hurting it. It's sorry. It didn't mean to eat those people and my *goatig*. He's old and can't really tell the difference between thinking things and non-thinking things."

It was Dacquon's turn to be puzzled. "Thinking? Non-thinking?"

"It eats only animals that don't have higher brain functions. It says many years ago when it was young, there were a lot more thinking things like us here, but they haven't been around in a long time."

Trevion picked up on it before Dacquon, who was engrossed. The eldest elbowed his brother and nodded toward Karlus, who continued.

"He can tell us a lot about the planet, if we want, but he says his fruits may be too volatile for our needs. He suggests the younger fruit of a seedling will be better."

"Karlus, have you gotten smarter?" Dacquon caught on that the dullness that seemed to cloud his little brother's mind had lifted.

"Not really. It was hard, y'know, hearing all those voices and trying to keep track of them. They've always had so many interesting stories to tell. I find them much more fascinating than math."

From under the brain, a third type of vine extended. It was pink and raw and pulsed like blood flowed through it. It hovered about half a meter off the ground and exuded a green and orange seed, but unlike any other seed Dacquon had studied, it was warm to the touch and something moved inside it like a chicken embryo in an egg.

"He says she needs to be placed in water soon or she'll die."

The scientific team gathered water from the underground river and secured the *vorarous* spawn while Trevion and Dacquon drew their brother into a hug.

\* \* \*

### Epilogue

Jaleasa Roundtree couldn't have been happier if the moon showered chocolate down on her nightly. Her middle son had returned to their farm, though he brought a whole contingent of scientists with him. The colony government had built a lab next to her house, and Dacquon stayed in an apartment on the second floor. Sure, he wasn't "home" home, and she didn't see him every day, but he did show up for Sunday supper, which usually happened on Wednesdays.

Trevion would come, when his position allowed. He coordinated several joint teams of explorers and soldiers. He was tasked with finding remnants of Eurynome's original inhabitants. Not wanting a repeat of their past mistakes, he checked in with his younger brother Karlus often.

Karlus spent most of his days talking to the new *vorarous* plants. The five, so far, were already twice his height. He accepted that some animals eat other animals, but wasn't happy about it. Together, he and the *vorarous* brood worked with the harvesters to pick the petro-fruit, so that no one accidentally got eaten.

Jaleasa had become Eurynome's first oil baron, but that didn't matter to her so much. Having her children healthy and happy, beat just about everything.

Well, everything but her having own personal airship. Mama Roundtree's got to ride in style, after all.

# WILLOWRUNNER

## B. J. Beck

A S IF THE gentle rolling on the living tracks wasn't enough, the hum of the magnets always put me to sleep. It was warm in the conduit, too, from the spin of the gears and the steam of the pipes, and that didn't exactly help me remain conscious. I couldn't say how many times I'd finished checking connections and pressures, lying there on my stomach in the half-light, and decided just to close my eyes for a minute or two, either flipping onto my back or staying face-down and tucking my arms under my head to keep the grill from making an odd waffle pattern on my cheek. Invariably I'd awake sometime later to the irritated sound of my brother's voice echoing through the intercom tube, located at the conduit's entrance. Today was no exception.

"Viola? Damn it, wake up."

God. I stretched and craned my neck in the direction of the sound. Why I thought I'd see something other than the conduit's entrance and a glimpse of the engine room was anyone's guess. After a couple of breaths, I turned over, pulled myself slowly towards the opening, and stuck my head out. The crackle of burning coal and the hiss of steam increased, and I had to make sure I talked loudly enough into the tube for Digg to hear me.

I reached over, extended the copper tube to my mouth, and almost pressed it against my lips.

"What?" I demanded.

"Finally." His voice sounded tinny. "We're coming up on Shorlias. I thought you'd want to know."

"Did you tell Weverlin yet?"

"Yeah. If you don't move your ass he'll probably beat you up here."

"Then I'll move my ass."

I let the tube retract and, after a little maneuvering, I jumped out of the conduit. The temperature of the engine room was higher than the conduit, and it wasn't the pleasant level I found so relaxing. I'd thought about insulating it better plenty of times, but that took money I currently didn't have. This job was supposed to take care of that, but like an idiot I'd agreed to only partial payment up front and the rest upon completion. My mistake was assuming that the job wasn't going to take months to finish. Naturally, my brother Diggrey was a pain about it, but since he was a pain about everything else, I didn't really notice it all that much. I just marked it up to the fact that brothers weren't being proper brothers if they weren't harassing their sisters.

I checked the pressure gauges one more time and, satisfied, I left the brass and copper gleam of the engine room and headed to Control at the front of my train. I'd named the Elberton after my deceased father, and it was both the source of my income and my home. I used it to run supplies, cargo, and all kinds of useful items around the different islands of the world. Rarely though, did I take passengers, since we weren't well-equipped to satisfy the needs of most people who could afford to travel that extensively. But, Weverlin wasn't exactly a luxury passenger.

I slid the door to Control open and was bathed in the cool glow the sunrise. The windshield stretched across the front of the train, which both aided in navigation and gave us an appreciation of the world upon which we lived. The creeping rays of the suns were crawling upwards, stroking the wispy clouds with gentle fingers of light, and our current height gave us such a clear view of a horizon I almost expected to see the planet's curve.

Before us, and all around us, lay the ocean that coated our world in its rich dark blue. The blue was broken by the occasional island, varied mounds of land that dotted the water and disappeared into the distance. In addition to the islands, a network of silvery green trees rose from the waves, their smooth trunks growing straight as pillars to spread out a thick green canopy of branches and leaves. The strongest branches connected one tree to the next to form the tracks for my train, and the trees themselves grew in paths that reached each land mass and made travel between the islands possible. If I looked hard enough, I could see other trains like mine gliding among the treetops, diving into and out from the branches, heading to destinations connected by a complex pattern of living rails.

The metallic composition of the trees we rode upon made them perfect for the magnetic trains, providing tracks that were meticulously woven together and maintained. The trees had been grown centuries ago, and their branches bonded and originally prepared for use as foot bridges. As technology advanced, the government had adapted them for a more practical, if more expensive use, and on our trips I would often spot workers making repairs or trimming new growth. As many times as I'd seen the horizon from the treetops, I never tired of the sight, especially at dawn or twilight. It was a constant reminder to me as to why I'd chosen this life, even when I had to deal with its less-than-pleasant aspects.

Digg was seated on the right in front of the secondary panel, lounging in the leather chair affixed to the floor. He swung it partway when he heard me enter, and his eyes were hidden by a pair of sungoggles.

"Glad you beat Creepy," he said. "Now I don't have to talk to him."

I took the driver's seat on the left and said, "Don't call him that."

"But he is."

"I don't care as long as he pays." I checked the clock on my panel to make sure it was wound, and I added, "It's also not his fault."

Digg shook his head and stated, "It's not his looks, you know that. Something else is going on there, I swear. Law enforcement, my butt..."

"I don't want to hear this again. You don't like the job, you find us one next time."

Digg fell silent and turned back to his panel. I checked the arrival time against the distance to Shorlias and then took a moment to fix my brown hair. It had gotten slightly mussed with all my crawling (and napping), and I quickly removed the band that held it out of my face. With a quick smoothing of my fingers, I wrapped it in the band again and let it hang behind me. Digg had the occasional lapse but I strove to keep an air of professionalism, even with someone like Weverlin who couldn't really afford to be picky about appearances.

Weverlin was suffering from Amal's Leprosy, which was an incurable condition that was spreading through the islands. You were either immune from it or you weren't, and fortunately neither Digg nor I had ever had any problems with it. Weverlin, however, kept himself covered from head to toe; he needed to, otherwise his wounds would seep and drip and get easily infected, hastening his death. Amal's had become so common and its sufferers so desperate that anyone promising an alleged cure was immediately brought to the attention of the government and inspected. If the claim was found to be fraudulent, the punishment was life imprisonment, causing a black market to arise that kept touting various treatments away from the government's oversight. Weverlin was one of the official enforcers, and he had a very personal stake in catching frauds. Unfortunately, the government didn't pay very well.

I heard the door behind us slide again, and I looked over my shoulder. As expected, it was Weverlin, and as usual, he was covered. The style of his clothing was pretty much the same every day, but he varied the colors of each suit, probably to keep from boring himself. Today, he was in a set of brown cotton wrappings and leather with not one square inch of skin showing. Atop his head was a matching newsboy cap, pulled down over the forehead of the mask he wore.

His mask. The only item that was always the same was the brass mask on his face. The first time I'd seen it, it had caused a bit of a shock, but by now I'd gotten used to it and hardly took note of it anymore. Parts of it were polished but most of it was dull, and it had slits for his eyes, nose, and mouth. On the temples and by the corners of the mouth were sets of tiny gears connected to intricate tubes, and the tubes wrapped up to disappear under the hat and feed into a hidden container of water. The tensioned gears were powered by weighted pulleys that traveled in slots just in front of the ears, and the weights would slowly climb upward throughout the day as the gears worked to spray timed gusts of mist into his eyes and mouth. The mist took the place of his missing eyelids and lips and kept those facial features moisturized. Even as he stepped forward the mist went off, and the wet gusts momentarily fogged up his dark gaze.

"Good morning," Weverlin slurred.

I could see a flash of his teeth through the slit. It wasn't always easy to understand him, but I'd gotten used to that, too.

I nodded and said, "Eight minutes and we'll be at the station. You sure you know where we're headed?"

He nodded once in return.

"Gun cartridges," he said, although I knew it was more of a question.

148

"They're full," I answered, referring to the pressurized air capsules we used to power our weapons. "We will need to do some shopping while we're here, I'm running low on combustibles—"

"Business first," he interrupted and turned away.

I watched him as he went to the cabinet by the exit door and rummaged through it, retrieving his guns and knives. While Weverlin worked, Digg pulled down his goggles and rolled his eyes at me. I glared at him and focused back on getting us to the station.

The offloading station was busy but well-managed, and it didn't take us long to be directed to a set of branching tendrils that took us to a docking port. I had to take manual control and steer it into place. Once it was docked, I stood, stretched, and informed Digg to stay with the Elberton. He didn't mind.

Weverlin initially went on these stops by himself, but after he'd come back with a wound from an arrest that had gotten out of hand, he laid down some extra money to take either me or Digg along. I was hardly equipped to get physical with anyone, and I wasn't a great shot, but I knew I was better than Digg at both, and I worried less when it was me instead of him anyway. So, I would grudgingly accompany Weverlin while keeping a hopefully-safe distance, just in case he needed back-up ... or a drop-off to a morgue.

With our cartridges in our guns and our holstered weapons under our jackets, we left the Elberton in search of a man who was selling hope in the façade of a cure. The island had sparse but groomed vegetation and was packed with glass towers that took advantage of its limited land area. The pleasant people were of different shapes and races, and most of them seemed healthy. There was also a segment of people dressed and wrapped like Weverlin, a few of whom were in the early stages of Amal's and hadn't taken to covering their faces yet. Those people had patches on their cheeks, foreheads, and mouths that were a sickly pale green in color and looked slimy. I didn't avoid eye contact, but it was hard to keep from looking at them with pity, and I knew pity could be considered just as insulting as turning away in disgust.

It was in a moment like this that I could not help but feel a little sympathy for the diseased man next to me, although I wasn't completely convinced that what he was doing was altogether right. Quashing the attempts to cure people could potentially discourage those genuinely trying to search for an answer, while at the same time it prevented the sick from receiving a little comfort, even if it was only perceived and not real. Weverlin never seemed to doubt his job, though, and he never discussed anything other than the last fraudster and the next.

We ended up in the part of town that wasn't as clean as the rest, and with a turn into an alley Weverlin stopped at a faded blue door. He gave a knock that was quickly answered. The pudgy woman in the doorway was unaffected by his appearance.

"You lost?"

It was an innocuous question, but Weverlin was expecting it as if it was code. It was all part of the information he'd gotten about this particular con man.

"Here," he said, and he pulled out a piece of paper.

The woman glanced at the message and stepped aside.

"Hurry," she said, and after we entered she shut the door.

She led us down the hallway and into an office on the left. Unlike the corridor, it was well-lit and nicely appointed, and there was an adjoining room in the back with its door open. Against one of the walls was a machine, and if I hadn't known what it was used for, I would have guessed it was a cross between an engine and a coffin. There was a vat of red liquid attached to it and the coffin's interior was lined with tiny needles.

After seeing so many weird contraptions that were touted as being the cure for Amal's Leprosy, this one didn't appear to be particularly notable, but for some reason Weverlin seemed to react to it. I couldn't really tell what he did, but I just felt something

150

odd from him, almost as if he recognized it.

"Dr. Jarls," the lady called, and I saw the shadow of a man in the other room move.

A moment later and a man came into the office. He was middle-aged and unremarkable, wearing a lab coat and goggles. The only thought that occurred to me was that the goggles were a bit much, likely more of a prop to make him look like a doctor instead of just a chubby man with no credentials.

"Good morning…" he began, and that was all he had time to say.

Weverlin pulled back his jacket, yanked out his gun, and shot the pudgy woman where she stood. She crumpled and fell, hitting the floor before the puff of steam from the gun dissipated.

"What?" I nearly shrieked, falling back against the wall and pawing for my own gun.

Without even looking my direction, Weverlin pointed his gun at me. I froze in place, almost in shock from what had just happened. Carefully, Weverlin pulled out a second gun and pointed it at the doctor. Jarls looked to be in worse shape than I was, the lenses in his goggles making his glazed stare even more pronounced. The three of us just stood there, unmoving, for several seconds. The mist went off on Weverlin's mask a few times in the silence.

Finally, I found enough courage to voice a question.

"Why?" I managed to whisper.

Weverlin ignored me and instead said to the doctor, "Sit down."

Jarls blinked his magnified eyes and sat gingerly in his desk chair. Weverlin withdrew the gun he had pointed at me and holstered it. He then stepped to the desk and reached up to the mask he always wore. Slowly, he began to flip the buckles that held it on.

I could have shot him right then and there, but I didn't. I wasn't a killer for one, and I didn't know what in all of Heaven was going on for another. I continued to just watch, fascinated and repulsed, trying to decide what, if anything, I should do.

The mask came loose, and with a quick jerk, Weverlin pulled it from his head. He set it onto the desk with a hollow *clunk*. His hat fell softly to the floor.

I squinted in puzzlement at the sight, my mind not really piecing together what I was seeing. Weverlin's skin was whole and smooth, except his lidless eyes were bulging and his mouth was in a fixed grimace. Weverlin reached up again and removed the clips that kept his lids and his lips pinned out of the way. He then blinked and licked his lips and smiled quite deliberately. There wasn't anything wrong with his face.

Dr. Jarls swallowed hard and gasped painfully, "You..."

Weverlin lowered his gun slightly but still kept it pointed.

"Hello, partner," he said with perfect enunciation.

"Son of a bitch!" I hissed, recalling Digg's skepticism over Weverlin's occupation. "Your partner? Is that what you've been up to all this time, looking for him?"

Weverlin shook his head once, still keeping an eye on Jarls.

"I could care less about him," he replied. "I'm here for the cure we found."

I glanced at the strange machine.

"You mean that works? It really works?"

"Ask him," Weverlin said with a gesture of his head.

"Of course it works," Jarls said.

"My god," I managed, my mind struggling to understand both of the men in front of me. "Why hide it? Expose it, let everyone use it —"

"Because he stole it," Weverlin said, "from me. It's why I had to wear that damned mask, take some law enforcement man's identity, because if he knew I was coming for it—"

"Liar!" Jarls said, gripping the arms of his chair angrily. "The idea, the research, it was all my doing." His goggled eyes, full of fright, turned upon me, and his tone held the sound of a man desperate to justify himself, as if it were his deathbed confession. "The government doesn't want a cure, they'd destroy it, or they'd hide it, use it to control the rest of us, just like they control the search for it. It gives them opportunities to deal with the population they wouldn't otherwise have. I've been able to cure others, not for money but just to … *help*." His scared gaze flicked back to Weverlin. "That's why I needed to leave him."

I looked at Weverlin's perfect face.

"What are you going to do with it?" I asked, not really sure if I wanted an answer.

Weverlin's smile returned.

"I think I'll benefit humanity," he announced and, raising his gun, he added, "starting now."

He pulled the trigger, again and again, and Jarls' dying throes were obscured by the steam. I watched helplessly, expecting that I would be next, readying to defend myself, assuming I was pretty much dead whether I fought back or not. But, once he finished, Weverlin looked at me and put away his gun. He casually picked up his face clips and pinned back his eyes and lips with the ease of a daily routine. A minute later his mask was back in place, the mist operating as it had before he'd turned into a killer.

"Let's get this machine to the station," he slurred as he bent over to retrieve his hat.

Shock is a numbing thing that obscures the clock and wipes away thought, because it didn't seem to take any time or effort to get back to the Elberton with the machine. However, it was dusk before I guided my train up and over the canopy of trees, headed to our next destination with Digg at my side, and my brother was scowling at me.

"I'm still waiting for an explanation," he said. "You ready to talk?"

The statement seemed to snap me out of the near-trance I was experiencing, or maybe it was the feeling of safety I got from the familiar surroundings of my home. Another feeling emerged as well, a twist in my stomach from seeing two people getting shot dead right in front of me while I did nothing. The resulting shame was tempered only with the fact that I could not have stopped it if I tried. I wasn't sure how to phrase the experience, what words would fit to convey my gut wrenched by unexpected violence, and as I struggled with the beginning, I heard the Control door sliding and knew that Weverlin was in the room with us.

I also knew why he was there. I don't know how, considering the way he'd fooled me for months, but I knew exactly what he was thinking. Maybe witnessing his murderous personality revealed the monster he was in so much detail that he could not deceive me again.

I slipped my hand under my jacket and, as I swiveled my chair around, I pulled out my gun and shot Weverlin in the chest. Digg yelped in surprise and leapt up.

"*Holy gods!*" Digg shouted. "Why did…?" The question died on his lips when he saw the gun in Weverlin's hand.

I stood and looked down at the still body. "Make sure he's dead," I then said, stepping over and kicking away the gun.

"At that range?" Digg asked. "Not only is he dead, I think you just damned him."

"You know I had to do that."

Digg stood and stared at me. He then nodded once.

"You okay?"

I shook my head and looked down at Weverlin.

"I don't know, Digg. I don't know what we can do. He's a killer, but we've been helping him for months now. If we turn him in, if we turn that machine in, I just don't know what's going to happen to it or to us. I think we're screwed no matter what we do."

Digg sighed.

"Well, we're not going to figure out what to do until you're thinking more clearly. Come on, sit down."

I managed to sit and I noticed I was shaking. Digg sat in his chair and the two of us looked at the sunset. It gilded the trees and the ocean with warm shades of gold before the suns dipped below the line of blue water.

"That's really pretty," I said, indicating the view, and my brother nodded.

# VENERIAN TWILIGHT

## DJ Tyrer

THE STILL of the shadowed swampland was shattered by the sudden sounds of wheezing and groaning: the respiration of pistons. Something large, like a gigantic brick built of bronze and steel, about the size of a locomotive, appeared from nowhere in a shallow pool and settled slowly into the mud. Twin stacks belched dark billows of smoke, whilst steam escaped other orifices with a hiss of effort. A multitude of unearthly flying creatures took wing in startlement at the commotion.

Slowly, the sound subsided to a background hum, as if the thing were no longer straining to produce energy. A periscope rose from atop the object and turned slowly as unseen occupants observed their surroundings. The scene again seemed peaceful; the flying creatures—strange beetle-things, enormous dragonflies and winged reptilian-seeming creatures—began to settle back on their perches or in hidey-holes within the trunks of tree ferns and other peculiar, unearthly flora.

A door, like a bulkhead door in a warship, opened in the side of the object with a sigh. Three figures stepped out, gingerly seeking a dry footing on whatever clumps of land rose above the water, ready to explore the strange and alien world.

The first figure to exit the vessel was a woman of about thirty. She stood a few inches above five feet in low-heeled, black-leather ankle boots, and was slim and athletic-seeming. She wore a divided grey skirt, a white ruffled blouse with a bow of black ribbon tied at her throat, and a dark-green jacket that left the ruffles of her blouse exposed. Her long, dark hair was hidden in a bun beneath the small dark-green hat perched atop her head, which was decorated with a small white flower. A pair of goggles was pushed up above her eyes and her leather-gauntleted hands held a heavy gun; the head of a harpoon protruded from the head of the weapon. From her demeanour, it seemed the strange world held no fears for her and that she was in command of the expedition.

The second figure was a skinny man several years younger than her, poorly shaven with longish, unkempt dirty-blond hair. He was dressed in faded blue jeans and a t-shirt with a goofy visage and the words *What, Me Worry?* written on it, and had a pair of angler's waders covering his legs. His rimless spectacles were already steaming up in the humid air.

The third figure stood taller than either of them and seemed even taller due to the fact that it was possessed of a pair of very long ears that rose even higher. This figure was a humanoid rabbit. A white rabbit with red eyes, with the angled legs and twitching whiskers of its kind. Barefoot, it wore black knee-britches and a bulky brown leather jacket of the sort known as a bomber jacket where he had found it. It also wore goggles, tinted ones intended to protect its eyes from glare, although they were not so necessary here. An enormous revolver was strapped to one hip and a machete to the other.

"Welcome to Venus," the woman said to her companions.

"Bally hot place! I'll be rabbit stew in a minute!"

"I'm steaming up," the man said, taking his glasses off to wipe the lenses clear.

"It's the atmosphere," the woman said. "The dense clouds keep the heat in. They're also the reason for this Venerian twilight."

"Venusian twilight, surely," said the man.

"No, Venerian," she replied. "Don't you know your Latin, Doc?"

"Sorry, Letty, it's not really my speciality." He changed the subject: "This world is utterly different to the Venus of my timeline. That's a dead world of acid rain and no signs of life."

Doctor William Jones, Doc, had found himself thrown together with Letitia Dane and her lagomorphic co-pilot Hopper when their Steam-powered Astral Traveller or SPAT had mis-jumped sideways in time and accidentally picked him up. The adventuress and her ally used the vessel to explore far and wide and, having been unable to replicate the accident that took them to Doc's world, had invited the eccentric young genius to join them in case they ever did.

"It's alright for you in those great big galoshes," Hopper said, glancing down at Doc's legs, "but I don't much fancy wading around barefoot in this primordial ooze. How about we break out the bally old exo-suits, me little lettuce, eh?" he said to Letitia.

"Why not? Besides, we don't know what the dense jungle holds. Just because we have seen no sign of anything nasty lurking about doesn't mean it isn't out there."

"Excellent observation!" the rabbit replied, enthusiastically.

They went back inside the SPAT, closing the door behind them before lowering the rear ramp. A few minutes later, they marched out in three matching exo-suits. The ten-foot tall constructions of chromed iron and steel into which they were strapped were each equipped with a pair of powerful pincers, one of which could be quickly exchanged with various tool attachments, and the other of which concealed within it a self-loading rifle of a calibre fit to fell elephants. To the rear, groaning with effort, was located the smoky steam engine that powered the suit and allowed them to lurch across the landscape at a fair speed.

Letitia slipped her goggles down over her eyes and led the way.

Unlike Letititia and Hopper, Doc seemed inexpert in piloting the clunking machine and he stumbled and nearly fell, barely remaining upright.

Hopper turned his exo-suit and called, "What's up, Doc?"

The man scowled and the rabbit chuckled, then said, "One day, you must tell me why that question riles you so, wot!"

Doc ignored him and Letitia asked Doc what was wrong.

"The foot of this thing sank into some mud," he replied. "Could one of you stop smirking and help me out?"

Letitia crossed to him and helped tug the leg of his exo-suit free, saying, "Do try and be more careful."

Their progress through the treacherous waters and mud of the twilit swamp was slow and the noise of their pistons and the ejaculated steam and the smell of smoke gave ample warning to much of the wildlife to take flight or take cover so that they saw little of it as they took their progress.

They hadn't gone far when they heard a low, languid snorting ahead of them and as they rounded a clump of enormous toadstools they saw before them a herd of large creatures with brownish-grey skins, long necks ending in small heads, and whip-like tails wallowing in the depths of a primal Venerian lake.

"By Jove!" Hopper exclaimed. "They're gigantic blighters, wot!"

"Brontosaurs," Letitia observed.

Doc grinned. "Much better than Apatosaurs."

"Pardon?" she asked him.

"Oh, nothing.... Are they safe?"

"Well, I think we'd have a hard time hurting them," she replied.

"That's not—"

"I know! Honestly! No, they don't seem dangerous. Look, they're feasting on the weed that chokes the waters of their lake. Hmm, unlike the Brontosaurs of our Earth's distant past, they don't appear to be reptiles; see, their skins are smooth with a sheen like that of a frog. I think these creatures are some sort of amphibian."

Her suspicions about the local wildlife were confirmed a little later when something like a crocodile, only with feathery gills reminiscent of an axolotl and mottled blue and black in colour, lunged from red-thick shallows to seize the leg of Hopper's exo-suit. Its teeth, designed to pierce the thin skins of amphibians, found the metal of the suit quite impossible and the creature quickly let go.

"You were lucky there," Letitia commented. "Had it been able to lunge up out of the water, it might have caught hold of your leg rather than the suit's." Strapped onto the front of the walker, the vehicles being intended for peaceful purposes, the pilots were unprotected.

"Yes," Doc added, delighting in Hopper's misfortune, "you really ought to be more careful."

Hopper snorted in irritation. "If the blighter had tried to munch on me, I would've have blown his bally brains out, wot!"

Some distance on, they were surprised to spy a collection of huts amongst which cowered beings like humanoid amphibians in a variety of bright colours.

"Salamander-men!" exclaimed Hopper.

"I'd always imagined Venus would be home to Lizardmen," said Doc. "I guess I read too much science fiction."

"Really?" asked Letitia. "I'd always half-expected a race of Amazons."

"You would," muttered Doc, hoping she couldn't hear him.

"Well, what we've got are Salamander People, so let's deal with what we have, eh?" Hopper said.

"I think our exo-suits are scaring them," Letitia observed.

"They are only small." Not a one of them stood higher than five feet in height.

"Probably think we're bally gods, eh?"

"We should dismount. Put them at their ease, if we can...."

They clanked over to the raised ground where the village was located and climbed down from their transports. With what they took to be confused expressions, the Salamander-men advanced cautiously to look at them. One, a little larger than the rest and possessed of a headdress of leaves and flowers, stepped forwards and spoke.

"That sounded like Polish," Doc said, bemused.

"Russian, actually," Letitia told him. "I speak the language. It has a poor grasp of the tongue and a most peculiar accent, but I think it is asking if we have come to take more of their males away to labour for us."

"Ask them about these other people," Hopper told her.

"Yes, thank you; I was about to do so." She spoke to the Salamander-man, then said, "These other humans came from the sky and have established a base in the highlands to the north of here. Russians."

"Russians," Hopper echoed. Their arch-enemies. "The dastards are obviously here enslaving the natives. We ought to put a stop to this transplanetary colonial cruelty!"

Doc agreed heartily, loathing slavery even if he had no problem with Russians on principle, and Letitia expressed her own disgust at such subjugation, before explaining to the clustered villagers that not only had they no intention of taking any more of them away as slaves but that they would go free their captured kin.

Doc shook his head at her volunteering them like that with no knowledge of the forces they faced.

A guide was volunteered to lead them to the Russian encampment, apparently a young female with pale yellow skin and large dark eyes, and whilst she remained wary of the exo-suits, her belief they were some sort of liberating gods reassured her, and she led them with alacrity through the marshes to where the land rose towards mountains capped with cloud.

"We're getting near," Hopper told them, ears twitching. "I can hear the thrum of machinery growing closer with every step." It was quite the miracle that his hearing could discern such sounds over the noise produced by their own mode of transport.

"Aha! And, I can see plumes of smoke," added Letitia, pointing to where the clustered columns of dark smoke rose cloudward, as out of place on Venus as their own exo-suits were. The planet was so damp that the natives seemed to have no concept of fire at all.

Pausing only to dismiss their guide, they approached the encampment with caution.

Silhouetted against the clouded sky, a hundred-foot-long dirigible was tethered in the midst of a collection of ramshackle huts. Three pairs of simple wooden rails led from the buildings to a mine entrance in a nearby cliff side; Salamander-men—from what their non-captive kin had said, the term was entirely accurate here—toiled to drag loaded carts of ore from the mine to huts acting as storehouses. Russians, in the tan uniforms worn by soldiers posted to warmer climes than Siberia, slouched around with rifles on a lax form of guard duty or stood ready with the vile knout whip to encourage slacking workers. A large vehicle, halfway between a bulldozer and a combine harvester, sat in the far corner of the camp.

"How did they get here?" Doc asked.

"By dirigible, of course," said Letitia, rolling her eyes at his ignorance. "Surely someone as educated as you knows about dirigibles."

"Yes, of course; but *how*? As the Earth's atmosphere thins, surely the balloon should burst, and even if it didn't, how do they pilot it here through the vacuum of space?"

"Vacuum? Whatever do you mean?"

"Well, um, a vacuum; nothingness."

Her eyes widened. "You mean to say that in your ... reality there is no aether?"

"No. People once believed in it, but, eventually, discovered that it doesn't exist."

"Really?" Hopper asked. "And, I'd thought your world jolly strange enough, wot!"

"So, the aether exists and allows zeppelins to fly through space?"

"Yes, if by what-a-lins you mean dirigibles," Letitia replied. Doc kept forgetting how so many common words and expressions meant nothing to her.

"So, my lovely little lettuce, what's the bally plan?"

"Well, Hopper, my love, I think you and I should go take a closer look and leave Doc here out of the firing line."

"Sounds good to me," Doc commented.

So, they left him there and, having clambered down from their exo-suits, crept into the camp. With the guards' blasé attitude, thanks to the Salamander-men's bewildered subservience, Letitia and Hopper found it easy to wander around unchallenged. Even when one of the natives, ludicrously dressed as a servant and carrying a tray of vodkas, spotted them, he made no attempt to alert his erstwhile masters; whether unable to differentiate humans, too browbeaten to care, or unwilling to assist the Russians more than it had to, Letitia had no idea.

"A right rum do, eh?" Hopper observed.

"Indeed. It seems they're mining something, that much is obvious, and also collecting the guano of some Venerian beast, probably to produce gunpowder for more of their militaristic ventures," she said, indicating where yet more slaves toiled.

"Lovely! So, how do we stop the blighters?"

"Ignite the refined guano, perhaps? That might upset their plans. Depending upon the gas they've used, the dirigible might be flammable. The only problem with that is that it will leave the dastards stuck here."

"That first idea, then, shall we?"

"Hold fast one moment, Hopper. Do you see who I see?"

"Where? Oh, dear, yes...." His gaze followed hers and he spotted Professor Zaroff of the Tsarist Scientific Fleet; a short man with wild hair, a diabolical goatee and a pair of pince-nez spectacles perched upon his nose. "I would rather not have encountered that bounder again, wot!"

Unfortunately, as they stared at him, he stared back.

"Intruders!" the Professor cried in Russian attracting the attention of the bewildered guards, who levelled their guns at them.

"So," Zaroff said, switching to heavily-accented English, "if it isn't the lithesome Letitia and her bloody bunny come to interfere once more with my plans! If you will lay down your weapons and surrender, I guarantee that your incarceration shall be no more than mildly uncomfortable for the next few weeks until we ship you back to Earth. Otherwise, I shall have my men shoot you down like ... rabbits," he sneered.

"Unfortunately, this cad does rather have us at a disadvantage, my dear." Hopper still had his gun holstered, meaning that Letitia's slow-firing harpoon gun was their only weapon. The situation didn't look too good. "It seems we're on rather a sticky wicket, wot!"

"Well, you know how I feel about such odds...."

"Enough talk! Lay down your guns!" Zaroff shrieked in English.

Exchanging a glance, the pair prepared to make an epic last stand. Then, the odds changed: Doc burst into the encampment in his exo-suit, firing his gun. Hardly a skilled marksman even when standing still, his sudden appearance nonetheless threw the Russians into chaos. Taking advantage of the confusion, Hopper hopped high over their heads, drawing his gun as he did so, blowing away a startled Russian as he landed.

"'Owzat!" Hopper cried.

Letitia fired her harpoon gun at Zaroff, but he was already moving, and the short, chunky harpoon slammed into the chest of one of his henchmen who tumbled backwards with a surprised and bloody gurgle.

Hopper leapt back over to Letitita, grabbed her as she fired another harpoon, and bounded away with her slung over his shoulder to the tree-line where their exo-suits were waiting. Doc sprinted quickly after them, firing a few more unaimed shots.

"This thing really could do with a ... Gatling-gun," he said as he reached them. "I don't think I've many shots left!"

"Well," Letitia said, strapping herself back into her suit, "it's not as if they were designed to be weapons of war."

"A redesign might be a fine idea, wot!" Hopper told her as he finished strapping himself in.

Despite such thoughts, the large-calibre bullets were extremely effective at felling Russians and allowed the trio to wreak havoc upon them and their flimsy buildings. Something ignited the processed guano and the storehouses exploded in flames, scattering the remaining Russians.

"Time to go, I think, wot!" Hopper suggested.

"Yes—and it looks like Zaroff is after blood!"

They followed Letitia's gesture and saw what she meant: Zaroff had powered-up the big industrial vehicle they had spotted earlier, which was now sputtering clouds of smoke and was slowly lumbering towards them with whirling blades.

As quickly as they could, they retreated back down to the marshlands. Unfortunately, whilst their exo-suits were swifter than the Professor's vehicle, its bulk and blades meant it could plough straight through trees and other vegetation they were forced to detour around. Soon, it was growing perilously near to them and they could hear Zaroff's maniacal laughter over the sounds of pistons and blades.

"The dashable dastard certainly seems intent on mischief, wot!"

"Indeed," Letitia agreed. "Still, we did ruin his plans—and not for the first time!" Then, she shouted, "Head for the nearest lake—I have a plan!"

At worst, marshy ground and deep water would impede the Professor. At best, she had a plan to tip the odds in their favour.

"You will not escape me, now!" Zaroff shrieked at them.

They were in luck: reaching the water, they saw, as Letitia had hoped, that it held a herd of brontosaurs. As placid as the creatures had seemed, they were now rather perturbed by the noisy intrusion into their munching-fixated lives.

"Right, fan out and herd the beasts at Zaroff!" Letitia shouted at her friends, who did as she ordered. Between them, they prodded and poked the creatures so that they lumbered out of the water and towards Zaroff's machine, which had been forced to halt impotently on the lakeshore where it was already beginning to sink into the muddy ground.

Zaroff swore in Russian and threw himself from the machines moments before the brontosaurs smashed into it, reducing it to so much smoking scrap.

Letitia walked her exo-suit over to where the Russian lay stunned in the mud and plucked him up using one of its pincers. Holding him at arm's-length so that he couldn't kick her in his struggles, she carried him back up the slope to the encampment, followed by the others. She unceremoniously tossed him onto the ground before his shell-shocked fellow survivors.

"Right," she told him as he stood and futilely attempted to dust himself clean, "I'm giving you the chance to get in your dirigible and return, empty-handed, to Earth."

"And, if I refuse?" he huffed.

She levelled the arm that contained the gun at him. "I blow you away, Zaroff. Please do not make the mistake of thinking the idea holds no temptation for me."

He swallowed hard. "You make an elegant point, Miss ... I accede to your, ah, request." He bowed stiffly.

With that, he turned and led his dejected men to the craft and took to the air and aether, his mission to Venus an inglorious failure.

"Another job well done, eh?" commented Hopper.

"Indeed. Right, well, I think we've done enough exploring for today. Twilight seems to be deepening into night. Let us repair to the SPAT for a well-earned rest, and we can resume our safari tomorrow."

Doc nodded, glad the danger was over.

"Excellent idea, my lovely little lettuce," Hopper agreed as they followed her once more down the slope.

"A job well done," she nodded with a satisfied smile. "A job well done, indeed."

# KEEPING IT FRESH

**R. Joseph Maas**

IT'S BEEN exactly six years and seven days since the generation ship launched. I'd like to claim it's because of my superior intellect and eidetic memory I remember exactly how long we've been in space, but I can't. I know how long this ship has been wandering the solar system because they won't stop talking about it! The parties they throw celebrating the marvels of their creation have spiraled out of control. The drinking and incessant feasting is far beyond reasonable. It's like they've forgotten why we had to leave Earth behind. They seem to think that this ship is a natural salvation. A gift from god to ferry us to another world we can destroy. Not the false triumph that it really is.

I've been trapped on this damned thing for six years and seven days. At first I thought it was a punishment. I thought they had all planned the death of our planet just to get me on the ship. But making the Icarus II just to trick me would have been crazy. Making me think it was all about me is crazy. They're making me think I'm crazy. I'm not. I'm not...

So I'm on this ship with a thousand two hundred and forty-nine people. I can't remember if that number includes me or not. I think it does. For now.

I'm not being punished. I can't be punished. What are they going to do? Put me in a chamber against the hull? Send me loose into the vacuum of space?

They've done it to people before. Of course, no one talks about it. It makes no sense. If it's in the vacuum of space where no sound can be heard, why is it no one talks about it from inside the ship? They have to do something with the criminals. When someone goes wrong, they must go somewhere. Where will I go? Will they speak of me instead of to me? Will it all be hushed in whispers said to family members only around place settings at a dinner table with bent pronged forks, tarnished spoons, and dulled knives...?

What I need is for Edward to stop talking to me. He hasn't stopped blabbing on since I killed him last week. He'd been at the party, drinking and eating with the same carelessness that got me trapped on this ship six years and seven days ago. If he would just stop telling me I'm wrong, I could get back to being right...

The engines were perfectly raucous and I couldn't resist. He had been contradicting me for weeks, telling me plenty of supplies exist for the party. Rationing wasn't going to be a problem and hydroponics would recover quickly enough no one would notice any difference in portions or how food was divided amongst families. Their tables would sit as full of food as ever.

He was just there. Staring at her. He had his back to the access way I was crawling through. I couldn't resist. She moved in to kiss him and I caught him in the side of the neck just below the ear. The jagged piece of copper insulation plating ripped into his skin more than cut.

I can't imagine the look he must have had on his face. I didn't have to imagine hers. I saw it. The wavering, flickering lights lit up her face just in time to see her eyes widen, her smile disappear, her cheeks flush.

The thoughts that must've raced through her mind when that first splash of arterial blood jetted out onto her porcelain cheek. What she must've thought it was...

It makes my hands shake with righteous fury just thinking about it.

I held his hair tightly, and refused to let go. The Ætheric generators pulsing loudly behind me must've drowned out her screams as she ran from the dying Edward because I heard nothing. But I know he didn't scream at all. Probably couldn't. I had gotten him good. Just below the ear.

I held him tightly until he dropped the glass of wine he'd been holding. It made an incredible shattering sound that was perfectly muffled by the sanguine liquid it had contained. The glass sparkled reflections onto the wall until his lifeless body fell onto it. And then he started talking again.

I can't understand why I could hear the shattering of the glass over the rumble of the steam engine, but not her voice as she ran, screaming away from him. But I know exactly why I can hear his voice now. He always told me I was wrong.

But I'm not wrong dammit! These people have to learn their excess will destroy all of us. Over a billion some people on a planet six years and seven days behind us wasn't a good enough example! What more is needed to show them the folly of their ways? There is no other planet this ship will get us too. The planets and stars are too far away. This isn't our new home. It's a prison.

I put his body in the cold sink in the engine room. The noise of the governor should keep anyone else from hearing his nagging voice. Always telling me I'm wrong. Always talking...

I went there yesterday, climbing over the pipes to get to where I had left him. The poor lighting made it hard to see the puddles of blood that he left on the wood floors as I drug him to his corner. I know I stepped in a puddle of him at least once. The steam keeps the blood from drying. It keeps him fresh.

I asked him to shut up. I told him that if he didn't leave me alone in my head, I was going to find that stupid little whore of his who had watched him die. The one who hadn't screamed when I cut his throat, just below the ear. I told him that I would kill her too, and put her somewhere else on the ship, far away from him, and he would never get to see her again.

He told me I was wrong. He told me he couldn't see her anymore anyway.

He was right. But only this once.

After I had dropped him into the cold sink, I ripped out his right eye and dropped it into the boiler. I can't remember why now. But I did. When he told me he could still see me, I jammed the handle of a wrench in the other eye.

I broke one of his fingers too. But that was an accident. I mean it. Who breaks a dead man's finger on purpose? Only someone who is losing their mind would do that.

I saw her that night. She still had his blood on her face. She was talking with the constabulary. She saw me too. She saw me and had no idea I knew her. That it was my fault her left cheek was dripping with his blood.

She saw me...

I kept my hands in my pockets, and just walked right on by her. I made a great effort to not gawk at her any longer or any less than any of the other people who walked past her.

But the lighting had been perfect. I hid behind him perfectly while I tore him open. And the only light in the room was the one that went across her eyes as she saw him sputter out the life blood from his neck. What she must have thought, partially blinded by the light dancing across her eyes from the fans in the corridor. The vague sight of him held fast to a darkened wall, bleeding to death, gasping for air that wouldn't come. She must have nearly lost her mind when she got out into the light and saw the blood on her hands.

That's right! The blood was on her hands. Over a billion some people dead on Earth. All of their blood was on her hands. I was merely reclaiming the life from someone who had left our world to fall into ruin. It's all so very clear now.

But still, Edward tells me I'm wrong. He says. I can't save the lives of those on Earth by killing the people of the Icarus II. He thinks this ship is the only way to ensure humanity continues. The only way for mankind to spread its ways to the stars. To keep us from ending.

I tell him it's crazy. He's crazy! I tell him any creature that destroys its own home is past redemption, and should burn with its own hive. Go down with its own ship.

This damned ship is a sign we have refused to learn the lesson. Adorned with carvings of kings and queens, decorated with gold and silver, the ship weighs twice what it should.

Edward tells me it's important to preserve our culture too. We need busts of dead patriarchs and matriarchs to remind us of who we are as a people; where we came from....

I promise to make a molding of him and to leave it in the cold sink with him so he can remember who he was, not who he is.

I tell him we are saving a people from a planet destroyed by excess by remembering the people who caused the waste, and not changing from their excessive ways.

He tells me I'm wrong.

Four days ago, I cut out his tongue. I broke his jaw doing it. I wanted to make sure to get it from the base. To leave none of his nagging tongue in his nagging mouth. He talked to me through the whole ordeal.

I thought if I could just get his tongue out of his head, it would get his voice out of mine. As I made the last slash at the muscle, silence had enveloped me. It had been such a relief. The sound of the water pumps, decks below, were even audible. I hadn't heard them since I went into the crawl space to try sabotaging the engines. To make everyone go down with the ship.

It was a whole thirty-two seconds after I made the final jerk to rip his tongue out that he told me I was wrong. He said I would always hear him now, and he didn't need it anymore.

First, I took his eyes.

Two days later, I took his tongue.

That was four days ago.

But he knows where I am. He sees me everywhere. He talks to me always.

It's funny, but he's never mentioned that I broke his damned finger.

Maybe I didn't.

Maybe I should.

I remember how the bobby even tipped his hat to me as I walked past the four of them. Three coppers and one crying, blood soaked whore. On her black bodice, the blood was drying. What had been white laces were turned dark red on the left side. Her cheek was drying, and the blood was crusting and flaking off. If she'd have stayed with him, he wouldn't be drying on her face. The steam keeps the blood flowing. It keeps it fresh.

Maybe it's too cruel a thing to make him sit in the cold sink all alone. Maybe that's why he's so damned noisy all of the time. Maybe that's why he thinks I'm wrong. Maybe he doesn't know what right is!

I think I will have to get him some friends. Some other people he can talk to. Maybe I should get him some new eyes and a new tongue too. I can bring them to him. I can have them sit with him in the cold sink. I think I can fit thirty, maybe forty more people in the cold sink with him. They can all hold court, and discuss why I'm right. Why I'm always right.

I might need to turn off the engine so they can hear each other. That governor is so loud. The water pumps are so loud. It's really amazing I can hear Edward at all. Even more so that I can hear him everywhere.

I think he just needs friends! I still have that copper insulation plating somewhere nearby. I'm going to find it, and then I'm

going to bring him some friends.
I'll start with that little whore...

# THE PERFECT PASTRY

## J. A. Campbell

"SHE'S too young."

Overhearing First Mate Nikiru, Aly paused next to the open hatch. She was the only one who could be described as too young on this ship. At sixteen, she was ten years younger than the next oldest crew member. That was the pilot, Ethan.

"She's a full member of the crew. We can't deny her leave," Captain Shelena replied.

"Shelena, we don't know her past. What if she gets into trouble?" Nikiru protested.

"Do you want to babysit her? She's earned her leave. We'll make sure she understands what parts of the station to avoid. She'll be fine. Besides, it's only for a day while we resupply."

Nikiru sighed. "You're right, as always. She just looks so young."

Captain Shelena laughed. "It's the blue hair. You'll get over it. Come on, we have a few minutes before we need to meet with the crew."

Aly scampered away from the hatch, not wanting to get caught eavesdropping. She didn't want them to think she was just a kid and too young to go on leave. They'd been hesitant when Aly had signed on as navigator a few months ago because of her age, but she had the necessary skills so they'd taken a chance on her.

Unfortunately, she'd have to move on soon. Keep moving, or get caught. At least that's what Kitty always said. So far she'd managed to evade capture by following her AI's instructions, but she really liked it here. She liked the crew; Ethan and his intensity, Tai and his expansive knowledge about the Aether powered engines. Even Joy, who was a little scary with her mech parts, was really nice to her. She'd never had a family before, and she almost felt like she belonged on this ship. Captain Shelena and First Mate Nikiru were also really nice to her and they never asked her about her past, although Aly was sure they wanted to know. It simply wasn't safe to tell them, or anyone.

That was a problem for another day, however. There wasn't much of a chance for her to pick up a job here anyway. Being a frontier station, there wasn't a lot of traffic. Not to mention, it was far too close to the Lab. The closer she was to the Lab, the more likely it was that she'd get caught. One day of leave shouldn't matter though.

She bounced into the conference room. Everyone but Captain Shelena and Nikiru were there. Ethan mussed Aly's hair as she squeezed past in the small space.

"Hey! I just styled that."

"Couldn't tell, sorry." Ethan smiled at her.

Aly sighed dramatically and slumped onto the bench.

"If it makes you feel any better, Aly," Tai, the engineer, said, "Ethan has the fashion sense of a space slug. He's the whole reason Captain got us jumpsuit uniforms in the first place. She couldn't handle the chaos from Ethan's clothing." He tugged on the black coverall he wore.

"Really?" Aly glanced at Joy, certain the two men were teasing her.

Joy nodded, winking with her natural eye. The other, mechanical, one didn't have a lid to wink with. She'd had a bad decompression accident years ago from a micrometeor strike on a small outpost, and a lot of her body had to be replaced with gears and cogs and metal parts to save her life. Joy was their quartermaster and their muscle when they needed it. Aly always thought that the woman must have been beautiful before the accident, with striking blue eyes and space-pale skin. She was tall but most people couldn't see her past the gears and metal. It had taken Aly a few months before she'd been able to see the woman behind the mechanical parts too, and she was grateful that her own artificial parts for her AI were hidden on the inside.

"Hey, she gave in when I demanded some accents. All black is, well, boring." Ethan grinned.

"At least silver trim doesn't clash with much." Tai shook his head.

"So, your first leave. What are you going to do, Aly?" Ethan asked.

"Um…" She had no idea, she'd never had the freedom to do whatever she wanted before. "Probably explore, I guess." Even after she'd escaped from the Lab she'd had to avoid detection until she could get off world.

"Well, while you're exploring, avoid the living quarter decks, they're mostly for the locals, and make sure you check out The Pastry Prophet on Deck Two. They have the best donuts in the outer system."

"What's a donut?" Aly shrunk away from the combined, incredulous stares of her three crewmates.

"You've never had a donut?" Ethan leaned back in his chair, eyebrows raised.

"Ethan, she doesn't even know what one is," Joy said a little more gently.

"How?" He shook his head. "Never mind. Make sure you get one. You won't be sorry."

"What do they look like?" Aly was almost afraid to ask, but she wanted to make sure she got the right thing.

*I know what they look like,* her AI, who she'd named Kitty when she was a kid, said.

Tai, still looking surprised at her lack of knowledge about something that was obviously common held up his hands in an O shape. "About this big. Round, hole in the center. They usually have icing on top and sometimes other stuff. It's a pastry."

She knew what pastries were, stomach rumbling a little at the memory. They'd been allowed one treat on their birthdays every year at the Lab, and she'd always looked forward to it. Lab food was usually extremely boring.

"Okay, thanks." Aly's heart raced. She was afraid they'd start asking about why she didn't know what a donut was. Questions she wouldn't be able to answer, and then they'd ask more questions, and then they would turn her in to the Lab and she wouldn't even get to try a donut. Obviously normal people all ate donuts, and she desperately wanted to be normal.

"Hi, Captain. Hi, Nikiru," Joy said as Captain Shelena and First Mate Nikiru entered. The room quieted as the small conference room became crowded.

Aly breathed a quiet sigh of relief when the crew's attention turned away from her.

"We've been granted clearance to go on station. Joy, make sure we get the supplies we need before you hit the bars. Tai, Ethan, Aly, help her. Aly, no drinking."

Aly grinned. She didn't want alcohol. She wanted sugar. Pure, wonderful, sweet sugar, like a normal person. "Yes, Captain."

"And, Aly, be careful. Stay on the main decks. I should remind you all, this is fringe territory. They don't always take to outsiders well, so watch yourselves. I don't want to bail any of you out of the brig, or worse."

Tai laughed and nudged Ethan. "Got that?"

"Hey, what is this, pick on Ethan day? That wasn't my fault."

Aly wondered whose fault it was that Ethan had ended up in the brig, but she didn't ask. If they wanted to share the story, they'd tell her.

"Okay, troops, move out."

Aly tried to contain her impatience while they helped Joy load a few crates of the supplies they'd already arranged. A few more crates arrived, and Aly danced. This was taking forever!

"Hey, jumping bean."

It took Aly a minute to realize that Tai was talking to her.

"Yeah, what, Tai? What's a jumping bean?"

"You, right now. If you bounce anymore, the station will shake apart. Get out of here. We'll take care of this."

She glanced at Joy and Ethan for confirmation. They both made shooing motions.

Grinning, Aly waved and ran for the lifts. "Thanks!" She called over her shoulder. Aly dodged around a scruffy man wearing stained gray coveralls with the words 'maintenance' on the back. His loader full of crates shrieked vented steam as he slammed on the brakes to avoid bumping her. She stepped out of the way and nearly ran into someone else. Aly spun around, trying to find a clear path in the chaos. She wasn't used to this sort of environment.

Kitty, always helpful, gave Aly directions to the lift.

"Thanks," she whispered. Her footsteps rang on the metal decking as she jogged along the clear path and she almost expected her breath to fog in the chilly air. Most of the people she dodged around were fully human, but she saw one other mech like Joy, and she thought she caught a glimpse of a non-human, but she wasn't sure what species. Nonhumans were rare in this sector.

"Kitty," she said quietly. "Do you have the location of the donut shop?"

If you would touch the computer panel, I will pull it up.

She couldn't speak to her AI without talking, but Kitty had no external speakers so she could only reply in Aly's mind.

Aly stared at a wall map, searching for the pastry shop. After a moment she found the shop and keyed the floor into the lift. The panel lights lit up and the lift hissed and clanked into motion as gears spun in response to Kitty's directions.

The Pastry Prophet is on the second deck. Go left once we exit the lift and it will be twenty meters past the first intersection.

Aly and danced with excitement. Her first donut was mere minutes away.

Rushing out of the lift when it opened, she almost ran into a beautiful woman with skin as dark as Shelena's and Nikiru's. The white lab coat she wore contrasted sharply with her complexion. That and her scowl made Aly jump quickly away, her heart racing. Lab coats reminded her too much of her past, though she was certain she'd never seen the woman before. Aly was glad when she went into the lift.

Watch where you are going. I doubt they serve donuts in the brig.

"Sorry, Kitty. I'm just so excited!"

I know. I am too. I have never tasted donuts either.

"Silly, you can't taste things. They didn't put sensors in my mouth."

No, but I can experience it through the reactions in your brain.

"True."

Aly, not used to running, was out of breath by the time she ran down the hall, past the first intersection and skidded to a halt in front of The Pastry Prophet.

"No!" Aly clenched her hands into fists in frustration.

It was closed.

"No, no, no!" The best donuts in the system were on the other side of a wall of glass. She could see them, right there, sitting on a tray next to other delights, exactly as described. Sugar cookies, cupcakes, croissants, things she didn't actually know the names of. She'd never tasted any of those either.

She put her hands against the glass and leaned on it, trying not to cry. She wanted to be normal. She wanted a donut.

*Aly, might I direct your attention to the sign?*

Aly glanced at the sign on the glass. 'Back in thirty minutes. Out for lunch.'

Heaving a sigh of relief, Aly stepped back, and remembering she was in public, glanced up and down the hallway to make sure she hadn't attracted too much attention. No one seemed to have noticed her.

"We just need to wait. I can wait a few more minutes." Looking around, Aly saw a small alcove with tables and benches. A porthole showed the starscape beyond.

*That would be an excellent place to wait.*

Other shops lined the hallway, though, now that she looked, many of them were closed or closing for lunch. They sold everything she could possibly want: from clothing, to food, to entertainment. Some of the entertainment showed scantily clad adults doing things that made Aly blush, and she averted her eyes.

"Okay, half an hour. I can do this."

Kitty laughed. *You will survive.*

She'd survived a lot worse than a half an hour wait, so she knew Kitty was right, but still, the minutes dragged. She didn't need a chrono to tell her the time, though there was a display on the wall across from her. Kitty would tell her when the time was up, if the store opening didn't alert her first.

To pass the time, she played chess with Kitty. She could whisper her moves and the AI would keep track in case Aly got confused. She almost never lost track anymore. It was one of the first games they'd been taught at the Lab, how to play chess with the voice in your head. She'd been so young she'd barely understood what she was doing, but after years of daily chess matches with Kitty, they'd both grown very good at the game.

She lost track of time and was startled when Kitty interrupted the game.

"Kitty?"

Quiet.

Glancing up, Aly's eyes went wide as she saw a familiar set of shoulders and dark head talking to the woman behind the counter at The Pastry Prophet. She was the same woman Aly had almost run into. She'd mistaken the woman's chef frock for a lab coat. However, there was no mistaking the other man, even if he wasn't wearing his lab coat.

"Dr. Olson...."

Kitty enhanced Aly's hearing implants so she could hear the conversation.

"She has light brown hair, dusky skin, dark eyes. About this tall." He held up his hand to approximately Aly's 1.7m height. "You haven't seen her?"

"He's looking for me." Aly whimpered. "How does he know I'm here?"

Kitty was silent for longer than normal.

I do not know. However, we are not far from the Lab. Perhaps he is here often?

Dr. Olson was the only adult to survive having an AI implanted in his brain with his sanity intact, though Aly thought his sanity was debatable. She vividly remembered him randomly losing his temper at small things; split milk, a book in the wrong spot in their library, the time Bekka had dropped the stylus jar in class.... She shied away from that memory.

Once experiments with adults had failed, the Institute had switched to children. That had gone a little better, but ultimately the last gen AIs had proved too intelligent. Essentially, the Institute had succeeded in their goals to create a true AI, but had failed in being able to control them. The AIs had tried to control their human hosts, so the Institute had decided to terminate the project.

Kitty, a later gen AI, but not the last gen, had woken Aly in the night with the news. Aly had barely escaped with her life and she was fairly certain she was the only one who had escaped. Obviously, Dr. Olson was trying to tie up loose ends.

Quick, look out the porthole. He's not searching for someone with blue hair.

Aly twisted until she stared directly at the porthole. The beautiful starscape was not quite enough to distract her from her racing heart as she heard Dr. Olson's purposeful steps click past her on the metal decking. If she hadn't been completely sure before, she was now. That precise cadence of steps had comforted her as a child and haunted her nightmares since her escape.

Waiting until she couldn't hear his footsteps anymore, Aly whispered. "Is he gone?"

Yes. For now. We should get back to the ship.

"I want a donut."

Aly, what if she recognizes you from his description. She could call him back.

Ignoring her AI's very sound advice, Aly stalked up to the counter.

The woman raised an eyebrow. "How can I help you?" She didn't exactly sound unfriendly, but Aly guessed she recognized her from the lift earlier. Her nametag said Nia.

"Hi, uh, Nia, first, I'm sorry about almost running into you, but I was so anxious to get over here. My shipmate said you had the best donuts in the area." Aly tried out her best charming grin.

Either the compliment or the smile worked because the Nia's mouth turned up into a fantastic smile. "I hope they don't disappoint." She hesitated, her expression turning back into a frown. "Was that man from earlier looking for you?"

Aly didn't reply. Turning to bolt, she hesitated, a small, frightened sound escaping her mouth. Dr. Olson was coming back.

"He hasn't seen you yet. Hurry, come around the counter and duck down over there."

She pointed and Aly wasted no time ducking through the

small opening in the counter and hiding under the shelf Nia indicated. Shivering when she could hear Dr. Olson's measured stride, she pushed herself further under the shelf.

"One more thing, Ms. Prophet. I wanted to mention that she is very dangerous, and there is a substantial reward for her capture. Don't try to apprehend her yourself, but please let me know if you see her." His voice sounded smooth, and oh so reasonable.

Aly remembered that voice telling her to take her meds, and telling her that it would be all right. Soothing her at night, even the night before they'd killed everyone. The night she'd accidentally spilled her medication. That had probably saved her life, along with Kitty's warning.

"Yes, thank you, Dr. Olson. If I see a young brunette woman of that description I'll be sure to let you know."

Despite her racing heart, Aly had to grin as she touched her blue hair.

She is a clever woman, Kitty said.

Aly nodded since she couldn't speak.

"Is that all, Dr. Olson? I have baking to do," Nia said after a long pause.

"Yes, of course. Have a nice day, Ms. Prophet."

Despite the clear dismissal, it was another long moment before Aly heard Dr. Olson walk away. Nia ignored Aly for a long time, moving about her bakery and finally starting to make something.

As her terror faded, Aly's nose reminded her that she was surrounded by sweet, wonderful sugar, and her stomach reminded her that she hadn't had any yet and her body mentioned that it had been shoved into a corner for far too long.

Nia glanced at her. "You should be safe now."

"Why are you helping me?"

Frowning, Nia glanced down the hallway where Dr. Olson had gone earlier. "Dr. Olson comes out this way about once a month. He always stops by the store and always gets something, and he always complains about it. And, occasionally he mentions his work," she hesitated, expression darkening further. "He says he works on lab creatures, but some of the things he does. Well, if a girl were running from him, I suspect there's a good reason. Not that I've seen any brunettes like he describes, mind." She smiled at Aly.

A little more confident, Aly scooted out from under the counter, brushing some white dust off of her pants.

"Now, you mentioned wanting a donut." Nia glanced down the hallway and cursed. "That man. He's coming back. I'll stay quiet, but next time you're through this system I want to hear your story."

Aly's heart raced again. "Sure."

"Out the back. Through that door!"

After one last longing glance at the tray of donuts, Aly slipped through the double swinging doors and went to the back of the shop where she found a service entrance.

"Kitty, do you remember the map?"

*Yes.* Kitty gave her directions.

"Great, thanks." She started down the corridor and then stopped, a chill of terror trailing icy fingers down her spine. "Kitty, what if he knows what ship we're on?"

The AI was silent for a short time before she replied. *It is possible he saw your name on a manifest.*

"Damn, I thought Aly would be different enough."

*He didn't seem certain you were here. Maybe he was simply, ah, what do you call it? Playing a hunch. However, we should hurry just in case. He won't be able to do much once we're on the ship.*

*Yeah, except tell everyone I'm an escaped experiment,* Aly thought to herself as she ran down the hallway and out the door Kitty directed her toward. She slowed, knowing the hallway she was about to head out into was in the public corridors. The service hallway she'd been in didn't go all the way to the docking bay.

*Just walk normally,* Kitty said when the door clicked open.

Taking a deep breath, and hoping she could pull it off, Aly walked out into the hallway and tried to slip into the flow of foot traffic. It wasn't that busy, so she couldn't hide in the crowd.

*Keep walking normally.* The AI sounded alarmed.

It took her a moment to see what her AI had already noticed. Dr. Olson walked toward them.

"Kitty, what do I do?" She whispered.

*It is too late to do anything except hope he does not notice you. Keep your eyes forward, and walk normally.*

Heart pounding in her chest, blood roaring in her ears so that she could barely hear, Aly did her best to keep her terror from her face as she walked down the hallway.

It seemed to be working. He glanced at people, obviously looking for her, but his eyes slid over her face as if he didn't recognize her and he walked past.

She didn't allow herself to feel relieved, and her shoulder blades itched as she imagined him turning around and seeing her. She waited for the shout of discovery, but kept walking, not knowing what else she could do.

*This lift.*

Aly turned and stood in front of it, waiting for a small eternity before the doors opened. She filed in with several other people, turning to look out the door.

Dr. Olson had turned around and was coming back this way. He frowned when he looked at her, and Aly desperately tried not to panic, tried not to meet his eyes, tried not to let her fear show.

In a moment of inspiration, she glanced up at the man standing next to her and smiled. "How are you today?"

He was a younger man in his twenties wearing local clothing. He smiled back. "Not bad. Thank you for asking."

The doors finally whooshed shut and she hoped that she'd fooled Dr. Olson.

The young man got off at the next deck along with most of the other passengers. Aly clenched her fists, knowing Dr. Olson's AI could stop the lift and bring it back up. She wanted to get off, but it wasn't her deck yet and she didn't want to end up someplace where she'd get into trouble. That would get her caught for sure.

Taking a few deep breaths as the lift vented steam and slowed, she forced herself not to bolt when she reached the docking bay. Aly walked calmly across the metal decking, not wanting to attract attention by rushing. She tried to look around without being obvious about it, and she didn't see Dr. Olson anywhere.

The door was closed when she arrived at her ship, and she keyed in her code, glancing over her shoulder once to make sure no one was watching. Clear, she ducked inside and sagged against the bulkhead, hands shaking as the adrenalin fled her system. Tears leaked from her eyes and she fled to her cabin, not wanting anyone to see her cry.

No one was on board anyway. Everyone else was enjoying the station like normal people did. Why couldn't she have a normal life? Why did the Institute have to ruin her life even after she'd escaped? Why couldn't she have a simple donut?

\* \* \*

"Hey, Aly," Ethan called through the door's intercom. "Dinner."

"I'm not hungry." She tried not to sound surly but ship food, while good and much better than Lab food, could hardly compare to the treat she'd missed out on and could now only imagine.

"You'll like it, I promise. Captain got take out."

Well, that would be a little better than ship food, she thought. "I'll be there in a minute."

Everyone had gathered in the small galley and plates of different colored dishes in sauces were scattered around along with flatbread and some grains. She dug in along with the rest of the crew, and the rich spices and delicious sauces made her forget, somewhat, her sorrow at missing out on the donut. Recovering from her terror at seeing Dr. Olson, however, was going to take more than interesting food. Momentarily, her sorrow that she was going to have to leave this ship sooner rather than later made her want to leave the galley. She liked it here too much, but it wasn't safe now that Dr. Olson was on her trail.

"Why'd you come back to the ship early?" Tai asked.

Shrugging, Aly ducked her gaze. "I was tired, maybe a little overwhelmed." She couldn't think of anything better to say. She couldn't say she was an escapee from what she thought was an illegal experiment and now they'd caught up to her. Now she'd have to run again. Sheer determination kept tears from her eyes.

"Ah, well, that happens." Tai gave her a sympathetic grin.

"Got a surprise for you. It'll make everything all better." Ethan grinned. "Close your eyes."

Hesitantly, Aly did as she was told, not certain anything could make her feel better. She heard gears grind as the door whoosh open, closed, and then open again, and then a familiar sweet scent tickled her nose. She snapped her eyes open and stared.

Ethan held out a white box with the words The Pastry Prophet on the side. "When I went up to get a donut, Ms. Prophet, the owner, asked me if I was the one who said she had the best donuts in the area. When I said yes, she gave us this entire box but said you had to have the first pick."

Aly held out her hands, took the box and carefully put it on the table. She lifted the lid, savoring the sweet smell and stared at the treats inside. Nia had sent more than just donuts, but there was no question as to which treat she'd try first. Carefully, she lifted out a chocolate frosted donut, holding it for a moment, savoring the event that she should have experienced as a young child. It was a step toward being normal, this donut, this thing that everyone else had already tasted by the time they were her age. It gave her hope that maybe someday she could completely escape the Institute's reach.

She closed her eyes and bit into it.

The donut melted in her mouth, coating her tongue with sugary bliss. Groaning in pleasure, her fears and worries fled, pushed away by the absolute ecstasy of the moment. It was everything she could have possibly imagined.

The perfect pastry.

# BURYING ENGINES

**Marilyn K. Martin**

"I HATED TO you to make this dog-leg on your circuit, Judge, just for this one case. But we didn't have a choice," said Sheriff Cal, spitting tobacco juice on a small, six-legged blue lizard that had stopped by his boot. He was tall and broad-shouldered, clad in a long-sleeved, lightweight shirt and replica-jeans, over ranch-style boots with a flat heel for more walking than riding.

"Well, I'm glad you called me, Cal," said the portly Circuit Judge standing a few meters away. He was preoccupied with looking around at the mounds of graves in the orange dirt, with their solar-patch and electronic-ID buttons glittering on their concrete stump markers.

The Judge was a short, stocky man in an Old West Earth suit, the collar of his white shirt already stained yellow with sweat all the way in to his string tie. "Especially since this engine case has a human family involved," he continued matter-of-factly, as he fetched a neatly folded absorb-o-matic handkerchief from a pocket, and watched it pop open.

"We've got to be especially careful with human families, since this Colony's never going to get more industry and immigrants if we don't get our 'Decent Place to Live' ratings up," the Judge panted as he lifted his bowler hat to wipe the perspiration already beading up on his balding head. "Especially since most folks love to read stories about places that extend human rights to non-humans, for some reason."

"Well, it's really just a big misunderstanding, Judge," continued the tall Sheriff uneasily. The huge Stetson cowboy hat on his head kept his face in shadow, and let his eyes dart around unseen. "My deputies are rough men, but they're brave and mostly reliable, Sir," he intoned solemnly, hooking thumbs into his gun belt. The Peace-Maker on his hip was all business—a fully working replica—the replacement handle of blue marble made to fit his large hand. And the top of his holster opening was already stretched and worn from too many quick-draws. "I've never heard any complaints about my deputies ever hurting any law-abiding citizen, let alone killing anyone who didn't deserve it. Although how much respect you're supposed to offer engines is a big point for debate, ain't it?"

The Judge didn't answer, continuing to look around as he mopped up sweat on his cheeks and neck, so the Sheriff jutted his chin out toward the back of the cemetery hill they were standing on. "Besides, lots of 'em implode every year from melted circuits like that. Me 'n the deputies done the best we could to smooth things over, but the widow wouldn't have it." Cal looked down and kicked away the blue lizard with the tobacco stain, still hugging his shadow as cool solace from the oppressive heat of the triple suns overhead. "Sometimes you just gotta call in a higher law to satisfy people and stop all the grumblin'."

"You made the right decision, Cal," answered the Judge, stuffing his handkerchief in a jacket pocket. "Even if trials are considered nuisances to a lot of folks, without justice you just have anarchy. And there's already been a half dozen Old West Steampunk colonies like AriMex that were shut down, what with all the people running around killing each other. Too many 'Daily Deaths from Violence', and Earth shuts off all supplies. And then the colony dies if they don't have enough Big Industry to order in supplies, which they always sell to the citizens for a huge mark-up."

The Judge looked around at the heat-shimmering mirages in the dusty orange distances on all sides of the hill. Even the odd shaped boulders, covered in blue lichen, seemed to waver in the rising heat of mid-summer. And everywhere, small desert critters scampered or slithered from one cool spot to another, seeking ever-shifting shade beneath the triple suns overhead.

"AriMex Colony already has this blasted summer heat and desert landscape to battle against, in our promotional media," the judge murmured, suddenly patting down pockets as he searched for something. "Plus we're already battling the popular misconception that Old West Steampunk colonies aren't proper places to raise families. Just places for wild hooligans to ride round on mecha-horses, shooting anything that moves."

He finally located a small video camera in a pants pocket, and took it out to transfer to a jacket pocket for quick retrieval. "OK, so show me where the engines are buried, Cal, so I can start recording some evidence."

The Sheriff straightened, unhooked his thumbs from his gun belt, then pointed. "Over here, Judge. The back part of Boot Hill is where we bury 'em."

The pair walked thru prickly black ground cover, orange dirt and speckled granite rocks glittering with bits of quartz. And the back part of Boot Hill was indeed covered with the graves of robots. Metallic and plastic human-like heads were visible in ragged lines, only a few feet apart, more like an unholy crop for cannibals than a cemetery. Buried standing up for both space and to prevent any toxic leaks, only the robots' heads showed above ground. Plastic markers glued to the top of each robot head carried a manufacturer's barcode with model information, and minimal identification.

"Marcus Motherboard - Saloon Dishwasher," read the Judge as he passed the first marker, on a plasto-metal head with several bullet holes clean thru it. "Forgot to duck" was all it said under robot-Marcus' name. The Judge slowed down to read the other robot-grave markers as he walked past. A rusting, seriously dented head nearby had a marker which read "Tommy Dell - Stagecoach Driver", and under that was written "Run over by a team of horses."

"You've got a sizable number of engine graves up here, I'll say that," agreed the portly Judge in the suit. "I don't know of any other town on AriMex Colony that buries their engines intact like this."

"Exactly!" spoke up the Sheriff, spitting his entire syntho-bacco wad aside to free up his mouth for more important matters. "I wanted you to see our Boot Hill first, Judge, so you'd notice that," nodded the Sheriff. "Most towns on this Colony, well, they ain't too fond of engines. Just as soon cut 'em up for parts and be done with it.

"Heck, we're risking ground-poisoning citations by burying 'em whole!" gestured the Sheriff. "Something about acid leaks and energy overloads. Like that explosion over in AbiDallas last year. They don't even have a hill anymore. It's just Boot Crater now."

The man in the suit smiled. "Yes indeed, Sheriff," he agreed. "You took on substantial risk to bury all these engines, I can clearly see that. So why exactly did you start burying them at all?"

The Sheriff straightened, his titanium badge glinting from all angles, due to the oppressive glare from the multiple overhead suns.

"Well, 'cause some people here in Mesquiteer got feelin's for engines," he shrugged. "Ol' widow Larsen bought herself an engine manservant from Smarty City a decade or so ago. Had him about ten years. Then one day he pushed her outta the way of a runaway cattle drive thru town, and that engine got stomped so bad he looked like a golf ball. Some kids even counted all the dents: a hundred and forty three."

The Judge turned to look up at the Sheriff, whose back was to the triple suns, just a Stetson shadow over his stern, leathery face. The Judge saw this ploy a lot as he traveled his circuit around this quarter of AriMex Colony. He dealt with a lot of local 'Men Of Some Importance' in small towns like this, back-lighting themselves to look more imposing as they announced something important.

Maybe that was part of the lure of living in an Old West Steampunk colony, the Judge figured. Where strong and brave men with Stetsons and gun belts loomed large, taking care of anything that the steam-powered machinery couldn't. Where a man's word was his bond, and no one was allowed to harass or harm innocent people. Although, as a Circuit Judge, he'd also seen some corrupt Sheriffs and Mayors who only followed the law when and where it suited them.

The Judge didn't quite have a handle on Sheriff Cal yet, but the Justice Department in Smarty City hadn't logged any citizen complaints about the lawman. "So kindly continue," offered the Judge now, as he turned back to the sea of robot heads marching down the back slope and away from Mesquiteer.

"Well, that ol' widow Larsen cried so hard that we kinda had to do something different for her dead engine, especially after she got the Preacher involved," continued the Sheriff, a hand gesturing roughly, almost dismissively, at the engine heads surrounding them. "Then, once we got that golf-ball-dented engine in the ground up here, all sorts of folks suddenly wanted to bury their dead engines too. It became a status thing, I guess. Suddenly no one wanted to just chop up their destroyed engines for parts, they wanted to bury 'em up here."

The red-faced Judge pulled out his 'kerchief again, noticing a few ever-fresh flowers and plastic cards filled with romantic hearts by some of the engine heads. "And where is the dead engine in question buried?" he asked, mopping his face.

The Sheriff shifted and took a deep breath. "Well, he ain't up here. The family insisted on burying him behind their house. Nobody in town objected, 'specially since that family lives on the outskirts by the Big Gully that always floods when it rains. Land out that way is undesirable but cheap. So we let 'em bury that engine in their back yard. Weren't anything left of the engine's head anyway, after those circuits blew."

The red-faced Judge continued wiping the sweat now running in rivulets down to his neck. He looked uncomfortable and overheated, but also determined as he pocketed his handkerchief. Then he fished the video camera out of his jacket pocket.

"Well, I'm very glad you started up here on Boot Hill with the engine graves, Cal," he said, turning on the video camera and raising it up to his eyes. "All part of the Discovery Phase. Let me get some video of these robot graves, to show how the townsfolk value their engines, even the destroyed ones," he murmured, slowly turning to pan the engine heads with his video camera. "What do you understand the charges to be, Cal?"

The Sheriff's jaw clenched and unclenched, as he cleared his throat. "Wrongful Destruction of a Robot, your Honor," he answered grimly. "I know it's all poppycock, we all know that engine died of a circuit meltdown. But the family he was livin' with insisted on filing charges and gettin' a court date.

"All you really gotta do is dismiss the case for lack of evidence, Sir," the Sheriff suggested in a strong tone as he watched the Judge videotaping the engine heads. "There was just that robot's body to bury, since most of the pieces from his head got washed down that Big Gully in that next Every Other Sunday Rainstorm.

"Or … you could just downgrade the charges to Destruction of Property," the Sheriff continued boldly. "And let the Colony Financial Department throw some credits at that family. That's probably what they really want anyway. Then you can get back on your circuit goin' after REAL crimes. You know, against decent folks."

The Judge lowered his video camera to stare up at the angry Sheriff. He was getting the distinct impression that there was more to this case than just one accidentally destroyed robot. "Well, thanks for the suggestions, Cal. I'll take those into consideration once the trial begins this afternoon."

Fifteen minutes later, the Judge again pocketed his video camera. "I guess we can retire down to the courthouse now, so I can make some notes on my laptop. I'll go record video of where the engine is buried behind that house later, once I've rested and rehydrated with some ice water." He again fetched his damp handkerchief to wipe beneath his bowler, and soak up the rivulets of sweat running down his cheeks. "But first I've got to get out of this heat before I have a stroke. You did say that you've got the air conditioning turned on in the courtroom?"

The Sheriff nodded. "Yes, Sir. Rev'd up the steam-pumps this morning, before you arrived. Should be a cool sixty-five degrees in there by now, ready for the trial and a roomful of onlookers."

"Good", panted the red-faced Judge. "So now please lead me down the best and safest path off this hill, Sheriff. So we can get out of the glare of these triple suns."

*　*　*

Sharply at one o'clock, the now cooled-off Judge entered the courtroom in fresh clothes. The hum of the ceiling A/C was briefly overridden by the scrapes of wooden bench legs on the aluminum floor, as everyone stood up. The courtroom was packed with men, women and children in their Sunday finery, standing quietly, their faces calm but expectant. Some robots stood along the walls, brought along by the families who owned them, their faces blank as they guarded steaming dinner-packs on the floor, or arm-rocked sleeping babies. Everyone knew that these one o'clock trials could sometimes go on into the night, so they had come prepared.

A packed audience was normal in most of the small town courthouses the Judge rotated through on his circuit. Court Day once a month was dramatic and emotional entertainment, since everyone knew all the parties involved. Although betting on trial outcomes had been outlawed, there were always a few people who jumped up cheering after the verdict was announced, even if they had no ties to either side on trial.

The Judge calmly took in the courtroom scene after he climbed up to the high desk, studying faces, especially those seated on the front benches, Prosecution on the left, and Defense on the right. The on-lookers seemed randomly seated wherever there was space in the crowded courtroom, and no one appeared to be sitting behind the side they most favored. So the Judge had no immediate sense of who most of the townspeople were rooting for, if any. He was not only sensitive to meting out a justice that the townspeople considered 'fair,' but also because he occasionally called audience members as witnesses in extreme circumstances. Mainly when one or more had eye witness testimony that had been overlooked—or suppressed—by the Prosecution or Defense.

The Judge now gestured. "Please be seated, ladies and gentlemen." Usually a deputy announced this, as a substitute bailiff. But this town's deputies were both Defendants in this trial, so the Judge handled the announcement himself.

He placed his steampunk laptop on the high desk before him, all polished wood with power bellows in small tubes on each side, then sat down himself. He opened his computer and angled the laptop so that he could glance at the people facing him, as he typed in a few notes: "Town of Mesquiteer, July 9, 3917. Widow Harriet Plempkin versus Deputies Slim Dozier and Taylor Trot. Charge is Wrongful Destruction of a Robot, named Proud Tom

Apel. Discovery Phase notes in file A1, accompanying video evidence the Trial Judge shot this morning in file B1 ..."

As he typed, the Judge kept glancing at the people in the front benches. On the Prosecution bench sat the widow Plempkin, a middle-aged woman with a lined, sad face, staring stoically ahead. Her long hair was done up in a back bun that was already coming undone, loose graying hair on her shoulders and around her face. She wore her best Sunday dress she'd made from patterned flour sacks, a small message on one lower hem reading "Best Flour West Of Smarty City!" Her hands firmly gripped a tablet computer in her lap, one corner cracked and bent, like a large animal had stepped on it.

To her side, in descending order, were an older boy, a girl, and a smaller boy. The boys wore pants six inches above their ankles, over scuffed shoes with holes in the soles, and frayed string ties on their best Sunday shirts. The girl in the middle sat barefoot, stuffed into an outgrown dress, the waist up to her ribs and the cloth stretched and strained around her shoulders.

He'd glimpsed this family earlier, anxious faces at a back window, as he had arrived behind their house with the Sheriff. The Judge knew he couldn't have any contact with Civilian Prosecution before a trial, in order to keep everything proper and legal. So the Sheriff had stood by the house while the Judge had videotaped the grave of engine Proud Tom, the orange-dirt mound decorated with fresh flowers and little mining car toys that someone had played with, tiny wheel trails all over the grave.

Seated now on the Prosecution bench, the Judge could more clearly see that all three children had metal plates on different parts of their heads, their remaining hair growing in odd spurts from bits of their original scalp. Both boys had one robo-eye apiece, glinting red as it zipped back and forth on its own, scanning the room whenever they looked up. The children too all had small tablet computers in their hands. The oldest boy, most of his head covered in riveted robo-parts with a geyser of white hair on the top of his head, was already typing notes. While the little girl in the middle had to elbow the youngest boy, madly working his thumbs on only a few keys, and loudly whisper, "Mama said NO vid-games in the courtroom!"

As a few people chuckled, the Judge checked out the Defendants' bench on the opposite side. A couple of hard-faced men sat shifting nervously in their Sunday Best, which consisted of their nicest shirts, jeans and string-ties. They also wore rough leather vests with black and grey animal hair still attached, as background for their titanium deputy badges. Well shined ranch boots were on their feet, worn cowboy hats in their twitchy hands.

The Sheriff sat on the crowded bench behind his Defendant deputies, at the inside corner beside the center aisle. He was dressed in his usual attire, his big Stetson on his lap and his white forehead denoting where the big cowboy hat usually sat. He studiously avoided even looking at the dour deputies in the row ahead of him.

He'd planted what seeds he could in the Judge's head while atop Boot Hill, and that was as far as Sheriff Cal was prepared to go. 'Cause now it was show-time, and the Sheriff had no intention of losing his job—nor being seen as covering up for his deputies—in case they were found guilty. Both deputies had already sworn several times to the Sheriff that they were innocent of engine Proud Tom's destruction, but he'd caught both in lies before. And the Sheriff was determined to hang onto his titanium badge, even if it meant laboriously having to train new deputies.

Finally the Judge hit his Send button, and cleared his throat. "This court is now in session. All real-time proceedings are now available thru CaseProudTom@Mesquiteer, for those of you with porta-comps." There was a shuffling noise as the on-lookers with computers logged in to the official recording of the proceedings. Overhead, a dozen small domes of surveillance cameras were now blinking and recording in all corners and in the ceiling of the room

"I received messages from both Prosecution and Defense that

you were going to represent yourselves, rather than wait for lawyers from Smarty City. Is that correct?" asked the Judge, adjusting his laptop toward the witness box. It was now recording all voices, but taking video of the witness box only, for crucial back-up of the overhead surveillance cameras. As everyone on both front benches nodded agreement, the Judge gestured toward the thin woman. "Since both sides have agreed to waive opening remarks, since I am under some time constraints to wrap this trial up today, I now ask the Prosecution to call their first witness."

Seconds later, the oldest boy, his head covered in riveted metal plates and a shock of white hair, sat in the witness box. The thin woman stood to the side, facing the stand and the Judge. "So tell the Judge here what your Pa meant to you, Johnny," she coaxed her oldest son. "And how he ended up on AriMex Colony."

Johnny looked down a moment to take a deep breath and gather his thoughts. "He was the best Pa there was, Your Honor," he said, looking up. "He was an old retired Apel Silk Model 96. He'd been built as a miner, with big strong hands that could lift my sister and brother at the same time, one in each palm. And all those old Silk models had social-cohesion programming too, so they were friendly and really nice to be around.

"My Pa was brought to AriMex Colony to work in that silver mine in Stun Valley, until the cave-in closed it," Johnny continued. "Then the mining company that owned him couldn't find another mine here on AriMex to rent him too. And they didn't want to pay freight on an older engine to send him to another mining planet. So they gave him a few thousand credits to settle somewhere on AriMex and just ... set him free."

"Keep goin', Johnny," urged the woman. "Tell 'em how I adopted all of you. How our family got started."

Johnny nodded at his mother, then faced forward again. "My Ma here is a widow who could never have children naturally. All of us kids were from Smarty City back east, where we got tore up bad in the 'Quake of '10. We all got put back together again, but ...

well, some of us didn't have any family anymore. Or the family we had did ... didn't want us no more the way we looked. So they put us on a Hybrid Orphan Train headed west." He nodded solemnly at the thin woman. "This nice lady, our Ma, met us at the big train stop over in Rio Rancho. She picked us out 'cause no one else wanted us, and signed the adoption papers for all three of us right there in the train station."

There was a ripple of comments thru the audience now. The thin woman cocked her head, noticing, but refused to turn around and look at the audience. "And how did your Pa come into our lives, Johnny?" she asked strongly, again facing the boy squarely. He nodded and glanced at the Judge with his one brown eye, as his red scanning robo-eye continued its own movements.

"Our Pa just knocked on our door one day, Sir, asking for work," continued the boy. "My Ma laughed and said, 'You know how to raise young 'uns?' And Pa, he just said ... he answered "Ma'm, I'd be right proud to help you raise young 'uns. I'm plumb wore out workin' with rocks and things that ain't alive." So that kinda ... well, it melted Ma's heart. So she took him in right then and there. She put "Proud" in front of Pa's name, which was Tom Apel. 'Cause she was right proud of all of us, no matter how we looked.

"And then we all went lookin' for a preacher willin' to marry a woman and an engine. But we couldn't find nobody, especially when they saw that us kids looked part engine too. So Ma and Pa just filed court papers as Unmarried Parents Raising Children, and Ma kept her last name of Plempkin."

\*　　\*　　\*

Deputy Dozier squirmed in the witness chair like he didn't belong there, his face set and defiant. As the loud murmuring from the audience died down, Deputy Trot, who was doing the questioning, tried to reword Dozier's answer to the last question.

"But you don't hate ALL engines," Deputy Trot announced loudly. "Don't you mean that you just ... don't like engines that try to act like decent folk? Pretending to have families and all that?"

"That's leading the witness!" announced the judge sharply. "But I'll allow it, as long as Deputy Dozier confines his answer to why he specifically disliked engine Proud Tom."

"I ... I didn't hate him," sputtered Deputy Dozier. "I'm a deputy sheriff, after all, so I gotta protect everyone in Mesquiteer. I mean, we got us a nice little town here, and the Sheriff and us try hard to keep everything peaceful and safe. Most of what we do is break up bar brawls, arrest drunks and petty thieves, and find lost kids. Maybe catch an occasional passer-by criminal we recognize from a Wanted List on the internet. Like the last time you were here, Mr. Judge. Remember One Eyed Pete? Kilt ten people in that range war a few counties away. And we caught him in a bar here in Mesquiteer!"

"I remember," answered the Judge flatly. He seemed unusually tense today, the Sheriff and some audience members noticed. Uncharacteristically, the Judge was snapping at the witnesses without his usual smile or softening humor. Somehow, this case was disturbing him on a deep, visceral level. "So what was it about engine Proud Tom that you didn't like, deputy?" the Judge now prodded sternly.

"Well, 'cause all of a sudden we were gettin' complaints," continued the Deputy, clenching and unclenching a fist as he tried to mute his hatred. "We got this engine walking around giving people orders. The widow here let him go into the general store and order groceries. Next thing you know, that engine's in the schoolhouse, askin' the teacher why that youngest boy there is so slow in readin'. I mean, he was arguing with folks just like he was people too! A lotta folks started to get a real hate-on for Proud Tom, I tell ya'. And us deputies and the Sheriff were the ones they all complained to."

"So what did you do?" prodded Deputy Trot.

"Well, you and I tried to talk to that engine, as well as Mrs. Plempkin," went on the deputy. "You know, tried to ask her to handle any problems with the school, or whatever, instead of her engine. But people were angry by now, and whenever Proud Tom came into town, people started yelling at him. You know, reminding him that he was just an engine and a servant, and couldn't be ordering real people around. Last time I seen Proud Tom before he was destroyed, I had to stop a bunch of boys from throwin' rocks at him on Main Street."

"That's a lie!" burst out the widow Plempkin's youngest boy, jumping off the bench angrily. "You saw our Pa when you kilt him!"

BAM! The Judge hit his fist on a round circle on his high desk labeled 'Gavel Hit.' The Widow Plempkin jumped up to grab the boy while saying, "Sorry, your Honor. Sorry." The courtroom was stone still now, the only sounds were the widow Plempkin on the bench, soothing her youngest son by telling him that he'll get to tell his part soon, and a few puffs of steam escaping as the depressed 'Gavel Hit' wooden circle piece rose and rejoined the rest of the high desktop.

"I, uh, got no more questions, Your Honor," said Deputy Trot.

"Do you want to cross-examine this witness, Mrs. Plempkin?" asked the Judge. When she shook her head no, the Judge turned to the witness box. "You may step down, Deputy Dozier."

Deputy Dozier stood up and faced the Judge. "Just so you understand, Judge, that both of us tried talkin' to that engine and the widow. We did what was right, after all those townspeople complained to us about that robot, Proud Tom."

He then turned to glare menacingly at the audience as he stepped down from the witness box, finally focusing on the little family sitting on the Prosecution bench. "And there ain't NO witness worth spit that can say I did anything to destroy that engine!"

\* \* \*

Soon the courtroom was hushed, like an indrawn breath, everyone waiting and watching. All eyes were on the thin woman's youngest boy, sniffling now in the witness box, his feet dangling a foot off the floor. The thin woman was nervously beside him, arms wrapped around her ribs, torn between wanting to comfort her youngest son, and standing her ground to treat him like the crucial witness he was.

"Come on now, Little Tom," she coaxed. "Tell these nice folks how those deputies kilt your Pa. Sit up straight, and speak out."

The boy wiped his runny nose on the sleeve of his shirt, then brushed away his tears with dirty fingers that left dark streaks on his cheeks. He shifted in the chair to sit up straight, then spoke out in a quavering voice. "It was ... I was on the shady side of the house, playing with my little mine cars Pa made me. Pa was in the back yard, pulling the clean laundry off the line. Everyone else was inside. You had supper on the stove, Ma, and was in the front of the house checkin' on my brother and sister.

"Those two dep'ties," he pointed angrily, "snuck up on Pa at the clothesline, and started talking real mean to him. They had their hands on their gun belts, sayin' they were tired of all the 'plaints—"

"Complaints?" clarified the Judge.

"Yes, Sir," nodded the boy, half of his head a metal plate, and the other half full of shaggy brown hair. "Them two dep'ties said they had ... com-plaints that Pa was still running around town acting like a real person. Giving orders and even arguin' with folks. They said engines ain't s'posed to act like that. That engines get kilt for acting like that!"

The audience rustled, murmuring darkly with disapproval. The deputies on the Defense bench stopped glaring at the little boy on the stand, and suddenly swiveled around to glance at the audience. The Sheriff continued to ignore them, sitting stoically on the bench corner behind them, a twitching shoulder and frowning face indicating that he was already distancing himself from this lying pair on the front bench. It was also beginning to occur to the deputies, as they mumbled to each other while turning slowly back to face forward again, that they might not have jobs when all of this was over, if the town was turning against them.

"So what did you do, Little Tom?" prodded his mother. "Did you come 'round to find me in the front of the house?"

"N-no," answered the boy, his bottom lip quivering. "I didn't want to stop watchin' Pa, in case they ... they did something to him. So I put my back up against the wall of our house, and crept closer, so I could see the back yard better. Then I seen that Deputy Trot there, kick my Pa to his knees."

"And ... and why didn't Pa defend himself?" asked the thin woman, choking back tears.

"'Cause he told us it was part of his ... proga-rammin'," answered Little Tom, as the thin woman nodded. "He couldn't never harm a live person, no matter what they did to him."

"And then what?" pressed the thin woman in an unsteady voice.

"Then ... then Deputy Dozier grabbed Pa's head and shoved something in his mouth. I didn't ... I couldn't figure out what they were doin', since Pa didn't eat," continued the boy. "As an engine, he never put anything in his mouth. He sat at the table with us for meals, but said his mouth was just for talkin'."

The thin woman had a trembling hand over her own mouth now, and was quietly weeping. But Little Tom didn't need any more coaxing.

"Then the dep'ties ran off the other side of the house. I hollered at Pa, and he looked over at me. He was still on his knees, and there was this sparkin' light coming from his mouth.

He shook his head No! pointin' his finger at me to stay put," continued Little Tom. "Then he ... he just stood up and turned, walkin' away from me and the house. He kept going until ... until his head exploded, and his body just fell over."

The boy, tears now streaking down his own angry cheeks, pointed defiantly at the seated deputies. "Them bad dep'ties tried to tell us Pa's circuits melted, and he just died all by hisself. But they kilt him! I saw it!" The boy then buried his face in his hands, sobbing.

\* \* \*

The frowning Judge walked solemnly back into the courtroom, and took his seat on the high desk. Only a few people stood up, then quickly sat back down, embarrassed. The Judge didn't even notice, since he was so focused on announcing his verdict. He'd actually made up his mind before the testimony had ended, although he'd struggled during the recess to temper his deep anger and be guided instead by both the letter and spirit of the law.

The Judge also realized that he had to be careful, as he stared out to study the audience. He'd misjudged audiences before in serious trials. Even though weapons were forbidden in the courtroom, he'd witnessed on-lookers rushing forward when a ruling was read, with sneaked-in guns blazing, aimed at people on either side—or aimed at him, as the Trial Judge. And with this particular case, he wasn't convinced that the town's on-trial law enforcement would even try to defend him if bullets started flying. So the Judge quickly adjusted his jacket to make sure his holstered revolver was within quick reach.

On the Prosecution's front bench, the thin woman sat dabbing her eyes. Little Tom sat in her lap, exhausted and hiccupping from crying too much. Beside her, the oldest boy had his arm around the little girl, who was trying hard to stop crying, wet streaks down both cheeks.

On the other side, the accused deputies sat frowning angrily, their arms folded. They kept glancing at the prosecuting family or back at the audience, with quick whispers to each other. The Sheriff, in the row behind, also sat with folded arms, but only stared at the Judge.

The judge tapped a few things into his laptop about starting the Verdict and Punishment Phases, then pushed it aside and folded his hands on the desktop before him. "Ladies and gentlemen," he announced solemnly. "As you probably know, we can't use a murder charge in the event of a destroyed engine. Wrongful Destruction is the only charge allowed, although the Punishment Phase is at the judge's discretion.

"I am hereby ruling FOR the Prosecution, that engine Proud Tom Apel was willfully destroyed by the defendents for purely selfish, negative and unwarranted reasons," the Judge continued in a strong voice, as gasps and a chorus of murmurs arose from the audience. "This robot was unarmed, like all engines, and at no time posed any threat to anyone in this town, beyond bending some inflexible expectations and challenging some prejudices. Proud Tom was instead a decent and loving parent to these three children, and a caring and helpful husband to this woman."

The courtroom came to life, amid a smattering of approving applause. Starchy women sat nodding their approval to those beside them, as mothers bent their heads to explain the verdict to their confused children. Crusty men were smiling one second, and then glaring daggers at the deputies next while swearing under their breath.

"Therefore both Deputy Dozier and Deputy Trot are to be taken into custody immediately by the Sheriff, and locked up in the town jail until arrangements can be made for their punishment," called out the Judge over the courtroom noise. The Sheriff was on his feet and quickly around the front bench, as both surprised deputies jumped to their feet. The Sheriff grabbed the closest one, a dazed Deputy Trot, and quickly handcuffed him. While Deputy Trot sputtered protests, the Sheriff shook his head angrily and murmured something.

Men from the audience were suddenly rushing forward to grab Deputy Dozier, who was making a run for the door. Surrounded and grabbed, his revolver was taken away as he lashed out, screaming at the Judge. "You gotta be kiddin' me! Punishing us for killin' a loud-mouthed engine? There ain't no justice in that!"

The Sheriff then moved to put Deputy Dozier in handcuffs too, while telling him angrily, "Now I know why you suddenly had to go visit your uncle who worked in a mine! You came back with a blasting cap, didn't you, Dozier?" As he yanked off the convicted deputies' badges, the Sheriff loudly addressed both of them. "I TOLD you both repeatedly not to harm that engine! Didn't I?"

When both men were handcuffed and restrained by the Sheriff and a half dozen townsmen, the Judge signaled for the audience to sit back down. "And now I'll announced the Punishment Phase," he said loudly, as all eyes again turned toward him.

"Since the silver mine in Stun Valley that engine Proud Tom worked at has now been reopened, I sentence both deputies to hard labor in that mine, for a period not less than sixteen years. They will be paid full miners' salaries, locked up every night, and under armed guard in that mine at all times. And seventy-five percent of both their salaries will be forfeited to this widow and her family. In sixteen years these children will all be grown and on their own, and Mrs. Plempkin will be receiving Colony Retirement benefits. Case closed." BAM!

\*   \*   \*

The next morning, the Judge stood waiting on the resin-coated wooden sidewalk in front of the General Store. He wore his overnight-cleaned and ever-present suit and little round city-hat, his bag and closed laptop resting on the sidewalk beside him. Squinting into the distance, as his grandfather had taught him on Earth, he could barely see the rising orange dust to the East that indicated that the morning stage was on time, and that the day would be fair and little humid by the low sluggishness of the dust, possibly indicating an incoming natural rainstorm.

"S-sir?" came a timid voice from behind him. He turned to see the thin woman, widow Plempkin, surrounded by her three children with their robo-part heads. "I ... we just wanted to thank you," the woman said, as all the children solemnly nodded. "And, well, my youngest boy here, Little Tom, his Pa bought him a calf to raise just before he ... he was kilt. And Little Tom wants to name his calf after you. But ... well, we didn't know your name."

The judge smiled broadly, as the distinct rattle and thundering hooves of the arriving stage could now just barely be heard echoing in the distance. His Honor smiled, tipped his round hat and nodded. "Judge TallFeatherSioux, at your service."

# CRYSTALLINE CLOUDS

## Sam Knight

THE INKY blackness of space was oppressive. It made Prudy feel small and insignificant in a way that looking up at the stars had never been able to. Looking out the portholes of her sphere-shaped space capsule into the depths of nothingness, she wished she could see even one star.

The interior of her little capsule was lit by a small glowing filament above her head that gilded everything as it reflected weakly off the brass and glass of her instruments. The light would fade and go out every fifteen minutes and Prudy would have to turn the hand-crank to recharge the battery. Every time she did, her eyes would unwillingly flick back to Roger's body, making sure it was still there.

He looked undignified, strapped into his seat with arms and legs floating upwards, and pieces of cloth, torn from her shirt, shoved into his mouth and nostrils.

Prudy felt guilty about that, but she had needed to stop the blood from dripping out and floating around.

*It's all right, Prudence, you did what you needed to do,* Roger would have said— had said to her hundreds of times before. But it didn't help knowing that. It was different when he couldn't actually say it for himself. She never should have let him come along. He was a good friend and a great financial backer, but he just wasn't made for adventure.

Hadn't been made for adventure...

Prudy sighed and looked back out into the blackness that she never had imagined could exist in the realm of the stars. If she had even remotely suspected the ether of the universe was so full of ... nothing, she never would have bothered building a ship to launch into it, no matter the potential to get rich harvesting the aether.

How had there been stars to see from below, but not from above? All four of her windows into darkness showed only that; darkness. It was so complete, the viewports might as well have been painted with pitch. Where was the moon they had aimed toward? Where was the Earth they had left behind? She couldn't even see the stubby wings she had put on the ship to help steer it. It was as if nothing existed outside of her little cockpit.

She was no fool who would think she had blasted through the gates of Heaven without permission and this was her punishment, but nonetheless, enough people had warned her that the idea now niggled at her thoughts. The fact that she seemed to be flying in her little enclosed space didn't help diminish the silly idea that she might be dead, too, no matter how hard she tried to convince herself it was just because she was completely surrounded by the aether of the universe.

The light dimmed again, and Prudy used the hand-crank to bring it back. Her eyes went to Roger, again. She didn't know what happened to him. She wasn't sure what had happened to her. As soon as she had given the signal for the launch, everything had gone dark. Perhaps being fired out of a giant cannon hadn't been the best way to initiate the journey after all.

Prudy had awoken in the dark and had to feel around for the crank to make light. The first thing she had seen was a marvelous shiny ball floating in the air in front of her. When she reached out to touch it, it had proven to be a liquid that wanted to stick to her finger, to follow her hand as she moved. Her first thought was that it was a liquid aether of some sort. Her wonder had faded when she realized it was blood.

She didn't know if it was hers, or Roger's. They both had suffered bleeding from the mouth and nose. Roger's had been considerably worse, though.

It had been morbidly fascinating to watch the floating balls of blood slowly soak into the rent pieces of fabric she held up to them, and she felt guilty that she wasn't more upset over Roger's death as she played with them.

In the past, he was the one who would point out that she was not responding appropriately to social norms, that she needed to pay more attention to what she was doing and what others thought of her. Without him to tell her how to feel about his death, she knew she was reverting to her habit of putting everything in its own time and place. Death was something she knew well and was familiar with. She could deal with it later, at her convenience. But being in the Heavens, or wherever she was now, well...it was a first, and possibly a one-chance only, experience.

Roger would have understood.

She wiped perspiration from her lip with the torn sleeve on her arm and then looked down at herself, self-conscious here, alone, in a way she never had been in public. *What would Roger have to say about this?* Scandalous enough that she wore trousers and men's shirts, but to tear the sleeves off and bare her arms? She almost chuckled at the thought of the way he would have acted: flabbergasted because it was expected of him, yet obviously with no personal qualms about what she wore.

Enough tomfoolery, she chided herself. Time to figure out what to do.

Prudy pushed away from the useless viewports and floated back to her instruments. They were useless, too. She had managed to devise a compass that could point on any axis, in hopes that it would point back towards north, and Earth, but the needle now lazily spun in a corkscrew pattern. Her altimeter had moved to the maximum setting she had placed on the dial, telling her only that she was not on ground—something she was already well aware of as she floated in front of the instrument panel. The pressure gauge on the boiler was below the line for a reading, and the thermometer was showing the water was near freezing in spite of the thick insulation.

She wondered how cold it must be outside her little bubble of brass and iron. Even in the deepest of winter, as she had readied to leave the confines of the Earth, there had been no hint of an insulation problem. She would need to re-heat the boiler before the water froze. Had her heating element gone out? That didn't seem possible.

She had designed the boiler to run on electric heating elements that it provided energy to itself. It was by no means a self-sustaining or perpetual motion machine, but it was as close as she could build, balancing fuel and energy requirements for the trip, and in all of her tests it had run for a week before needing outside help.

Holding on to the pilot's seat, she twisted herself upside down until she floated with her feet pointed up at the ceiling and began working at the hatch that led to the boiler. Experiencing a moment of vertigo, she had to stop and close her eyes to keep her gorge down. When it passed, she discovered she had to use the chair as leverage against her body to be able to open the hatch.

The change in air pressure caused her ears to pop and pulled her body gently towards the opening as she fought the door. It also caused Roger's limbs to sway, catching her eye and momentarily filling her with false hope. When she got the hatch open, the darkness below her was revealed to be only slightly less complete than that outside. She was grateful for having installed a cranklight here, too, and in a moment the ruddy glow filled the round, metal plated room.

A sphere with a smaller sphere, the boiler, set inside, the room was more a curving tunnel than a proper area. A bicycle pedal and chain powered generator that worked on the same principle as the cranklights, but was used for recharging the batteries for the boiler, sat below her as she drifted down without bothering to use the ladder. She allowed her fingers to trail along the outside of the boiler plate, knowing she wouldn't feel any warmth, but hoping anyway. Prudy had almost removed the manual crank for the boiler, for weight purposes, but was now glad that caution had won out.

As she neared the cycling apparatus, Prudy grabbed it and pulled herself in, trying to settle onto the seat. She quickly discovered that, while she could stay on the seat with little problem, it certainly was not bearing her weight, and the slightest use of the pedals pushed her off.

*Propriety be damned*, she thought as she took off the remainder of her shirt and tore it into strips. If Roger were still alive she wasn't sure if he would be grateful for, or shocked by, the revealing of the homemade half-corset she used to keep her breasts out of her way while she worked. As she tied her feet to the pedals, she was grateful for it, having become aware of how her body tended to continue moving in various ways in this strange gravity-free environment.

Unable to tie her legs down to the seat and still peddle, Prudy finally tied a slipknot through the belt she wore on her trousers and pulled it tight to secure herself to the seat. Even affixed to the contraption as she was, she found it difficult to pedal and charge the batteries. After only a few minutes, sweat beaded up on her forehead, and when she wiped it off with the back of her hand, droplets broke free and drifted away, glistening in the glow of the weak electric light.

She was still watching the jewel-like liquid baubles when the overhead light faded and died, leaving her in the total darkness again. The light in the cockpit had also gone out.

Rather than go through the effort of untying and re-tying herself again, Purdy peddled on in the dark.

With no curious floating things to distract her, her ears became sensitive to the squeak of the pedals, the slight grinding of the chain, and the hum of the electric generator she was working to spin. Other than the occasional popping of metal, from contraction in the cold she assumed, the only other sound was her own breathing.

She peddled on until she became aware of another sound, and she realized it was her own quiet sobbing. In the darkness, some part of her had finally allowed itself to break free, and she cried for Roger.

He had been there for her for years, supporting her in whatever crazy endeavor she fixated on. Not only as a friend, but financially, too. He would get people to invest money in her projects, businesses to sell her contraptions, banks to loan her money...

As she felt the hot tears on her cheeks, she admitted to herself the real reason why Roger was always there for her. He had loved her. And she had taken it for granted. She taken his gifts, his attentions, and his friendship, and returned so little.

Guilt flowed through her as she finally allowed herself to think, not only of his death, but of the relationship they'd had. Or rather the one they hadn't. Prudy had never bothered to think about it before, to classify Roger as a suitor, as a friend, as a companion, or at all.

He just was.

Had been. He just had been.

She was always obsessed with her next project, and he was always...her assistant. Her second. Her sidekick. She sobbed. *Good God, did I really think of him like that?* She hung her head as she peddled on.

She had never overtly rebuked or rebuffed him, but then she

had never needed to; Roger was always the perfect gentleman. But she had known that he loved her, and she had never warned him off, never told him he was wasting time better spent courting someone who wanted to be courted.

And now he had blindly followed her out into the nether regions of the universe. And it had killed him.

How selfish she had been. How foolish to take him for granted. She had never once thought about him 'in that way', and even now the thoughts were uncomfortable, but she had at least owed him the respect to have let him know that. Didn't she?

Ah, Prudence. You worry over the wrong things! Why can't you worry over the things normal people do? Money, food, family? It's always aether or electricity or the ratio of something or other...

When had Roger said that to her? She remembered hearing it, but she couldn't remember having responded.

*Am I worrying about the right thing now, Roger?* She wiped at the tears and peddled on, alone in the darkness, until her legs ached too much to continue.

When she was exhausted, Purdy fumbled at the knots in the darkness, finding it hard to locate ends that floated instead of falling down. Finally freeing herself, she gave a gentle push off in the direction of the ladder and held her arms out, feeling into the black ahead of her. When her fingers touched the ladder, she grabbed hold and pulled her body into alignment with it.

She gently guided herself up the ladder, wondering if 'up' meant anything in this place, and found the hand crank for the light.

As she turned it, and the glow grew brighter, she winced at the light, surprised such a weak light could seem so strong in a black darkness such as she now resided in. It offered none of the warmth or comfort a light that color usually seemed to exude.

She pushed away and floated back down to the batteries and the heating elements to restart the boiler. Under normal circumstances she could have the boiler up to pressure within an hour, but here, wherever here was, she hoped she could do it at all.

When she had done all she could to rekindle the boiler, she busied herself by checking the other equipment they had brought to gather and compress the aether. Everything seemed to be in working order, but without the power from the boiler, she would have to use a hand crank to operate things.

Having nothing left she could do while she waited for power to build up, she decided to start working manually. She worked her way around the curved hallway of a room to the small compression room with an airlock that lead out into the aether and the darkness of space. She double checked the seal on the inner door and began turning the crank that opened the outside hatch. It wasn't so much that she was afraid of the aether outside, as everyone knew aether wasn't poisonous, it was more that she was worried about diluting the air inside so much that there wouldn't be enough oxygen left to breathe.

The purpose of the compression room was to let the aether in, where the machinery could then gather it and compress it into tanks that could be taken home and sold. Pure tanks of aether would be worth a fortune, as Roger had convinced their backers.

As the outside hatch cracked open, she experienced a pull, much stronger and quicker than she had when she had opened the hatch to the boiler room. The inner door, which she had already checked the seal on, clanked shut tighter, startling her, and then bowed outward, as though kicked by a giant.

Through the thick glass, Prudy saw the room fill with light and a crystalline haze that swirled in rainbow sparkles and rushed out the crack in the exterior door. In the blink of an eye, the haze was gone, leaving behind only a few dancing, shimmering shards that floated lazily about in the light.

Prudy squinted into the light. It streamed in like a sunbeam, but was a pure blue-white, not the warm gold of sunlight. As she stepped closer and touched the door, she hissed and pulled her hand back. It was so cold it burned. Frost crystals had already formed all over her side of the door. On the other side, the bellows that were to be used for collecting aether had all but turned themselves inside out, and were ruined.

She stared for a long moment, not sure what to think of what had happened. Her eyes began to adjust to the light and she became curious as to its origin. Returning to the hand crank, she fought to open the door more, but it was slow going. The gears seemed to not be working right and being weightless robbed her of leverage.

*Ah...They're frozen! The grease has frozen!* Prudy tossed back her head in frustration. How had she not foreseen this? Of course it would be cold in space! The higher up you climbed mountains, the colder it got. This was as high as you could get, so it must be as cold as you can get, too.

She would have to wait for the energy from the boiler to move the gears; her arms weren't strong enough in this situation. She realized she was beginning to feel heat coming from the boiler, and she was grateful for it and the return of power it represented.

A rasping noise came from above her, and she looked up into the darkness. The light had gone out again, but she hadn't noticed with the blue light streaming in from outside. She pushed off to glide up and investigate. Could it be Roger?

She shook her head at the foolish thought. She knew he was dead.

As she approached, the darkness ahead began to lighten and she could make out details. It continued to brighten to a gray, and then, as she entered the cockpit, a thin shaft of the blue-white light shot across her vision. Like a God Ray from the heavens, it shone in from one of the windows and illuminated Roger's face.

More of the rasping sounds, all around her, everywhere, and more light appeared. The single shaft expanded wider and new shafts manifested. The black was being scraped off the windows, letting light in.

Prudy pressed close to see. Outside, a crystalline cloud swirled about the ship, tiny crystals sandblasting away at the windows as they collided and rubbed across the ship. She put her hand on the window and desperately wished she could help remove the black faster.

*Carbon scorching?* She wondered. *Gunpowder residue?* Whatever it was, it had completely obscured the outside until now.

As the little sparkling flakes worked on the outside of the portholes, the heavens opened up for Purdy to see, and she forgot to breathe. Too many stars to take in, too many to see. She couldn't even try to focus on just one, and below…Earth.

Purest blue and white, and green and brown, it was the most beautiful thing Prudy had ever seen. She had thought she could cry no more, after sitting in the dark alone, but tears came again. A different kind of tears.

"I wish you could see this, Roger. It really is the Heavens. As beautiful as any Pearly Gate anyone ever imagined. But you already know that, don't you?" Her voice trailed off.

She spun around and looked out the other windows, now all mostly clean of whatever black stuff had covered them. The sun seemed small and distant, yet it was brighter than she had ever seen it.

"There is no aether out there, Roger. We're not going to get rich. I guess we'll still go down in history, but we won't be rich. I also don't know how we're going to land this thing without aether in the ballast to slow us down."

The edge of the moon appeared in one of the windows and she moved closer to see better.

"My god, Roger. I had no idea…"

A creaking and popping noise brought Prudy out of her revelry. The boiler was up to temperature and she needed to set it to work before the pressure built to high.

The moon filled one of the portholes now, its silvery glow

filling the cockpit with light and Prudy with wonder. She glanced over at the porcelain mask Roger wore in the light and tried to ignore the ignoble rags she had shoved into his nose and mouth.

"I know we never really talked about this before, Roger, but how do you feel about going to the moon?"

# AFTERWORD

## Guy Anthony De Marco

THE words I had heard while sitting on a panel at AnomalyCon 2014 in Denver, Colorado gave me pause.

"I don't really like steampunk. I like science fiction," said the young man who was dragged to the convention by his corset-and-goggles wearing girlfriend. "If they had spaceships instead of airships, maybe I'd like it."

"Hmmm," I thought to myself. "Steampunk in space. Steampunk on other worlds. Why not?"

Indeed....

Almost all of the steampunk I've read involved things happening in an alternate reality version of the Victorian age – usually in England or the United States. Most of the characters were Caucasian, with plenty of college education to back up their intelligence and ability to tinker with things and make discoveries.

After talking with the folks at Villainous Press, they brought in their senior editor, Sam Knight, to gauge his reaction to having an anthology taking place either in space or on other planets. To say he was enthusiastic would be quite the understatement. Sam took on the role of soliciting stories and editing them, doing his usual job of professional cat-herding. He also brought in some ringers. Pro authors Peter J. Wacks and David Boop contributed stories that helped to elevate the anthology to new heights. In fact, Peter was so interested in the project that he did the original design of the cover.

Sam Knight had to go through many stories in the slush pile to pick out the best ones. Competition was fierce, and stories came in from authors ranging from those who lived down the block to those living an airship's distance away in Croatia.

Villainous Press hopes you enjoy this collection assembled by Sam as much as I enjoyed reading it. I'm thinking we'll have more "other worlds" anthologies in the future. I'm already hearing some talk of doing stories about folks who don't normally star in steampunk tales.

I'm waiting with excited anticipation to get more unusual steampunk stories to read and enjoy while sipping a cup of tea.

Earl Grey of course. Hmmm…who knew that Captain Picard from Star Trek: The Next Generation was secretly a steampunk enthusiast living in space.

## Other Books Available from Villainous Press

| | |
|---|---|
| The Adventures of Dr. Bird | Sterner St. Paul Meek |
| Giants on the Earth | Sterner St. Paul Meek |
| The Heaviside Layer | Sterner St. Paul Meek |
| Ancient Terrors 1 | Guy Anthony De Marco |
| Ancient Terrors 2 | Guy Anthony De Marco |
| Ancient Terrors 3 | Guy Anthony De Marco |
| Life & Everything Too | Guy Anthony De Marco |
| Odd Places | Guy Anthony De Marco |
| Tales from the Fleet | Guy Anthony De Marco |
| Golden Girl of Munan | Harl Vincent |
| Barton's Island | Harl Vincent |
| Purple & Gray | Harl Vincent |
| Vagabonds | Harl Vincent |
| A Princess of Mars | Edgar Rice Burroughs |
| Warlord of Mars | Edgar Rice Burroughs |
| The Gods of Mars | Edgar Rice Burroughs |
| Thuvia, Maid of Mars | Edgar Rice Burroughs |
| The Chessmen of Mars | Edgar Rice Burroughs |
| House on the Borderland | William Hope Hodgson |
| Grey Shapes | E. Charles Vivian |
| Pharos the Egyptian | Guy Boothby |
| The Gates Ajar | Elizabeth Stuart Phelps |
| Sorceress of the Strand | L.T. Meade & R. Eustace |
| The Thing from the Lake | Eleanor M. Ingram |
| Vendetta | Marie Corelli |
| Watcher by the Threshold | John Buchan |
| Steampunk: The Other Worlds | Sam Knight |
| Freakend Madness Vol. 1 | Sam Knight |
| Deathworld | Harry Harrison |